DEGRANON

Degranon is a science fiction novel that involves time travel, diversity, overpopulation, civil wars, and one family's struggle to remain a family. Welcome to the planet Valchondria, where speech and actions face constant scrutiny, the future offers no progress, and most people can no longer see in color. Those who want change will not only confront the rigid maintainers of tradition but also become involved with a violent religious fanatic from a war-torn planet called "Degranon."

The writing of Dr. Duane Simolke (pronounced "Dwain Smoky") has appeared in dozens of publications, including *Nightfire, Mesquite, The International Journal on World Peace,* and *Beyond: Science Fiction and Fantasy.* He was born in New Orleans on May 28, 1965. Majoring in English, he received his B.A. at Belmont University (Nashville, TN, '89), his M.A. at Hardin-Simmons University (Abilene, TX, '91), and his Ph.D. at Texas Tech University (Lubbock, TX, '96).

His home page (duanesimolke.com) includes some of his writing, as well as a variety of links that will interest readers, writers, activists, and almost everyone else. He lives in Lubbock.

Simolke wrote *Degranon* in increments from 1980 through 2001. Between those increments, he completed three other books: (1) *The Acorn Stories*; (2) *Stein, Gender, Isolation, and Industrialism: New Readings of Winesburg, Ohio*; and (3) *Holding Me Together.* He is also the editor of the fiction anthology *The Acorn Gathering: Writers Uniting Against Cancer. Degranon* is his first science fiction book. As this book goes to press, Simolke and Antoinette Davis are co-writing *The Return of Innocence,* a sword and sorcery novel about a young woman who stumbles into grand adventures.

Readers can order Duane Simolke's books at most local or online bookstores.

DEGRANON

Duane Simolke

Writers Club Press
San Jose New York Lincoln Shanghai

Degranon

Writers Club Press
an imprint of iUniverse, Inc.

For information address:
iUniverse, Inc.
5220 S. 16th St., Suite 200
Lincoln, NE 68512
www.iuniverse.com

Any resemblance to actual people and events is purely coincidental. This is a work of fiction.

ISBN: 0-595-21371-5

Printed in the United States of America

This book is for all people who dare to be themselves.

Thanks to the many people who gave me feedback on the drafts of this novel over the years and encouraged me to eventually finish it. I would go for months or even years at a time without looking at the manuscript, but my mind often wandered to the distant worlds I had created. It took living my own life for more years before I could fully explore the lives of these characters; it also took rejection from several publishers to push me into just writing the novel as I really wanted to write it. I hope you enjoy the final results as much as I have treasured constantly returning to this project.

Just a few days after I finished Degranon, I saw the results of real-life fanatics attacking a real-life city in my country, and destroying a popular landmark, which I once visited. I made only minor changes after the September 11 attacks: changes such as punctuation, clarification, or removing wordiness. Some people will find parts of this novel disturbing or offensive, but I refuse to water down the very self-expression that oppressors fear.

Though I wrote this novel as entertainment and focused on making it exciting, I hope it will also provoke people to think for themselves, rather than blindly following those who claim to know the way for them, and rather than fearing those who want to control or terrorize them. So I repeat the dedication that I wrote for this book years ago.

This book is for all people who dare to be themselves.

"*Everything would be so much better if suddenly a bell rang and everybody told everybody else honestly what they did about it, how they lived, and how they loved. It's hiding things that makes them putrefy. By God it's horrible.*"

—From the John Dos Passos novel *Manhattan Transfer*.

Contents

CHAPTER 1

*D*r. Lorfeltez couldn't help but feel nervous. At age twenty-six, she had already become a representative of the Supreme Science Council, a powerful branch of planet Valchondria's government. And she had already requested grants for her research into core energies and artificial environments.

Now here she stood in the amphitheater that welcomed people into Valcine Plaza, the apex of human achievement. But she wasn't here to represent the Supreme Science Council. And she certainly wasn't here to recite the Pledge of Legally Permitted Language. Despite working for the SSC, part of the establishment, she hated almost anything imposed upon her by other people. She even hated the name that her parents had imposed upon her, and looked forward to one day changing it to a name she chose: Taldra. She wanted less control from her parents. Yes, they helped her rise quickly in the SSC, but they also drove her rusted with their obsessively mindless following of Maintainer laws. Simply put, Lorfeltez wasn't maintained.

In fact, Lorfeltez and several other scientists had gathered to speak about a nearly forgotten subject: outer space. She listened to Dr. Hudza's speech on the subject. The beautiful black woman with the animated gestures and the wallscreen voice could easily energize a crowd, but her words hardly sounded like something that anyone would hear on the wallscreen. Most members of the SSC simply didn't take such views seriously, while the Maintainers saw such views as dangerous, and perhaps even treasonous.

Dr. Hudza explained, "After spreading humanity to much of the known universe, we eventually abandoned not only colonization but also the colonists. Supposedly, we had too many problems at home to bother with problems on other worlds, light years away. But the advent of the virus over the past forty years has quickly exacerbated a problem that had slowly developed after the colonizing ended: overpopulation. The solution seems simple enough to me, and to many others, even if the Maintainers disagree. We need to return to the stars, and we need to continue advancing scientifically in ways that would further promote colonization on seemingly uninhabitable planets."

Lorfeltez agreed with all the sentiments in Dr. Hudza's speech. She nodded as Dr. Hudza slammed her left fist onto the podium and the crowd around her continued to swell. Hudza insisted, "We need to start building our ships now!" Hudza's outfit oddly reflected her words. Like Lorfeltez and the other protesting scientists, she wore a dress with pictures of stars and planets. Such clothing marked them among the drab outfits that everyone else wore. Lorfeltez even noticed a blue planet in Dr. Hudza's outfit—not that most Valchondrians could see any colors but black, white, or shades of gray.

Lorfeltez could see colors. She could see the green vines hanging from the elevated ceiling. She could see the red of the awnings that surrounded a huge amphitheater that was normally reserved for speeches from Leader, the SSC, or the Maintainers. She could see the orange and silver stripes across the ceiling and the walls. For Lorfeltez, those stripes symbolized the Valchondrian banner of silver flames on an orange plaque, but they now appeared as simply varying shades of gray to most Valchondrians.

Unfortunately, Maintainer law forbade her from telling anyone about her colorsight. Supposedly, the Maintainers feared giving so-called "special rights" to colorsighted people, thus making them cultural elitists. Lorfeltez wanted no special rights, but she knew that she was different, and she only wanted to explore those differences. She wanted to tell other people about the colors that her eyes allowed her to see.

She hated concealing her true self in such a way, or in any way. No law could stop her from being different, so the Maintainers used a law to make her hide that difference. The Maintainers forced her to lie, in order to protect the common good. How could their way be right if it involved lying and deception? Why couldn't she let others benefit from her abilities, or at least let others know that those abilities existed? She hated the hypocrisy of the Maintainers. They warned against deceit, but passed laws that promoted deceit. They talked about protecting Valchondria from violence, while they used violence to keep people in order, to "maintain" them. Who was Valchondria except its people, the very people that the Maintainers claimed to protect?

And what were they protecting anyone from by denying her the ability to acknowledge her colorsight? It was a gift, and she wanted to tell others about it. She loved colors! Even the hideous green swirls in dethua wood looked beautiful to Lorfeltez, who longed for the pleasure of exercising her gift.

Her fellow human beings granted her that pleasure simply by virtue of their appearance. Never mind the gray headbands, hair clips, and body suits that most of the people at the amphitheater wore. Other than a stripe of green on some headbands or belts, and other than an occasional hint of red or blue, Lorfeltez rarely saw any color on clothing.

Instead, she could see people's skin of red, brown, or black—all in varying shades. She could see their eyes of green, blue, gray, or brown, and their lips of pink, brown, or red. Everyone had black hair, but those of red, light brown, or mixed race often had a gloss to their long, flowing hair that distinguished it from the hair of most black or dark brown people, which tended to grow outward or sometimes just upward. And the male children of all races loved their hair short, so that one could almost see their skin color through it. Together, the many people who crammed into Valcine Plaza that day reflected the diverse beauty of Valchondria's population.

Still, even with all of that beauty, the countless people in the audience began to unnerve Lorfeltez with their scents, their shouting, and their crowding. The infamous Dr. Tquil seemed to shout the loudest, accusing Dr. Hudza of danger speak that threatened Valchondria's children.

His green eyes bulging in his round, red face, Tquil dashed onto the stage as Dr. Hudza stepped down. He shouted into the sound-amplifying pores of the podium: "Go home, to the safety of your wallscreens. This is the sort of anti-glory that I warn about in my new computer chip, *The Video of Values*. If you care about your children, you'll hover to the mall now and buy a copy, before these dangerous perverts tear asunder the very fabric of Valchondrian society."

Tquil shook his fists with exaggerated desperation as his eyes bulged even further out and his black mane bounced around him. Like many red-skinned men, he always kept his hair near waist length.

Lorfeltez asked herself, *Why me, and why now? Why does he have to start his impromptu video tour when I'm the next speaker?* Then she realized the answer and whispered it to herself: "The gossip masters must be here."

A glance behind revealed a troupe of slender post-adolescents with too much white make-up above their eyes and too many of their grav-free microphones floating around them. The glass balls sometimes bounced lightly off a head or two, causing tempers to flare, but the gossip masters never cared about people getting hurt or angry; they only cared about wallscreen ratings.

Lorfeltez knew all too well that Tquil wouldn't appear in public unless it was wallscreened, so she assumed that he had contacted the gossip masters. She swallowed the taste of disgust that rose in her mouth as she pushed herself toward the stage, enduring bony shoulders, hands, and elbows along the way. The smell of sweat, cologne, and perfume mingled with the overpowering roar of voices, but she tried to ignore it all. Stepping onto the stage released her from a microcosmic reflection of an overcrowded planet, but experiencing all of that pressing and shoving only strengthened her resolve to address the population crisis.

"Young Dr. Lorfeltez," said Tquil, glancing at her but mostly looking at his audience. A fake smile split his thin, chapped lips. "It's good to see that the Supreme Science Council has sent their newest researcher and media representative. We need a voice of sanity."

"That's why I'm here to replace your voice," said Lorfeltez, as she stepped close enough for the podium to transmit her words. Tquil cut his eyes at her as she unsnapped her credit box from her belt and showed him a read-out. "I bought this podium time. You didn't."

"This is why the Maintainers are planning to ban podium time," he whispered, turning his face enough that the podium wouldn't pick up his voice. As he walked away from her, he added, "And I wouldn't want to be the one credit-boxed with being on stage when they disrupt the riot here."

Lorfeltez asked in an unbelieving tone, "The what?"

"Notice that I'm leaving the stage now. I suggest that you do the same."

"I certainly won't!"

As Tquil slithered back into the crowd, Lorfeltez began articulating her vision of Project Life Unit, a structure that would not only house people on other planets but also provide them with energy. She spoke of the colonies and of lost fragments of Valchondria's past.

And while she spoke, her eyes fixed upon one face, that of a handsome young man about her age, with red skin, shoulder-length black hair, and glistening blue eyes. His face seemed carefully sculpted by nature, not modified but simply perfect. And that cleft in his square chin: she just wanted to....

Something pulled her attention from the handsome stranger. In the midst of the crowd, five men began using holo-projectors to create lifelike but transparent images. No one could mistake those gray, padded uniforms with black headbands and black boots. The images represented Maintainers, and the men started slapping at those images.

One of the five men screamed, "Up with science! Return to the stars!" Such passion surprised Lorfeltez, and delighted her in a way, though the physical demonstration hardly seemed productive.

"We won't be maintained!" screamed another of the men, his face stretched and sweating, as if he were lifting some heavy weight, rather than slapping at an artificial image that floated in the air.

Lorfeltez kept speaking, but her gaze then moved from the shouting and slapping group of men to the bulky Maintainer cameras that locked on them from the corners of the amphitheater. Maintainer law forbade anyone from impersonating a Maintainer or replicating a Maintainer uniform in any way. Even wallscreen programs couldn't depict fictional Maintainers. At most, the gossip masters could follow the Maintainers around with their grav-free cameras, or even buy footage made by Maintainer cameras. Lorfeltez often thought about how such laws were supposedly for everyone's good, but she could never fully convince herself that the Maintainers always wanted everyone's good, or that they themselves were always "good."

Good or not, they would be nearby. They constantly patrolled the Valcine Plaza area.

Even as she described her proposed creation of Project Life Unit, she suddenly realized something: someone had tipped Dr. Tquil off about the demonstration. The arrogant son of a hiliate actually showed some concern for her by trying to warn her about the possible riot.

And his concerns made sense; he knew how people would react to the men's demonstration. Indignant at the lawlessness, trained from birth to obey all laws and respect the Maintainers without question, several men and women began slapping, kicking, and punching the five men who used the holo-projectors. Even people who would listen to speeches about colonization would not go so far as to tolerate the idea of desecrating the very protectors of Valchondrian values. The five resisted the crowd that attacked them, while a few others tried to defend the five. As Lorfeltez feared, a brawl quickly began. She thought, *it would happen right in the middle of my podium time, with a record on my credit box, matching the time of the riot. This day isn't going well at all.*

Lorfeltez suddenly realized that she had stopped speaking and that everyone had stopped listening, or even jeering. The Maintainers had arrived. They filed through the crowd like a swarm of insects, freely pushing and shoving with all the authority that their office granted them, elbowing several people, and pushing a few out the doorways.

Part of the crowd began disappearing, as if the weight of the entering officers forced them outside. However, many of them failed to move away in time, and the Maintainers freely grabbed at their collars or even punched at them, before finding the sources of the disruption.

A female Maintainer yanked the holo-projectors away, knocking them to the floor, then used the handle of her rifle to destroy them, sending hot metal parts and wires everywhere. One of the wires gashed a woman's arm, sending out a small spurt of blood. Before even noticing her, the Maintainers quickly managed to handcuff all five men, even while the crowd continued to shift madly about, trying to escape. But then one of the Maintainers assisted the injured woman, holding his hand over the cut on her arm while obviously calling a healer with the transmitter in his ear.

Dr. Lorfeltez saw an elderly red woman in the audience, frail to the point that she had obviously lived beyond the virus's benefits. One of the Maintainers waved his laser rifle around to scare away the remnants of the controversial gathering; he held the rifle at the center, his hand near the button.

It frightened Lorfeltez to see the Maintainer's barrel sometimes pointing directly at the old woman. At least the other citizens could move quickly from his senseless demonstration of power, even if some of them ran in too many different directions for everyone to escape. As he swung it around again, the handle struck the old woman on the forehead, knocking her to the floor.

Surely that Maintainer sees what's he's doing, Lorfeltez thought. Just as some members of the crowd almost trampled the old woman, the handsome stranger pulled her up and helped her escape.

Lorfeltez had wanted to intervene as well, but another Maintainer stood beside her, aiming a laser pistol at her. The Maintainer was an extremely tall black woman, but barely more than a teenager, with hair shooting out from her headband, reminding Lorfeltez of a docle flower, one of the few remaining flowers on Valchondria's overly industrialized landscape. The absence of stripes on her uniform revealed her as a trainee, but she carried herself like a Top Maintainer.

"Dr. Lorfeltez," she said, her voice brimming with Maintainer superiority, and her unusual height adding to that superiority. Lorfeltez had always hated being short, especially at times like this. The Maintainer continued: "I find you in conflict with the glory of Valchondria. To protect our children and our society, I hereby refrain you from public mobility. Any verbalization on your part will be considered heavy hazard. Do you recognize my guidance?"

Her dark brown eyes studied Lorfeltez. The self-confidence was real, but Lorfeltez could see that this Maintainer didn't actually want to arrest her or stop her from voicing her concerns. Something existed between them: a sort of sisterhood, if such a thing could exist for two young women in a world with no siblings below the age of forty.

But it was her job, her genetic destiny as someone with a Maintainer-quality genetic structure. That genetic structure reasserted itself. "I ask again, Dr. Lorfeltez: do you recognize my guidance?"

"I recognize it." Lorfeltez clasped her hands together behind her back, her slender fingers grasping each other. It was the proper motion of surrender, and she imagined one of her own hands as that of her mother or her father, reaching out to comfort her in this moment of crisis.

But they wouldn't be holding her hand anymore. They had warned her to avoid the rally. "Think of your career," her mother had said. Her father had said much worse: "Stay away from disruptive elements. If you don't distance yourself from them, we'll have no choice but to distance ourselves from you. Be maintained, if you want to be a part of this family."

Those words had stung Lorfeltez like nothing before. Her parents were the ones who had introduced her to science and discovery: her mother, the atmospheric technician, and her father, the Valcine University software archivist. They had become Maintainers too, not in the official sense, but in the sense of bowing to the same driving, blinding force of tradition. Everything was a certain way, and to question it was a threat to society. But how, and why?

"It will be all right!" Hearing that comforting male voice, Lorfeltez turned to see the stranger climb onto the stage from its center. He had returned, and looked even better close up. It seemed an odd thing to notice at such a time, but he was undeniably handsome!

"Who are you?" asked Lorfeltez, as the stranger stepped back from the Maintainers, careful not to upset them in an already tense moment.

His smile comforted her. "A friend. You'll see me again soon. I'll make sure of that."

The Maintainer who read Lorfeltez her rights stood between them and warned the young man, "Having the wrong friends can get you killed."

His red face grew a deeper red, and his features tightened. "I'll take that chance, Trainee." His voice resonated with anger and a confidence that equaled the Maintainers; he even mocked her by using the word "Trainee," and he said the word with a dismissive tone. Lorfeltez liked him immediately, and believed his assurance that they would meet again. But for now, she knew she must face Urloan Control, the one place all Valchondrians tried to avoid.

"Does 'Friend' have a name?" the angered trainee demanded, slipping between him and Lorfeltez. Before he could answer, she pulled a scanner from her belt and waved it in front of him. Looking at the read-out screen and sighing in disgust, she said, "Dr. Naldod. A healer, and third-generation SSC, on both sides of your family. Your parents served the SSC until they died, while you were in your late teens, but it says here that your father's twin brother just checked himself into hospital yet again. You'd best go see him. He didn't have a spouse or child of his own, did he?"

Dr. Naldod's blue eyes narrowed, revealing a violent beast inside. "He just had us. I know Leader, and I have many connections. I've also been following Dr. Lorfeltez's career via the wallscreen; she's very well-liked in the SSC, and by Leader."

The trainee gestured to the stage exit and tilted her head back slightly. "You should be tending to family, instead of interfering with justice."

Though he nearly responded to her comment, Naldod looked past her to give Lorfeltez a reassuring gaze. Something in those beautiful pools of blue convinced Lorfeltez that she shouldn't worry about her situation. He ran toward the exit, obviously torn by his determination to help Lorfeltez and his need to see his sick uncle.

Then Naldod was gone, along with the crowd. Only the Maintainers remained: dozens of them. Lorfeltez walked down the stairs on the left corner of the stage, into a sea of weapons and gray uniforms.

CHAPTER 2

When Dr. Naldod arrived at the hospital, he pulled on his healer headband, so he could rush to his uncle's room with less security clearances. A quick check during his trip there had already revealed the room letter, on the thirty-seventh floor. The black metal bubble of an elevator seemed to move up too slowly, its treads buzzing and clicking slightly from overuse.

Born long before the Supreme Science Council unveiled the virus or the Maintainers created the zero-population law, Naldod's father and twin brother grew up together in Valcine. One became a scientist, and the other an architect. Though K'Laar's work required constant and lengthy trips, Naldod always enjoyed spending time with his beloved uncle. After Naldod's parents died, K'Laar became Naldod's benefactor, father, and mother, even though he usually carried on all three functions over the wallscreen, from distant cities.

The elevator shook slightly as a thunderous rumble surrounded Naldod, making his stomach and chest tighten with nervousness. The lights flashed twice, as the elevator seemed to slow even more. "Now what?" Hachen asked, gripping the latch that could open the emergency stop box. But the rumbling soon dissipated, and Hachen finally reached the thirty-seventh floor.

Stepping uneasily and slightly dizzy from the elevator's sliding doors, Naldod stopped a passing healer. "Was that a quake?" he asked her. He often spoke with her, but had forgotten her name in all the day's excitement. Countless healers and patients strolled up and down the long, intersecting hallways every day, just as in that moment, so he often found it difficult to remember the names of the people he encountered during his brief shifts at the hospital. But today seemed worse; he felt fortunate to even remember his own name, or the name of his uncle.

"Yes," she replied, smiling in the forced "no, nothing's wrong" manner that Naldod learned in Valcine University's Healer Basics class. "Nothing serious, just the routine Valcine vibrations. To the side, your uncle designed this building, and his stabilizers prevented any damage. I'm just glad I wasn't in the elevator."

Naldod wondered if she meant that as a joke. He was in no mood for joking. "Yes, you should be. You know my uncle? Are you his healer?"

"I am." She nodded, proudly, suggesting a successful operation. "He asked about you, if you were working today."

But he forgot to wallscreen me, Naldod mused, before asking the healer his condition. After assuring Naldod not to worry, and that K'Laar only suffered from a mild heart condition, she pressed a button that caused K'Laar's door to rise into the ceiling.

As Naldod stepped inside and the door slid down, he saw his uncle: eyes closed, white hair matted and disarrayed. Like his twin brother, K'Laar aged and wrinkled almost overnight, going from a young man one day to an old man the next.

K'Laar represented a dying group on Valchondria: aunts and uncles. In fact, Naldod had already lost his aunts and his other uncle. Because of the zero-population law, few people could still find an aunt or uncle by blood, though many people functioned as aunt or uncle to the child of a close friend. Despite his constant absence, K'Laar remained a good uncle to Naldod: one Naldod couldn't bear to lose.

Tired eyes opened on K'Laar's long, thin face and suddenly sparkled with pride. That look of pride swept over K'Laar's countenance, making him appear more healthy, and making Naldod feel like the child who brought his pressure tournament trophies to K'Laar's apartment, or—more often—held them up to the wallscreen for K'Laar to see them.

"Dr. Naldod!" K'Laar exclaimed, emphasizing the word "doctor" as if Naldod had earned that title a day earlier, rather than nearly a year earlier.

Naldod rushed to his side and checked his readings. "K'Laar, why didn't you tell me you were in hospital?"

"You work here. I assumed you'd find out."

"I work here part-time, and I won't even tell you how I found out, or how much I panicked."

Laughing a hoarse laugh, K'Laar reached from under the sheets and grabbed his nephew's hand. "You're still too uptight! It was minor, but the healer gave me a synthetic heart anyway, just to be safe."

"Good." Naldod squeezed his uncle's hand, while trying to look calm. He hated when people called him "uptight," though he agreed with that judgment. "I think everyone should have synthetic hearts. They're more reliable than the real thing."

"Well, don't give up on humanity just yet." K'Laar released Naldod's hand, but continued to gaze approvingly at him. They hadn't seen each other in person more than three or four times since Naldod's graduation.

"It's just an organ. It isn't what makes us human."

K'Laar rolled his eyes slightly at Naldod's scientific mind. "No, I suppose not. To the side, I feel great, and forgiveness for giving you a scare."

"You, and that quake."

"My buildings can handle anything," K'Laar insisted, in a tone that suggested a sales pitch. "So can this tired old body. But my mind…. I don't know if my tired old mind can handle Valcine any longer."

Naldod motioned a dismissal of K'Laar's usual and expected complaints about the pollution, crowding, and corruption of Valchondria's capital city. "As if you're ever in Valcine! You're always away, for another building."

K'Laar's eyes widened suggestively. "And there will be countless buildings in the North Edge Project. I've accepted an indefinite series of contracts there, and a home of my own design."

"K'Laar! That's wonderful news!" The joy suddenly dropped from Naldod's voice: "But I'll never see you!"

"We'll find the future at North Edge: you and me, everyone! I'm building a hospital there. You could work at it full-time, and maybe find a spouse." K'Laar raised his white eyebrows in a joking manner.

Blushing, Naldod countered, "Like you ever found a spouse!"

"I'm still looking," K'Laar said, with a sly grin.

"You're rusted! To the side, there is someone I met today, after wanting to meet her for a long time. She's unlike anyone I ever encountered!"

"Why didn't you bring her? Where is she?"

"In prison."

K'Laar's eyes narrowed, revealing his paternal side. "Naldod!"

"She did nothing wrong. She's a dreamer, an idealist, like you. But she was part of a demonstration that upset the Maintainers."

"The Maintainers!" spat K'Laar. "Your parents loathed them, and they came to loathe the SSC, even though they belonged to the SSC. Politicians are all the same these days. They just want to control everyone, while they themselves are controlled by the Power Holders and the Wall System Conglomerate. And their self-righteousness is appalling! The more laws and sermons they give the public, the less fidelity they give their spouses."

Naldod smiled, but worried it looked like a forced healer smile. "Calm down, before you wear out that new heart."

But K'Laar wouldn't calm down. "Your parents wanted you to be a healer because healers try to help people by literally helping them, not by controlling them. You remember that."

Holding up his hands, Naldod said, "I'll remember. And you remember to tell me when something's wrong."

"I will."

Confident in his uncle's safety, Naldod's thoughts returned to Lorfeltez and how he could help her. He knew he couldn't move to North Edge, or to any place but her side. He believed in her words, in her vision, and he couldn't stop thinking of her perfect face.

❧   ❧   ❧

In the basement of Valcine Plaza, in an office much larger than most Valchondrian apartments and much more adorned with sculptures and paintings than any of Valchondria's neglected museums, two rather tall black men argued politics.

Leader was ninety-seven years old, and the most respected person in all of Valchondria, yet this upstart of a rebel dared to question his judgment and to dictate policy to him! He couldn't tell Dr. Geln's age, but he looked like an ugly, oversized boy. Thanks to the virus, most Valchondrians looked like teenagers until their mid-twenties and then like twenty-five-year-olds until their late forties. However, Geln was no Valchondrian, and he carried no virus to protect him from the ravages of disease.

Toying with his long, braided hair, Geln paced majestically around the room, basking in his arrogance and in the strength of the muscular body that bulged through his black body suit and even his black knee-boots. Only the light gray stripe across the black belt that held his credit box provided a distraction from the utter darkness of his drab clothing.

Geln wasn't a handsome man at all, not with the two scars just below his right eye, and not with the almost inhuman square-shape of his jaw or rectangular-shape of the sockets around eyes that seemed much too small for his hulking body. He looked like a character that had been poorly drawn by the wallscreen animators, not that many of them possessed the talent to justify their popularity or their constant presence on the wallscreen.

Yet, this ugly, brazen man somehow kept Leader's attention and respect. Geln was, after all, the chosen representative of Degranon, and his mind seemed ever sharp, ever crafty. He was, after all, Leader's secretly recorded choice for a successor, and no one could change Leader's chosen successor but Leader himself.

"Outlawing podium time might turn some people against you," Geln said, in his vile, scratchy voice, which often popped slightly near the end of statements. Despite learning to mask the harsh intonations of a Degran accent, Geln still sounded like a hissing hiliate.

"Gratitude for that acknowledgment," Leader quipped, with little sincerity.

"But the Maintainers would have done so eventually anyway. Upsetting the masses can work to our benefit. I have already seen the radical element forming beneath your walkways."

"The walkway people?"

Geln dismissed that thought with the swing of an oversized hand. "Not just your poor, though desperation could also turn them into soldiers. I've had contact with many dissenters, all searching for something to believe in, and I will give it to them. I've even kept up with their attempts to defy the Maintainers; I only wish that Dr. Tquil could have warned Dr. Lorfeltez in time about that absurd demonstration. Aside from those who simply want to attack oppression but offer no alternatives, there are many young idealists, like Dr. Lorfeltez. Of course, she's the one who interests me most."

Leader pressed the wrinkled tips of his slender fingers against each other. Despite the virus, he kept feeling pain in the joints of those fingers. But he said nothing to his healers about the pain; they would just give him placebos and assure him that the virus had eliminated arthritis. His body had already begun growing old before the virus, and before he met his former spouse; in fact, he rarely heard about other people his age. He wondered if their bodies hurt as much as his.

Still looking at his hands, Leader said, "To the side, she'll be here soon. I've arranged her release from Urloan Control."

"And you've arranged the purchase, at the exact location I gave you? It must be at the coordinates where my sensors found the doorway to the right time." Geln's eyes widened with joy, giving his scarred face a surprisingly childlike look of enthusiasm.

"Yes, I followed your coordinates. We had to vacate some families and demolish a low-rent housing complex, just like when we constructed this building above the doorway to your planet. But I'm willing to accept those sacrifices, for the good of both of our worlds."

"I know those were difficult choices for you, Leader, but gratitude for making them. My superiors never regretted their decision to contact you. Soon, I'll have the secrets of Degranon, as well as help from one of Valchondria's most brilliant minds."

Leader cleared his throat. "Make that two. A young man named Dr. Naldod is also coming to see us. He wants to join in Project Life Unit."

"And you know this young man well?"

"Yes, his parents both held seats with the SSC. They're dead now, but what a contribution they left in him! This boy is a genius. He's both a healer and a scientist—energetic, charming, handsome. Everyone likes him."

Geln sucked his upper lip into his mouth before responding. "Good. We need all the support we can find, if we want to bring the home world back to the glory of Degranon. Providing a doorway to the original Degranon will unite the factions of modern Degranon, and it will make this city a holy place for all Degrans. Who would shed blood over a city they consider holy? I speak clearly: no sane person would do that. Instead, they will trade here, negotiate here, and bring your world into the future. You and I will work together to ensure a better future for both our worlds. My people are destroying each other, and they long for the home world. We can give it to them, and give Valchondria gifts like space travel and trade with the colonies."

Having long since embraced the philosophies in his illegal copy of *The Book of Degranon*, Leader believed the Degran promises, but he also wanted his position strengthened, so he could truly lead his people into the future. He loved the Valchondria of his childhood, and hated the drab, oppressive world that the Maintainers had created. In all honesty with himself, he never really understood the concept of windows that allowed visions through time and space, or doorways that allowed travel through time and space. Still, he understood that Geln knew about such matters and how to use them for the glory of Degranon and Valchondria. If that meant a certain amount of deception, then Leader would take part in deception, even against people he admired deeply, such as Lorfeltez and Naldod.

The tiny transmitter that was clipped to Leader's left earlobe tingled as it came on. A young man's voice told him that Dr. Lorfeltez had arrived. "Send her in," Leader commanded, before the transmitter clicked off.

As the door slid into the ceiling, it slowly revealed the intoxicating form of Dr. Lorfeltez: her silky black hair pulled to one side, her chin slightly pronounced on her round face, her forehead free of the white make-up that some women liked, and her small body contoured without exceeding weight/height ratio. Leader imagined the light redness of her smooth skin, though the virus denied him that pleasure; he hated that he even imagined touching her skin. Perhaps more disturbing, Leader could see that her beauty also struck Geln, who had only seen a two-dimensional hologram of her before. Still, he wondered what harm could come of noticing a woman's beauty.

"Leader," said Dr. Lorfeltez. "Gratitude for my release."

Leader bowed slightly. "Your arrest was a horrible mistake. After checking the wallscreen records of those men against yours, the

Maintainers found that you'd never had contact with them." Though Lorfeltez winced at that intrusion of her privacy, Leader continued with his assurances. "You know that the SSC treasures you. In fact, they've given me the privilege of telling you the good news."

Lorfeltez smiled, and her smile seemed to nearly make Geln tremble. She glanced over to him then touched his shoulder. "I'm Dr. Lorfeltez," she told him, before obviously forgetting about him and turning back to Leader. "They're funding the project?"

"Yes, and if you accept the contract while continuing your media work, you'll make enough credit for a rather nice house that we're having built beside the property, just in case you want it. We'd like to keep you near the project, if possible."

"A house?" Lorfeltez asked, with disbelief. Few Valchondrians owned houses. Most of them lived in apartment buildings of sixty to ninety stories. "My house?"

"If you so desire. Though I know your parents would prefer that you remain in their apartment."

Lorfeltez hesitated, some of the enthusiasm leaving her face as her eyebrows sank down. "I don't think they'll mind completely. My house? And my project?"

"And your assistants." He motioned at Geln. "Dr. Geln, for one."

Geln touched her shoulder. "It will be a pleasure. I've heard all about the pro-colony video chip that you're making, and your plans for Project Life Unit. You don't know what an honor this is."

She bowed her head briefly, a common Valchondrian gesture of respect or gratitude. "And what's your specialty, Dr. Geln?"

"Core energy. I—"

After Leader pushed the remote for the door again, he saw a look of delighted recognition in Lorfeltez's eyes and a threatened look in Geln's eyes. The connection between Lorfeltez and Naldod began as immediately as the conflict between Geln and Naldod. Leader could already guess at the problems that might arise from that connection and that conflict, but he said nothing, did nothing to change his choice of team members. He would spend the rest of his life regretting that silence.

CHAPTER 3

*D*r. Naldod touched Dr. Lorfeltez's shoulder, forcing himself not to leave it there. It was really her! He was really going to work with her! From the time he had first seen Lorfeltez, he had been fascinated by the perfect shape of her face, the assertive inflections in her voice, and the obvious intelligence in her words. He loved everything about her.

Over the next two months, he saw her and Dr. Geln almost every day. To spend even more time with her, he gave up most of his duties at the hospital. The construction of Project Life Unit's prototype happened quickly, just across the walkways from Lorfeltez's two-story house, which went up even more quickly.

Both buildings looked remarkable because of their obvious newness: their lack of vines, crumbling, or hover-fume stains. Life Unit almost matched the house's prominence at its high point, and its triangular shape created an odd geometry with the house. A tiny triangle stood close to a tiny square below the maze of hoverlanes that connected the thin, towering apartment buildings and business buildings of Valcine.

Despite its limited size, Naldod often stood outside, staring at that pristine but lonely-looking house and wondering what it would be like to step inside it. One day, he finally learned.

Looking up at the consoles in Life Unit's cluttered control room, Dr. Geln breathed in deeply. "The coils for battery seven are wedged between two plates. I knew their lasers needed re-focusing."

"I never understood why we had to dig there in the first instance," Naldod told him. "Our scans showed easier pathways to the core energies."

Geln rolled his tiny eyes. "It's always easier with you, Naldod. What about better? That deposit of core energies is unlike anything recorded in the video archives."

"Yes, you've mentioned that two or twenty times already. I still don't see your aim."

Lorfeltez walked in from the battery room, wearing a flowing lab coat. Her hair was pulled back to the right and knotted around the stem of a plastic docle flower. The three earrings that dangled from her only exposed ear bounced as she walked.

Both men always froze when she entered a room. Sure, they had been watching her through the window as she checked the readings that displayed themselves near the tops of the seven batteries that towered above her. Their eyes never left Lorfeltez. But for her to be in the same room, that was another matter entirely.

To hear the subtle echo from the boots that tried a little too hard to make her look taller, to smell the bathing powder still fresh on her skin, to see the shiny gray eyes that glared defiantly at any challenge or obstacle, those were the moments for which Naldod lived. He kept hoping that he could accomplish more than just staring, and he kept worrying that his work might suffer from his preoccupation with Lorfeltez. But he needed to move quickly.

Naldod saw Geln always vying for Lorfeltez's attention. Anyone could have seen that. So he decided to become more aggressive in welcoming her advances. His winks and smiles simply weren't enough.

"Are you boys fighting again?" she asked, setting her palm computer on the console.

Geln suddenly straightened up in his chair, as if a Maintainer had entered the room. The lights of Project Life Unit's master control danced around Lorfeltez. She always referred to the computer that enveloped them as "Life." The abbreviation fit, since the project had become their life. They spent most of their time inside Project Life Unit, while it spent most of its time running calculations and poking its expandable tentacles around under the rocks and dirt of Valchondria's infertile surface layers, drilling for core energies.

"He's fighting," said Geln, in his smug, dismissive tone. His voice popped at the end of the statement, as it often did. "I'm trying to get battery seven running."

Naldod shook his head and leaned back in his chair. "I'm tired of this."

Lorfeltez placed her hands on his shoulders. "We're all tired. Notice, batteries one through six are functioning perfectly. All we lack is battery seven." She stepped back then spoke toward the narrow ceiling. "Life?"

"Yes, Dr. Lorfeltez?" The metallic voice surrounded them. Naldod hated that voice; it was almost as annoying as Geln's. Lorfeltez had once mentioned that they should try to humanize it, but they never had time.

"Continue digging in the same area, unless you read damage to battery seven's tentacle. Shut down when seven is fully charged."

"Yes, Dr. Lorfeltez. To the side, my collector reports inform me that, one day before the Maintainers ban podium speech, Dr. Tquil will have something called a 'protest' in regard to my existence. Should I stop existing?"

Naldod laughed before looking up and projecting his voice toward Life's audio receiver. "Ignore that hiliate, Life. He's probably just released another video chip and needs a publicity boost. You don't want us to become walkway people, do you?"

"No, Dr. Naldod. You are my creators."

"Then don't stop existing. We need this project. Besides, I like you."

"Gratitude, Dr. Naldod. Do you like me as well, Dr. Lorfeltez?"

"Of course," she replied. Her confident smile revealed the pride she felt when talking to the fruit of her genius. It almost seemed that she were a mother talking to her child. And Naldod couldn't help but imagine how much she would love and protect an actual child.

"And you, Dr. Geln?"

Rolling his eyes, Geln pushed back from the monitor and stood up. "I have a meeting. Tell Life Unit that I like her."

"You can tell her," said Lorfeltez. "She knows your voice print."

But he didn't tell her or look up at the receiver. He looked only at Lorfeltez. "Glory. Forgiveness if I've been temperamental lately."

"Can we help?" asked Naldod. "My aim is, if something's wrong—"

Geln creased his brow. "It's nothing you can help with. It's…personal. But gratitude." He looked up. "Life Unit, I like you very much. Please open the outer door."

"Yes, Dr. Geln. And, gratitude."

❦   ❦   ❦

As soon as Geln left, Lorfeltez asked Naldod a question she had often wanted to ask: "What do you think of Geln?"

Naldod's expression told her that he really didn't want to answer the question. "He's a brilliant scientist."

"And…?"

"And he's overly aware of his own brilliance."

"Agreed. And I also don't like him looking at me the way he does. I've caught him doing it several times, just today. But, Naldod, Geln has connections and alliances in the SSC that are stronger than ours, even with the blessing of Leader and the lasting influence of your parents. To the side, his grasp of core theory surpasses anything I've ever seen. We need him."

Naldod sighed, but in a much more attractive way than whenever he would resign to one of Geln's arguments. His look of annoyance seemed playful this time. "And, as Project Top, you're saying that I need to get along with him?"

She nodded. "We both do."

"To the side, you acknowledged that you've noticed Geln's lingering gaze, and that you didn't like it. Certainly you've noticed that I can't keep my eyes from you."

"Yes, but I like that."

Naldod blushed, just enough for it to show on his red skin. It struck Lorfeltez as charming, especially on such a confident and assertive man. "You've never said anything," he told her.

"Well, you know that the Maintainers suggest holding your feelings inside during the initial months of acquaintance."

"I've never thought of you as maintained."

"The Maintainers make sense sometimes, except when they're arresting me. Would you like to see what I've done with my house? I've almost gotten all the ceiling trunks empty."

He laughed. She had always liked his raspy laughter; it sounded like an amplified whisper. "After all this time, I should expect so. But, yes, that would heavy honor me."

The two continued to see each other outside work. Lorfeltez's parents had already pulled away from her before she moved out, so it wasn't like she would be spending time with them. Her only close friend was Dr. Hudza, who was busy with her own relationship, and with becoming married. Naldod had buried himself in studies and work from the time his parents died and never developed any close friendships. So, as soon as Naldod and Lorfeltez began dating, they quickly fell into becoming the center of each other's world.

Lorfeltez activated her wallscreen as Naldod sat down on the synthetically quilted couch. He crossed his hairy and muscular legs, which peaked out from under his witness robe. Lorfeltez also wore a witness robe, and the heavy material made her arms itch. Still, she took comfort in the fact that her underclothes kept the rest of it from her skin.

She thought of telling Naldod that she wanted to change into something more comfortable, but it seemed an incredibly forward thing to say. Rather, she asked if a glass of meda squeezings would delight him.

"Yes, I would like that," he replied, giving that tender smile he had given her countless times at work. Even with seeing him nearly every day—and now many nights as well—she never stopped taking great pleasure in seeing that smile directed at her, or his beautiful blue eyes sparkling at her.

After pouring two glasses of meda squeezings, she sat down with him, slightly closer than usual.

"Gratitude," he said, as he accepted one of the glasses. With his other hand, he tugged on his robe, obviously trying to stop it from pulling on the back of his neck.

"Unbearable, isn't it?" she asked.

"The robe?" He looked into her eyes for affirmation and then nodded. "I think witness robes were all designed by some hideous, spiteful little man who knew he would never graduate from university, never become married, and not care how people felt at his vaporizer ceremony."

Grinning at his imaginative humor, she realized something. "Forgiveness. You barely know Dr. Hudza. I shouldn't have pulled you to her wedding."

He touched her hand, not reluctantly but with deliberate caution and care, as if asking her permission while taking her hand into his. "Yes, but it was a beautiful wedding, and I was heavy honored to be there with you. I speak clearly: it heavy honors me to be anywhere with you."

Clasping his hand tightly, she leaned forward and kissed him on the lips, feeling the warmth of his embrace and smelling the scent of his cologne: a scent much like the one released by the environmental regulators during spring time. She knew at that moment that they would always be together, as long as they lived.

CHAPTER 4

*D*r. Geln asked Life the time again. Since Dr. Lorfeltez had given her a more human-sounding voice, he found talking to her more tolerable. To the side, it was better than talking to Lorfeltez or Naldod, who constantly talked about each other. Why had Lorfeltez fallen for Naldod, of all people? Geln hated seeing them, coming back from their dinners or their speaking engagements together. From that day a month earlier, when he had walked home with her for the first time, they had rarely been apart.

The way she doted on him was intolerable! No Degrans would ever put their romantic feelings on public display! That was the problem: despite her many admirable qualities, Lorfeltez was no Degran, and she never would be. And there was the other problem: Geln loved her. Her loved her so much that his mission on Valchondria seemed like a distant memory. He lived only to see her, and to impress her.

But there was still the matter of opening the doorway. He had collected all the doorway energies into battery seven, but nothing ever happened. Most doorways opened for long periods of time, but this one had never opened. He kept wondering if all his work had been pointless, if he were just there making himself crazy for no reason at all.

Life Unit told him the time then said, "Dr. Naldod has arrived."

Geln breathed out a noise of disgust. "Gratitude."

"Geln!" Naldod exclaimed, when he arrived in the control room.

"Naldod." Geln tilted his head forward.

"Please, use my chosen name."

No. I'm not ready for this. "Your chosen name?"

"Yes, I've chosen the name Hachen, and Lorfeltez has chosen the name Taldra. She's asked me to become married with her."

Geln looked away, fearing what his face might reveal to his coworker, to his rival. He wanted to reach into his shirt and retrieve the concealed laser pistol. He wanted Naldod out of the way.

And Hachen has to be the most overused of all Valchondrian names! The few Valchondrian men who aren't Hachen by birth will then choose that name when they become married! What insipid, unimaginative fools these Valchondrians are! What a waste of the home planet!

"I'm very happy for you," Geln said to the wall. "For both of you."

Hachen touched Geln's shoulder. "We knew you would be. You will attend the wedding?"

Shuddering, Geln reached into his shirt, but he managed not to grab his weapon. "Of course."

For Geln, it all became a blur from that moment: the wedding, the talk of renewed civil war among the Degrans, the discovery that battery seven had indeed absorbed the temporal element that Geln needed. However, one event slowed the blur: the news of Taldra's pregnancy. That was a clear, distinct moment. That was the beginning of a clear, distinct day.

Geln arrived for work that morning, just after an early meeting with the secret organization he had named the Youth For Valchondrian Reform. Granted, he chose a long and unwieldy name for them, but he saw himself as a reformer, and he saw his efforts as something positive for young people to join and celebrate, so he continued to use that name. He had considered names that used such words as "values" (Tquil's favorite), "crusade" (for a solid, military connotation), and "family" (because he liked exploiting the lack of extended family structure and what he considered its dilatory effect on the home world's society).

But he liked the name "Youth For Valchondrian Reform." It sounded noble. And Valchondrian children were as pliable as his superiors had suggested. He only needed to replace the wallscreen with a few slogans and a few drugs to make them his.

But he found no such fortune with Taldra. She wanted Hachen. Geln had thought that nothing could ever repulse him more than the thought of those two sharing a bed. He was wrong.

When Geln walked into the battery room that morning, he found Hachen staring at battery seven's monitor, comparing it to the graph chart he held in his hand. Hachen's flowing black hair had grown long, nearly to his waist, and it hung down into his face. He pushed it back with his long, thick fingers and looked Geln's way, but it was a while before he finally spoke.

"Geln, have you noticed something strange about the energy spikes in this battery?"

Geln wasn't sure how to answer. He had hoped that the doorway would open the day when he had first tapped into the special deposit of core energies that the Degrans had detected. He and Leader had already planned ways to keep Taldra and Hachen busy if needed, or remove them from the project if needed. Secretly, Geln had planned to simply kill them and make it look like an accident, a practice he knew well from his years in the secret branches of the Degran military.

But after all this time, there was no doorway. And even if the doorway appeared, he could never bring himself to kill Taldra. Hachen, yes, but not Taldra. He loved her too much. He hated loving her.

"Geln?" asked Hachen.

"Forgiveness. I just wasn't sure what you meant."

"The energy spikes are a mirror image of what they normally are. They're exactly the same, but in reverse."

Geln tilted his head. "I'll have Life run a diagnostic."

Hachen shrugged his shoulders. "Did that. She couldn't figure it out, either. Maybe we should shut down until Taldra gets back from the hospital."

Geln froze, and he feared that his tone might reveal his true feelings for her, so he spoke in a forced monotone. "Why is Taldra in hospital?"

"She'd been having some dizziness. I received clearance to run the tests myself, but I wasn't quite complete with my report."

Despite the efforts of Dr. Tquil, the Degrans had never managed to infiltrate or influence the Maintainers. Having never cared much for moralists, Geln saw the Maintainers as a stubborn, fanatical, and self-righteous lot. Therefore, the idea of Hachen doing something illegal and in defiance of the Maintainers mildly impressed Geln.

Setting the graphs on a worktable, Hachen explained: "She's pregnant, with twin boys."

Brothers. Like Geln and R'zrn. Geln thought of that day when he turned twelve years old. Though R'zrn was more than a year older than Geln, he had always been smaller and sickly. Geln could easily have dominated him, but chose instead to protect him.

That day, their father took them to the arena for the first time and showed them the dragon claw match. The claws were hollowed out, so they could be worn as gloves, with sharp talons.

The two women fighting wore protective padding everywhere but their faces. The taller of the two women, who looked at least forty, ripped her dragon claws through the padding on her younger opponent's shoulder. The crowd of soldiers cheered, many of them standing up and shaking their fists, as if the younger woman had somehow wronged them and was now receiving a well-deserved punishment.

Geln had heard about people cheering at executions in the same manner, and he wondered if this would lead to an execution. After all, no one ever talked about what went on in the arena. He could see why they went but never discussed what they saw: it was a shameful pleasure, enjoyed in crowds. Something about the cheering repulsed him while urging him to join.

R'zrn's thick lips trembled, his dark brown eyes wide with horror.

Their father—a tall, menacing force in their lives—acknowledged R'zrn's reaction with a grunt of disgust. He grabbed R'zrn by the collar bone and told him, "When this is over, boy, it's the two of us. You've been the weaker for too long."

The match soon ended. To the relief of both boys, the goal was simply for one woman to dislodge the other's claws from both hands. The older woman won, receiving further adoration from the crowd. As that crowd dispersed, Geln's father went and spoke to the two women, who left both sets of claws behind for him as they walked out opposite exits.

He motioned into the stands. "Come down here, boys." They looked at each other. R'zrn's eyes reflected Geln's fears. Their father added, "Now!"

They stepped over the benches slowly then climbed the railing to the dirt area of the arena. Their father put on a set of the dragon claws and glared at R'zrn. Those eyes always frightened R'zrn and Geln. They stared cold through the tiny slits that hid under a forehead that looked like an unfinished sculpture, a misshapen piece of core rock.

"Put the other pair on," he told R'zrn, his voice filled with challenge.

R'zrn's tiny body trembled, as he tried to speak. "But, sir, no padding," he finally managed to stutter out.

"Do you think you'll have padding when you must defend your home against the evil ones? Do you think the civil wars will stop because no one let you strap a pillow over the weak little heart that keeps you at the healers?" He drew closer, leaning his rock-like face down to the gentle, sweating face of R'zrn. "Do you?" he demanded, shouting.

Geln had always stood by when their father seemed too harsh with R'zrn. But he couldn't stand by this time. "Father, please don't do this."

Their father's head turned slowly and with slight jerks, like the setting knob on the laser rifle he had given Geln on Colonization Day. "Geln, your brother is going to be drafted, and so are you. The draft age is dropping from fourteen to twelve. There aren't enough soldiers left to fight the evil ones."

Geln stood dumbfounded, stuttering as badly as R'zrn. "But they'll station us together, won't they?"

He shook his head. "The military isn't a family place. You'll both stand alone: no brothers, no sisters, no friends."

For a moment, their father's eyes revealed a great sadness, but he spoiled that moment by using the dragon claws to slash the air just in front of R'zrn's face. As he swung again, R'zrn stopped fidgeting with the dragon claws and pulled his hands into them. They hung loosely and almost fell off.

"Grip the insides with your fingers," he told R'zrn. "Or you'll lose. And I'll not be as gentle as those two women."

He swung with his other hand this time, but Geln lunged between them, shouting, "Father, no!" The action was too sudden, too unexpected. If their father wanted to avoid what happened, he was unable. But Geln always doubted it was an accident. Two of the claws ripped through Geln's right cheek, nearly gauging his eye. He fell backwards, into his brother's arms. R'zrn screamed Geln's name, holding the claws outward so they couldn't scratch him.

"Why are you like this, Father?" R'zrn demanded, his soft voice suddenly defiant.

"So you can survive." He made the statement as if it were totally logical and indisputable. Then he tossed the dragon claws to the ground. "I want you boys to remember the things I've taught you."

"Oh, I remember, Father," said Geln, feeling a strange heat rise through his body and into the jagged scars beneath his eye.

"Forgiveness?" asked Hachen.

The battery chamber glowed and rumbled. Life's warning sensors buzzed.

"I remember your saying you want to be a father. I—"

Hachen shook him. Geln despised Hachen's touch. He almost felt like making use of his training and simply killing Hachen at that moment, just as he had wanted to grab one of those dragon claws from R'zrn and kill his father.

"Geln, the energy's affecting you too, isn't it? I have this strange feeling, like I'm being pulled backwards."

"Yes." The temporal doorway was opening. A blast of light emerged from the glass cylinder that housed battery seven. It began spinning around the room. Separate waves and sparkles of multi-colored lights danced inside the larger light. *What a pity for Hachen, to only see this spectacle through the limiting eyes of the virus.*

The battery itself turned into pure light, and the silhouette of a man stepped through it, his tall body a shadow in an explosion of incandescence. Hachen reached for a Maintainer button, but Geln urged him to wait. Someone was stepping through from the past, from the intertwined past of Valchondria and Degranon.

As the lights springing into his face and body allowed his features to emerge, they revealed a middle-aged man of immediately evident wisdom and confidence—his brown head fully shaved, his dark eyes gleaming with wonder, his simple robe stretched by a muscular body. But most surprising and impressive of all, he didn't look the least bit frightened or astounded. Instead, he merely looked delighted and curious, like an explorer who knew where he was going but not what he would find when he arrived.

Geln touched the man's shoulder, just to make sure he wasn't a hologram from the Wall System Conglomerate. He didn't even acknowledge Geln's touch; instead, he slipped by Geln and Hachen.

"Geln!" Hachen's hand again reached for the button. "He's a walkway person. He's probably been sleeping in here, and the explosion woke him. We don't know if he's medicated."

Geln pulled Hachen's arm away, though not as forcefully as he wanted. "Think, Hachen. How could a walkway person get inside Life Unit? Even with the hand panel and the voice recognition, we have trouble sometimes. Nothing can get through the entrance without Life's permission."

Hachen pointed at the man, who barely seemed to notice them. He was too busy taking in the sights and sounds of the battery room. "Then how did he get in here?

"Through battery seven."

Hachen's eyes narrowed. "Are you crumbled?"

"You've studied time/space dimension theory."

"With a stress on the word 'theory.' And the only research happened in space, which meant the end of that research."

"But what if we were looking above us when we should have been looking below us?"

"Forgiveness?"

Geln waved his hands about. He couldn't think of how to explain such matters to Valchondrians, with all the ignorance that their isolationism had caused them. Degrans learned about core energy and other scientific insights long before their teens, along with math, writing, and military strategy. The later part of childhood went to military service.

Geln's superiors had taken Leader through the Degran doorway to explain everything about doorways and what had happened to the colonists, and even that required a great deal of time. While Naldod surpassed Leader in intelligence, he had never benefited from such an experience.

Geln continued, "Valchondria is alive with powers that we all use daily and only pretend to understand. What if the powers include the ability to jump through dimensions of time and space? What if this man is—?" He was revealing too much too quickly when the stranger finally returned his gesture of greeting by touching him on the shoulder.

"You seem so real," the stranger said, his deep voice resonating in the room. Geln noticed that he had a large mole near his left ear lobe. Moles on an adult Valchondrian generally suggested extreme poverty, since facial modification could easily remedy such imperfections. "Is this a vision?"

"Sir, we're not involved in undermall vision casting," insisted Hachen, obviously shaking at the thought of Maintainer intervention. The Maintainers had been complaining a great deal lately about Project Life Unit and the goals of its creators. "I suggest you explain your presence here, rather than making accusations."

The stranger walked around him, eyeing him with the same curiosity he showed to Life. "Glory, my friend. I'm not familiar with undermall or vision casting, and I mean you no harm. I've seen fire sparks in the secret cave, but nothing of this magnitude."

"Sir, we are real," said Geln, touching his shoulder again to prove it. "Might I ask what time you're from?"

"It's the afternoon, of course."

"But what date? And on what world?"

"Forgiveness, but I know nothing of dates or worlds. Valchondria is the only world, and it's the afternoon."

Geln couldn't hold back the smile that disrupted his face. He had always teased R'zrn for smiling so widely, but he knew that he sometimes did the same. "Hachen, this man just walked through time."

The realization seemed to slap Hachen on the side of the face, but he soon became as comfortable and fascinated with the stranger as Geln was. The stranger introduced himself as Alom, one of the priests of a village called "Dalii." They quickly surmised that priests once held the same power as Maintainers, and that Dalii would one day become Valcine.

Since Alom knew nothing about even the crudest technologies, Hachen was the first to say that he probably came from thousands of years in the past. All that they learned of that past seemed to fascinate Hachen as much as it did Geln. But Hachen seemed much more saddened than Geln by the revelation that Alom's spouse had died without leaving him a child to serve as his apprentice.

It was then that a plan came to Geln, and he voiced it before thinking about how insane it sounded. "What if we kept the second child secret, and let him be apprentice to Alom? We could bring him back when he's old enough for facial modification, or sooner if colonization re-starts."

Hachen looked dumbfounded and stammered about. "Well, no, people can't…. Won't that defeat the purpose of giving Alom an apprentice? Who would become their priest if my child is no longer there…then?"

Alom's sense of wonder was fading into confusion, but he still managed to explain: "There's another priest, with another apprentice. She was just born this season. She would be next in line." While Hachen brooded, like a man lost in a fog, Alom tried to understand: "Gratitude for your suggestion, but I can't see your aim. You can only have one child?"

"Yes," said Geln, nodding solemnly. "The other would be destroyed, unless you would be willing to do this thing we ask."

Alom looked shocked by that revelation, even more so than by their request. "I see that you want to protect your child, but you don't know me."

Hachen touched his shoulder. "I feel that I do, somehow, as if we've been occupying the same space in two different times. And considering the alternative, I have no choice, unless you consider this task."

"This honor," said Alom. "I should return to my people, or they'll worry about me. But I wish to see both of you soon, and to meet Taldra."

"We look forward to that," said Geln. "But there is one other item. Perhaps it would be best for the child's safety, and for time's safety, if no one knew about the time doorway."

Alom flung his hand over his head. "All these words about time! Time means nothing to me, but I will honor your wish, for the child's sake. I only feel shame that it may cause me to lie to my people."

Geln said, "This is one of those cases where you have to deceive people." He felt absurd for making that statement. His whole life had turned into a case of deceiving people. But he couldn't just tell all the Valchondrians that he wanted to replace their entire way of life with the true way. They weren't ready for that. Instead, he needed to pose as Taldra's assistant to do his work.

Still, he wished he could be honest about one thing: his love for Taldra. At least he could do this one thing for her. Maybe one day, she would realize that he was the one who led her to the doorway, thus saving her son.

He wanted her to see that. He wanted her to love him.

Soon Alom was gone, and then Hachen went home, leaving Geln to ponder the madness of his own idea. His mission on Valchondria was to last indefinitely, but he feared that he might be abusing that freedom. He was supposed to take the journey back in time himself, not send someone else back in time. Maybe sending the child would make Taldra love him. Maybe it would give him some sort of victory over Hachen. Maybe it would help him gather more information about ancient Degranon. He wasn't really sure what he hoped to accomplish with this new scheme, other than separating two brothers so that both of them could live.

"No brothers, no sisters, no friends," Geln whispered to himself as he piloted his hovercraft down the hoverlanes, toward the barren apartment that awaited him in a secret area of Valcine Plaza.

Geln was only fifteen years old on the night his commander woke him in the barracks. Touching his forehead in an almost maternal gesture, she told him, "Your parents are going to contact you soon, but I thought you should have someone tell you in person first."

"Tell me what, sir?" He asked the question, despite knowing the answer. He could see it in her eyes, and he began crying. That was the last time he ever cried. "No."

"The entire red fleet was destroyed. All are confirmed dead. Your brother's firejet was leading the charge. He died a hero."

The tears burned the scars on Geln's face as he sat up, destroyed by the shock. "Gratitude."

"You're my best trainee, but I'm willing to give—"

He interrupted her, something he had never dared before. "Please don't give me anything but the hardest, most dangerous missions."

"Geln…."

"Please, I need to fight the evil ones, for R'zrn, for Degranon."

"For yourself?" The lines on her black forehead revealed the deep compassion she felt for him at that moment. She had told him about her three daughters. In fact, she had only recently returned to duty after taking maternity time for her youngest, Jase-Dawn. Geln could somehow tell that she was thinking of those children and of losing them to the evil ones.

"For myself, for you, for your children. Tell me what I can do to protect and strengthen Degranon. I'll do it." The tears dried, and the trembling stopped, but his father's words echoed in his mind: "No brothers, no sisters, no friends."

CHAPTER 5

❀

*T*aldra sat at the kitchen table, nibbling a gredga chip with total incredulity. Hachen paced around her in his usual excited fashion, nearly running into the plastic walls and cabinets at times, swirling about in the gray spectacle of a room. If she weren't afraid of getting caught, Taldra would have bought some red or blue paint in the undermall, just to brighten up at least the kitchen.

She asked Hachen, "So, your plan, which was suggested by Geln, is that we send one of our twins backwards in time, after concealing him throughout my pregnancy."

Hachen stopped pacing and turned his head back slightly. "It sounds much more reasonable when Geln says it."

"I don't know how. To the side, I thought you hated Geln."

"I never said that. He's just annoying at times."

"Hm!" She bit into another gredga chip, enjoying the intense, tingly sweetness of it, and trying not to think about the fact that the exclusive manufacturer of gredga chips often sponsored anti-colony programs on the wallscreen. The celebrities on those programs always bashed Project Life Unit. For that matter, they often bashed everyone and everything, even while their own ranks kept disappearing. Valcine's citizens disappeared all the time: into the walkways, into the hospitals, into the drug undermall, into the wallscreen parlors, into nothing.

Taldra almost wanted to disappear, not from Hachen, but from her own body. It already hurt all over from the pregnancy. But she considered the idea of her baby disappearing in such a way, and the idea of her baby becoming a new kind of explorer. Those ideas somehow made a bizarre sort of sense to Taldra, as they apparently had to her spouse. And she trusted Hachen, more than she had ever trusted anyone, just as she loved him more than she had ever loved anyone.

So she agreed to meet with Alom, and to return to the secret cave with him. The beauty of the spinning colors enraptured her as she stepped through them with Hachen, Geln, and Alom. Standing there in that strange, humid place, thousands of years in the past, she made the decision that would allow them to defy the Maintainers.

Still, she somehow knew that Geln's plan wouldn't come to fruition in exactly the manner he had proposed it. Something foreboding lurked beneath Geln's eyes, behind those scars he would never discuss. But she would have to confront that threat some other day. For now, she only wanted to protect both of her children, and this was the only way.

❧   ❧   ❧

Hachen watched his balding coworker, Dr. Geln, wrap the newborn infant into his robe, making his stomach look nearly past regulation weight-for-height guidelines. Hachen also watched his sleeping spouse in the hospital bed, and the other newborn in the pod attached to it. Taldra's eyes opened as the door slid shut behind Dr. Geln. Despite her long black hair clinging to her face from the sweat of delivery, she looked no different from the beautiful young woman Hachen had met a year earlier.

Her gray eyes sparkled like no eyes Hachen had ever seen. Actually, she had broken the law by secretly telling him that her eyes were light brown, but, unlike his gifted spouse, he couldn't see in color. He couldn't even see the redness of her skin, though he knew from history class that most people on Valchondria have red, brown, or black skin, and some of the people who had once lived there had yellow or white skin. To him, everyone simply looked white or black. He clasped the slender hand that reached toward the tiny person in the infant pod that was attached to the bed.

"I'll get him," said Hachen. He gently lifted the pale infant, who was wrapped in a white cloth as soft and warm as his skin.

"I was hoping to be able to say 'them.'" She accepted the crying child into her arms, and he grew quiet as she rocked him back and forth.

"We had to work quickly. It's bad enough we're violating the codes. We can't jeopardize Geln's career as well as our own."

"I know, Hachen. I just wanted a chance to see them both. I can't believe I passed out during the birth."

"I think those mind relaxants had something to do with it. I'm just glad no other healers came in. No one knows except for you, me, and Geln."

"Wouldn't the gossip masters love this story? 'Leading scientists discover a rift in time and transport illegal twin into the past. Check your collector for details.'" She rubbed the tiny infant's red face, and he seemed to smile. "Is this Argen, or Telius?"

"Argen," said Hachen, sitting down on the edge of the bed. They had agreed on given names for the twins long before Taldra even started showing. "They're identical. I performed a genetic scan; they're both healthy and of potentially high intellect. Telius will need that to survive in his primitive environment."

"But you said the village is peaceful. Hachen, where are we send-ing our baby?"

"Someplace where he at least has a chance." Hachen had never seen her look so vulnerable before, like anyone could crush her with a touch. Before, she always projected herself as brave and outspoken, sometimes even reckless, but he could tell becoming a mother would change her. Somehow, she seemed less courageous but more protec-tive. He tried to think of words to reassure her. "The village is peaceful. I just meant that he won't have all the luxuries and protections we have. He'll be like…well, like the people who live on the colonies."

The look of worry gave way to one of wonder. "I like that analogy." She smiled at the baby who slept in her arms. "Maybe one day, we'll all be on one colony together, the four of us."

"That sounds nice." He gently lifted Argen from her arms and returned him to the pod without waking him. He wished he could still share Taldra's surety that they would live in outer space one day, but the Maintainers fought all such notions. Still, he thought the video chip tour that Taldra had started might make renewed colonization a reality in the distant future, especially with her strong media presence. Even if they didn't live to see the day, they could at least know that the twins were safe, and had benefited from all their work.

"I have to turn in—" He decided not to finish the sentence. They had used Life Unit's advanced wallscreen capabilities to create records that appeared to be from the hospital scanners. That act alone could cause him to lose his healer license, and probably land all three of them in Urloan Control. It was best not to say it aloud; in fact, he realized that they should not have been speaking about the twins aloud. He had passed the Maintainer camera in the hallways constantly. What if they were now also putting listening devices in the rooms?

Even Leader and the SSC would not protect them from the Maintainers, not that the SSC was as pro-colony as they claimed. Their overpopulated world presented far too many problems for its governing body, when the simple solution for most of those problems was to relocate part of the population onto other worlds, like their ancestors had done. But few people listened to him or Taldra. Even the SSC made it clear that they doubted Life Unit would ever be used for its intended purpose: an energy source for colonies. Yet they still funded it.

He kissed Taldra on her forehead, tasting the salt from dried sweat. "Now get some sleep. Your part is finished, and Geln is bringing Telius into the doorway."

She motioned him away. "Go get everything else done. I'm not leaving for a while."

He smiled, almost laughing, then picked up the box of computer chips and palm machines that he needed for completing his task. As soon as he arrived on the control floor, another healer stopped him, but only to ask about the score from a pressure tournament. Hachen told him the score, and he moved on, without questioning.

Hachen slipped into the control room, passing a few computer technicians who were playing wallscreen games and eating gredga chips. They barely seemed to notice him, since healers went wherever they chose in Valcine Regal Hospital.

He walked around several corridors of video chip file cabinets before coming to the up-link wallscreen that led back to the computer where the technicians were supposedly working. Just before passing a Maintainer camera, he placed a device on its side that would cause the next ten camera sweeps to skip it.

Geln had purchased the device in the undermall, and they had decided not to ask about why he already had such connections. Sometimes Geln seemed incredibly sinister, and Hachen resented how much they needed him. But they did need him, so they said nothing to him about his undermall purchase.

After the device buzzed, Hachen removed it and walked past the camera, to the wallscreen. Just as he finished his work and stood back up, another healer approached him.

"What were you doing there?" she demanded. She looked near or slightly past her height/weight ratio. She only came up to Hachen's chest, but she easily passed his weight.

"I'm not accustomed to being questioned in such a tone, especially not by a healer who doesn't even wear an SSC logo. Do you think I need additional emotional torment while my spouse is in hospital? Are you able to deal with heavy-stress situations? I truly doubt your heart could survive it, especially considering that you're at least ten percent over regulation weight and probably will have to pay a fine at your next exam. Why, someone of your bulk would probably fall dead at the slightest stress. You look like you're hyperventilating now."

"There is no reason to threaten me with regulations, Doctor…Doctor…."

She would know he was a healer from the squares of his headband, and that he was an SSC member from the line through those squares, but he had hoped that she would recognize him immediately and walk away. He had almost forgotten his headband, and had driven back home to get it. The staff on his floor would have allowed him without any identification, but it just seemed like a form of protectively safe traditionalism, a way of not looking like a threat to Valchondria.

"Doctor Naldod," he said.

"Oh," she replied, tilting her head back slightly. "Dr. Lorfeltez's spouse." She walked away without saying anything else.

She used that recognition as an insult, a response to his insult, but he let it go, knowing he deserved it. He knew that invoking the height/weight ratio would unnerve any woman, but he still hated resorting to such tactics. After all, Geln and a lot of other men lived over the height/weight ratio without ever receiving a fine. The only men the Maintainers ever fined over height/weight were clean-ups, but that was usually just an excuse for deleting their jobs, leaving them to become walkway people. Hachen abhorred the hypocrisy and inconsistency of the Maintainers. Sometimes, he wanted to punch them all, knocking the smug countenance from their frequently modified faces.

Just after he pushed past the healer, he uttered a curse—not at her, but at the insanity of his situation. They were sending their baby through time, to a place without computers, hovercrafts, hospitals, or wallscreens. What would happen to Telius?

When Hachen's parents both died in hospital within two years of each other, it made him despise their insistence that he become a healer, for all the good that healers had done in his life. Now he was glad that he had at least obtained dual degrees, so he could pursue healing part-time. He really only wanted to be a scientist. The urgings of his parents had saved their grandson's life; if he weren't a healer, the plan never would have worked.

"Gratitude," he whispered to his mother and father, across the divide of life and death.

Hachen lumbered through the long white hallway, amid the sounds of emergencies and intercoms, amid the rushing of healers from one room to the next, wishing that his parents had lived to see their two beautiful grandchildren, or simply that they had lived. He lost them; he wasn't going to lose one of his boys.

CHAPTER 6

❀

$\mathcal{A}$s quickly as the hoverlanes would allow, Dr. Geln returned to the triangular machine/building that Taldra had so quaintly named "Life Unit." Once inside, he took Telius from the filtered blue box he'd been carrying him in and cradled him. The infant's tiny hands seemed to wave at Geln.

"Now, you have to be careful, Telius," said Geln. "We have to get you back one day. But don't wait around for your parents. I'm the one who will bring you back. With you, I gain knowledge of the original Degranon, and I gain so much more."

Geln laughed to himself, remembering the wedding Taldra had invited him to—her wedding. She looked so beautiful that day, disturbingly so, in her wedding dress. As a spy who had gained favor both with the military and with his circle's Control, he could have had virtually any Degran for his spouse. But Valchondria only knew him as a member of the SSC and as one of the assistants to Dr. Lorfeltez. On Valchondria, he was little more than a shadow, a clean-up with a doctorate—not that any actual clean-up would ever have a chance for a higher education in Valchondria's oppressive class system.

Geln had tried to capture Taldra's attention, but she didn't seem to know men existed, other than Hachen. Hachen, for all his genius, lacked the discipline and courage of his spouse. Besides, he looked painfully ordinary to Geln; unlike most upper-class residents of Valcine, Hachen had never bothered with facial modification.

Geln couldn't see why she would give Hachen a second glance. But she accepted Leader's request that Hachen become her other assistant on Life Unit. Then she fell in love with him, and became married with him. But worst of all, she invited Dr. Geln, her other dear assistant, to the wedding, where he had to pretend not to recognize all the Degran spies in key Valchondrian positions, where he had to pretend that he did not want to drain the life blood from Hachen's heart.

"I could just as easily kill the child and find someone else to help with my work," Geln said to himself. "I can even do the research myself. What does Valchondria need of another Hachen, or two more Hachens?" Telius began to cry, and Geln realized he was holding the infant too tightly as he walked toward the battery room where the temporal doorway had opened.

Just as he had planned, Life Unit's roots collected energy from beneath Valchondria's surface at just the right place, and they had pulled the doorway up through one of its batteries. What Taldra and Hachen had not realized was that such doorways often exist within planets, or that Degran technology had led Geln to choose where Life Unit would be built. With his access to Life Unit and his secret understanding of both temporal doorways and spatial doorways, Geln had managed to adjust the doorway enough to get it closer than any of his people had ever gotten to the time of the great kings of Degranon. And now he was taking Taldra's child there. Yes, he would let Telius live, but he would avenge Taldra's rejection, her insult.

The doorway opening presented itself via a swirl of colors, surrounded by man-sized battery cylinders and computer panels. Geln walked through it, into a glowing cave, where he saw Alom, who always wore a red robe when Geln saw him. Alom stood holding out his arms, looking like an athlete about to receive a trophy he knew he would have to return. Geln gave him the child.

"This is Telius."

"Where are Hachen and Taldra?" asked Alom. "Have your leaders harmed them?"

"No." Geln immediately regretted saying "No." He could have let Telius think they were dead. Then he would have less trouble getting Telius to go back with him instead of them. Then again, his true plans were still developing in his mind. He hated this confusion—this conflict—that Taldra caused him. Before his goals had been so singular and simple: serving Degranon. But now? Now he schemed for her benefit and worked begrudgingly with her pathetic spouse. "Taldra had some trouble with the birth, and Hachen is staying with her. But they're both fine."

"Good. When can I bring Telius to see them?"

"Well, you can't risk going to Life Unit again. But they have control over the doorway now. They told me that they're going to make it here once a week, at this hour and day, and they'll come here to visit Telius. Just keep bringing him to the cave."

"They can't visit more often? Why can't they stay here?"

"Because...they're very noble, idealistic people. They believe they can change the Valchondria of our time and help it return to the other worlds they told you about. But they will be here to see Telius; give him that promise. And they'll reward you for taking care of him."

Alom shook his head. "I want no reward, only the honor of doing so. I only wish he didn't have to be apart from his parents for such long periods. For a family to be divided that long seems...unnatural."

"You will raise him well, won't you?" asked Geln, touching Telius's chin. The infant looked so tiny against his hand! "It really hurts me to see Taldra and Hachen worried. Please assure me that there's no reason for them to worry."

"I can assure you of that. I'll teach him all I know, and I'll protect him."

"Protect? Is there anything in particular you would protect him from?"

Alom's eyes widened. "No. I chose my words poorly."

"There are no conquering people, no hostile armies?"

"No. Nothing like that. My people deal swiftly with violence."

"Well, be sure he is not ignorant of your history, or of any other peoples you know of. Our people see ignorance as dangerous. You would insult his parents by not seeing that he learns everything possible about your time."

"I won't fail them." A hint of annoyance crept into Alom's voice, as if Geln had questioned his competence.

"I have to leave now," said Geln. "Oh, I should mention that, because of the virus that protects us from all illness, my people see everything as white, black, or gray, and we might not hear every sound that you hear. You will have to explain to Telius that his perceptions are slightly different from yours."

"Is your aim that the sky is not blue to him?"

"Yes. Your robe is gray to Hachen and Taldra. I can see that the robe is red, but that's extremely unusual, and I'm not even supposed to tell anyone that I can see in color. It's unlikely that Telius will have the same gift."

"Red is the color of our village."

"How…pleasant," said Geln, as he stepped through the fading doorway, back into the darkness of Life Unit.

CHAPTER 7

Three days later, Taldra and Hachen were working on a ruptured battery tentacle when Life's dull lighting began to fade up and down.

Taldra turned off her laser drill and looked upward from the cramped utility room. The most annoying design flaw they'd overlooked was that a triangular building of Life's size would only give maximum space at its very center. So, while the battery room and its surrounding control room offered a break from the elbow-bumping work environment, the storage rooms and the utility rooms offered no such refuge. For that reason, Taldra tried to avoid being in the outer rooms with Geln. With Hachen, she usually didn't mind.

Hachen also looked up. "Life?"

"Yes, Dr. Naldod?"

"Battery three's tentacle should be off-line. Did we cause that power fluctuation?" He set his laser drill back onto one of the many shelves of the cluttered little room.

"No, Dr. Naldod. You told me to take battery three off-line completely, and you've never programmed me with the human traits of forgetting or willfully disobeying."

Taldra laughed slightly as she pushed away from the thick, metallic coil and stretched her arms above her head. "You're charming enough without those traits, Life. What caused the lights to fade?"

"The thing you call 'doorway' has reached its peak and is beginning to close. Should I leave a message in Dr. Geln's collector?"

"Yes," said Hachen. After saying that, he lowered his gaze to Taldra and tried desperately to look calm. She could tell that he really felt anything but calm.

They rushed into the battery room, only to find the doorway's sparks collapsing on the floor like the final snowflakes of a brief blizzard. Hachen squeezed Taldra's hand, but she could feel nothing.

"Taldra?" Geln was there in response to the collector message that Life sent for Taldra and Hachen, but the sensors in his secret office had just told him the same thing: the doorway had gone inactive. The temporal energies were still present, but they had stopped colliding at a fast enough rate to keep the doorway open or reactivate each other.

Taldra was working even more frantically than usual, running holographic projections of the energy deposits they had found. He could see from the red in her eyes that she had been crying.

"Taldra?" he asked again. "Have you had any success?"

She turned off the projections that surrounded them. "No. Hachen's in the back utility room. We've been working nonstop. I...."

"It's all right." He reached for her but forced himself not to make contact. She looked so vulnerable, so fragile, so unlike the fearless and tireless Dr. Lorfeltez that kept the gossip masters busy on the wallscreen.

It wasn't all right. Despite all his efforts and his hidden knowledge about other doorways, Geln couldn't think of how to make this doorway re-open. They worked past the point of exhaustion, but kept trying everything that might possibly help.

✤   ✤   ✤

Late that night, Hachen caught Geln dozing against the master control panel and insisted that he go home with them. The idea thrilled and repulsed him, but he declined. Hachen persisted, sincerely worried that Geln might crash his hovercraft, and Geln accepted.

To Geln's disappointment, Taldra never left the master bedroom, leaving Hachen to put Argen to bed in the baby room. It seemed that she wasn't there at all, in her own house. But she filled Geln's dreams anyway.

✤   ✤   ✤

The next morning, as the three of them were walking back to Life Unit, a holographic image sprang from Geln's credit box and started explaining options for upgrading his wallscreen package. Equally surprising was the sudden burst of laughter that came from Hachen. It was the first time Geln had seen him smile since the doorway's collapse.

"I'm not interested," Geln told the transparent woman, who floated beside them as they walked. She kept explaining anyway, though he knew that she was programmed to relay vocal responses to her controller at Wall System Conglomerate.

She eventually finished her presentation and disappeared, just before they reached Life's entrance. After he stopped laughing his whispered laugh, Hachen remarked, "Those holographic ads don't usually come up unless your credit box is top level. Do you have a side job now?"

Geln shook his head as he placed his open hand on the recognition box, letting Life check his fingerprints and his genetic structure. "No, the SSC keeps me busy enough. It was probably a computer glitch."

"How unfortunate," said Taldra, as Life said Geln's name and slid open the door. "You're on a holo-list now." She tried to smile like Hachen, but Geln could see how intensely sad they both were about the failure of the doorway. As much as he hated Hachen and felt betrayed by Taldra, Geln couldn't help but share in their sorrow. But he also resented them for bringing up those feelings in him, those feelings of lost family.

CHAPTER 8

A singular light in the corner of the baby room revealed only Argen's crib and the murals of outer space that Taldra had purchased during her pregnancy. As she held her five-month-old son against her breast, she couldn't stop thinking about the other son that they had sent through time. Sent through time! The whole concept was so bizarre, so unlikely!

Even after all that happened, she still couldn't quite pull her mind around the concept. Dr. Geln had calculated the trajectory for Life Unit's tentacles, after tracking a fault line that contained Valchondria's core energies. Valchondria held an abundance of such energies; they powered the hovercrafts, the lane-lights, the homes, the schools, the malls, the credit boxes, and everything else. They protected everyone from the harsh Valchondrian summers and winters. But Taldra, Hachen, and Geln designed tentacles even more elastic than those used by the Power Holders or the Wall System Conglomerate.

With those tentacles, Life could find the energies of any planet, protecting the colonists who used her. And Geln used them to tap into energies unlike anything that anyone had ever encountered before.

Geln.

Of course Taldra appreciated all the work Geln put into the project, and all of his constant support of her pro-colony efforts. But she couldn't stop regretting her decision to let him take Telius from them. He stole her child, sending him to that strange, primitive time.

Sure, Alom seemed like the strongest yet most gentle person she had met since her parents. But people changed. Her parents certainly changed! What if Alom grew weary of Telius or one day saw him as an embarrassment?

Argen pushed away from her breast, gurgling slightly. His green eyes sparkled like his father's blue eyes. She wondered if she should confess her long-standing fears to Hachen. Something about Geln scared her beyond measure. Though she liked that he shared their pro-colony views, she worried that he held some deeper, darker agenda.

And the way he had looked at her that day after she proposed to Hachen! He looked like he wanted to kill someone: maybe her, maybe Hachen, maybe himself, or maybe just the next walkway person who begged him for credits.

Hachen entered the room as Taldra closed her black shirt over her breast, fastening it with the buttons on her left shoulder. From the glimmer in the blue eyes she had just been thinking about, she could tell he had good news. They needed good news.

"The doorway energies are building back up," he said, excitedly. After kissing his spouse and his son, he added, "From measuring the spike patterns, Geln thinks the doorway is now working in cycles of five months, with an opening at the height of its cycle. He's worked out a formula that shows how it will keep repeating."

They had worked out formulas before, projecting every possibility, except for some unknown flow of nature. It sounded strangely plausible to Taldra. She set Argen in his crib then hugged her spouse tightly. "We'll see Telius again! We'll...." Her voice trailed off with a realization: "How will Alom know? He's probably given up by now."

Hachen stepped back, still holding her arms with his. "Alom said that he prays in the secret cave all the time, that it's his place of quiet. Maybe he's seen some activity there."

"And if there's no activity on that side? How will he know when to be there? How will we find him?"

Hachen's countenance announced his determination to not give up hope. "Alom also said that his village is near the cave. We'll find him. We're explorers. Why not explore the past?"

"You're right! That's what Telius is doing."

They stood together, comforting each other.

❦   ❦   ❦

Less than a week later, Geln's theory proved itself. Exactly five months from the day the doorway first opened, it opened again.

Taldra sat in the control room, trying to focus on the research she needed for her next status report to the Supreme Science Council. Geln's voice came to her over the intercom, asking her to join him in the battery room.

She looked through the glass, at the first few multi-colored sparks that bounced around the room. They looked even more beautiful than she remembered. After activating her wallscreen, she spoke into it: "Dr. Lorfeltez, chosen name Taldra. Urgency. Voice print: Valcine Regal Hospital, D5,281,965."

After a slight delay, Hachen's unshaved face appeared on the screen. "Forgiveness for taking so long. Argen's training hasn't quite…. Well, side that. Are you calling about the doorway?"

"Yes. How soon can you be here?"

"Well, Argen's having one of his moods, so I don't think I should bring him. I think he needs a nap. I'll call to see if the watcher is available."

The sparks grew more plentiful and started encircling each other. Geln darted about the battery room, checking readings, his scarred face vibrant with enthusiasm.

Taldra knew how difficult Argen could be, so she understood Hachen's lack of focus. With just a hint of impatience, she told him,

"I don't think I've heard an actual answer yet, Hachen. The doorway looks like it's about to open."

Hachen pulled his mane back. His wide-eyed expression revealed that her words and their implications had suddenly registered with him. "We're on our way, one tired father and one perturbed baby, ready for time travel."

Taldra laughed. "Just move your feet this way. We'll see if the boys still look identical."

"Glory," said Hachen. The screen went black before re-booting with collector headlines. But the news of the day held no interest for Taldra. She went to the battery room, looking for news of yesterday: the yesterday that protected Telius.

"Did you contact Hachen?" asked Geln. He set aside his hand machine in favor of simply watching the spectacle that swirled around them.

Taldra couldn't help but wonder if he could see in color. Even though it was illegal to talk about such matters, and even though she never liked Geln very much, she hoped that he could see what she saw at that moment. Still, she resisted telling him about her color-sight; it was bad enough that she had told Hachen.

"He's bringing Argen," she told Geln, whose beady eyes followed the sparks in their circles. "They'll be here promptly."

"Good. I hope it opens before they get here."

"So do I," said Taldra, her fingers locked together beneath her chin.

She felt a brief chill as the swirl of sparks grew more concentrated and danced around battery seven, which became a focal point of radiant white energy. Alom stepped through the light, wearing a long red robe and cradling Telius in a red blanket that almost looked like part of the robe. Taldra shouted her son's name.

"I knew I would find you again," said Alom, in that deep, majestic voice of his. Telius looked perfectly healthy. His guardian had kept him from harm. "Forgiveness for coming here instead of waiting, but I couldn't stand another moment!"

"Gratitude for not giving up," she replied, as Alom handed Telius over to her. He still looked identical to Argen, but no one had ever handed Argen over to anyone else without making him cry. "Gratitude for everything," she added, as she held her son and rocked him slowly.

Alom nodded and then looked over to Geln. "Geln, it is good to see you as well."

"And you," he replied. "How did you know that the doorway was re-opening?"

"I was there three days ago when the sparks starting rising from the ground, like embers from a buried fire. I told my people that I needed to go away and meditate for a few days. Telius and I have been living in the cave since then. I was so worried when the doorway faded before, but I never gave up hope."

"I only recently discovered that it's a five-month cycle, with the doorway only opening for a few days at a time. We—" Geln stopped talking when Life announced Hachen's arrival. "Well, there will be time for explanations later."

The reunion was joyful. Despite all the trepidation that Taldra and Hachen now felt about the plan, they decided that Telius should remain in the past. They would simply work with Valchondria's natural cycle.

Five months later, they all found each other again. Five months after that, the three scientists wrestled with their instruments, ran their calculations, waited for sparks that never came.

On the other side of time, Telius was speaking his first words and walking his earliest steps. He wandered about the cave while Alom kneeled, praying desperately.

Telius tugged on Alom's robe, his pudgy young face revealing no trace of the sadness it would later show whenever they visited the cave.

"Gone," said Telius, as if his parents were playing a game with him and hiding behind one of the boulders in the cave. "Gone."

Alom opened his eyes and stood up. "I hope you're wrong, Telius. Those people look at you like you're the brightest star in the sky. You need to grow up seeing that love, even if it's only for a short visit at a time. I hope they're not gone."

Telius shook his head and looked solemn. "Gone."

❦   ❦   ❦

The event seemed perfect. The entire Supreme Science Council and most of its local researchers gathered at a dinner to reward remarkable achievements. One achievement brought a thunderous applause. During its first year of operation, Project Life Unit proved that it could sustain human life in any environment, providing oxygen and power to the people that inhabited it. It also provided a laboratory for testing batteries, tentacles, and various other technologies.

Many people at the dinner spoke of Life Unit's applications underwater, in the desert, or in the still-unexplored South Edge. Hachen always found it odd that no one ever changed the names of North Edge or South Edge to something that suggested Valchondria's spherical shape; thousands of years had passed since anyone thought the world was flat. But this new discovery he assisted, it would change more than words.

He looked at his beautiful spouse in her newly designed dress, and knew she could only think of one place to use Life Unit: on other planets. Of course, she just couldn't say that aloud.

At times like these, he almost forgot the pain of losing Telius, and the nagging feeling that he would never see Telius again. He could almost forget all of his fears. But then something would disrupt his joy, something like the young man standing over him at the table, pressing gently on his collarbone.

The errander whispered, "Forgiveness, Dr. Naldod, but you were having your collector messages forwarded here."

"Yes," Hachen whispered back, turning to the young man while Taldra accepted an award. "Is it my son's watcher?"

"No, sir. It's your uncle, K'Laar. He's died in hospital at North Edge. He'd outlived the virus and…." The errander's dodging eyes suggested that he realized he shouldn't say anything else.

Naldod tried desperately to maintain his composure and not to disrupt Taldra's much-deserved moment of glory. Taldra recognized the assistance of Geln and Hachen, asking them to stand. The errander slipped away. As applause surrounded the trio from all the dinner tables, Hachen looked over to Geln. He wondered, *Geln, will you be uncle to Argen, and one day to Telius? I'm not sure I like you myself, but Argen does, and he needs someone to be there when we can't.* Then he looked over to Taldra, who bowed humbly and actually seemed to blush a little.

Their glances locked, and she knew. Somehow, she knew. One night during their courtship, she had accidentally revealed her colorsight, by saying she loved his blue eyes. But she saw in even deeper ways than color. Taldra's gentle soul and sharp mind could understand Hachen in ways that he never understood himself. Her countenance projected the comforting sympathy that he needed, but he still felt like falling apart, like screaming and running down the walkways.

Later, in their bed, Taldra held him against her bosom while he cried uncontrollably.

When Control contacted Geln through the inter-doorway wallscreen, she reminded him that he and the other Degrans must continue their work on Valchondria, even if something happened to her. He looked surprised and agitated at such a statement, but she somehow decided to remind him of that again. Even after her recent promotion from a commander in the Fourth Circle of Degranon to its Control, and even with the guards always near her living quarters in the capital building, she never felt safe. A bomb or missile could descend upon her home, just as upon so many homes, on every side of the civil wars; the missile-defense system only worked part of the time, mostly just providing credits for the scientists who designed it and the politicians who approved it.

She felt death hanging over her family. It took her spouse, and now her two teenage daughters had joined her in military service. Only one of her children remained innocent.

Control walked nimbly into Jase-Dawn's dimly lit room, not sure if the seven-year-old had already fallen asleep. Waves of long black curls shook as Jase-Dawn bolted up in her bed, pushing back the blue and orange blanket she loved so much. Her round little face bubbled with excitement as she said, "Degranon!"

Control sat on the edge of her daughter's bed and asked, "What about Degranon?"

"Tonight's story!"

Cocking her head, Control replied, "I didn't know you got a story every night. Don't you have school tomorrow? And your sisters will be here by the time you get home."

Jase-Dawn patted her mother's shoulder. "Tell me a story, and I'll go to sleep. I promise."

More than happy to share the wisdom of the book with her precious little girl, Control pulled the covers back up to Jase-Dawn's chin and began. "On the home world, Degranon fell to a great dragon that descended upon the castle, destroying it and nearly everyone inside. The dragon then leveled the rest of the kingdom. The only survivor was a little boy named N'Vaar, who had been playing in the castle's dungeon. That little boy was the son of the king, and he would one day become the last of the great kings. N'Vaar vowed to one day slay the dragon, but the years went by, and the last of Valchondria's dragons died from its own violent battles. Instead of slaying dragons or becoming a ruler, the little boy wandered aimlessly from one village to the next as he grew to manhood.

"Finally, N'Vaar decided to go home and rebuild the kingdom of Degranon. He brought with him people from each of the villages he visited. Many of them became his warriors. And one of the women would become his spouse, bearing him many children to continue his lineage."

Jase-Dawn interrupted, boldly. "Then he wasn't the last great king!"

Control touched her daughter on her flat little nose. "You're jumping ahead of me. N'Vaar ruled wisely, a powerful military leader who smote all the enemies of righteousness but befriended all of those who upheld the principles that are now gathered in *The Book of Degranon*. He saw to it that all of his wisdom and experiences were written down, including even his worst experience of all, but I'll save those for another time."

"But, tell me, did he ride in a firejet, like my sisters?"

Control laughed gently. "No, there were no firejets back then. Like all soldiers on the home world, he rode a hiliate."

"A what?"

"Hiliates were giant, six-legged creatures that walked on their back four legs but ran on all six legs. The arch of their back made them conducive for riding, their impenetrable armor made them conducive for protecting soldiers in battle, and their loyal nature made them conducive to control. They were remarkable creatures, and they never attacked people, but they were hateful toward each other, and rather putrid in their odor."

Jase-Dawn made a face and shivered. "So why did you always call Father a hiliate?"

"It's an old insult. I was only joking."

The little girl's dark brown eyes grew serious. "Do you miss Father?"

"Yes, of course, but he died protecting us from the evil ones, just as we all must do one day. Now, it's time for sleep, little soldier."

"I love books, Mother!"

Control smiled proudly at her youngest daughter, amazed by her curiosity and intelligence. "I'm glad you want to know so much about *The Book of Degranon*. From the time Zaysha transcribed it on the home world, it has been our most important book."

⚜ ⚜ ⚜

"It's only a book!" Alom insisted, pulling the blankets up to the three-year-old's smiling face. In the dim glow of the candlelight, Telius looked amazingly like his father, and Alom wished it were Hachen telling him stories or reading to him from his favorite scrolls.

"It's *The Book of Degranon*!" Telius proclaimed, in his squeaky but charming voice. "It's my favorite!"

"Yes, I've noticed." Alom knew that the amused tone in his voice would signal his resignation. "Very well. Do you want to hear about the war, and the promise that Degranon could rise again?"

"Please!"

Alom couldn't resist when Telius used those dimples, though he almost resented Telius's use of them. Alom couldn't remember being so young, and doubted he was ever so likable. After going and retrieving a bag of scrolls from his own bedroom, he returned to Telius's and gently unraveled one of them. Though he doubted most of his wisdom would help Telius in a futuristic world, he took joy in knowing that Telius loved to read and to learn, so he felt that Telius could adapt to the future, when that time came.

The passage Alom read came from the final scroll in *The Book of Degranon*. It seemed almost too dark and disturbing for a child so small, but Telius loved to hear of the last great king's final battles and of how he taught his now-adult children to fight mercilessly against their enemies. Eventually, no enemies remained for his children but each other, all of them consumed with a desire to destroy people that they saw as a threat to what Degranon should be. Just as he received news of how his final surviving son had perished on the battlefield, the king realized that his wine had been poisoned by that very son. Before drawing his conclusive breath, the king vowed that Degranon would rise again.

Rather than falling asleep as promised, Telius lay wide-eyed, enraptured by the violent tale. Geln kissed him on the forehead and told him not to stay awake too long.

As Jase-Dawn fell asleep, her imagination stretched across time and space, to the home world, and the time of the last great king of Degranon. She imagined someone there, in the midst of history, another child like herself, loving books and words. More than anything, she wanted to escape to a place of legend, instead of living in a world where her sisters must go off to war.

The collector message on Geln's inter-doorway wallscreen seemed casual and routine, like an update of predictable weather. A missile had destroyed the living quarters of the Fourth Circle's capital, killing Control and her two oldest daughters. Jase-Dawn was away at school. "Please continue with your mission."

No apologies. No remorse. No encouragement.

"Please continue with your mission."

Death seemed the only constant in Geln's life, and always the death of people he loved. Why couldn't it be some worthless nuisance, like Hachen or Leader? Why someone like Control? Why someone like his brother? Why even his parents? He regretted that his parents made him kill them.

But he would keep on killing. That was the Degran way.

Geln whispered bitterly, "Please continue with your mission."

❧   ❧   ❧

Taldra buried herself in her work and her family so much that she would not have noticed the years slipping by if not for Argen's constant growth or the SSC's constant demands for monthly status reports. She and Hachen had become increasingly comfortable with Geln, mostly because of Argen's comfort with him. Geln would sometimes help them look after Argen when they brought him to Life with them, and Geln would always entertain him with fantastic stories about strange worlds or bizarre creatures.

One night, as she was about to leave Life Unit, she noticed that Geln seemed unusually sad and distant.

"Geln, is everything adequate?" she asked, running her hand in the air near his shoulder, not quite touching it. She still wasn't quite that comfortable, where she would want physical contact with him. "You've been rather quiet today."

He stared into his monitor, tapping it lightly with two fingers as he awaited the final graphs they needed for their status report. "Forgiveness." His voice sounded incredibly weak and defeated. "I had someone who was something of a mentor to me. I received news yesterday that she and two of her three children had died...in an accident. She was very young. In fact, her surviving daughter is only a few years older than Argen and Telius. She was away at school."

Seeing the revealing twitch near the scars on his face, Taldra actually touched his shoulder. "I'm saddened to hear that. Was it sudden?" Taldra regretted asking that question and feared that it sounded insensitive. But she often heard of parents becoming ill, going to the hospital, then suddenly dying. It had happened to Hachen's uncle and both of Hachen's parents. Though Hachen found it too difficult to discuss those deaths, she knew that the suddenness hurt him more than anything else, so it seemed strangely appropriate to ask if the mentor's death was sudden.

"Sudden? Yes. It was those—" His voice tapered off as he caught his breath and clenched his giant fists. "I mean, it was one of those cases where no one expected it to happen to her. She was too strong to die so young." A series of graphs began flashing on his monitor, and he seemed relieved by the distraction, as if he regretted exposing his emotions to his superior. "Well, there it is. I'll wallscreen the graphs with your report."

"Gratitude. To the side, we're having supper with my old friend Lyjia—Dr. Hudza—and her spouse. They recently moved back to Valcine, and their son just turned four a few days ago, just a month ahead of Argen and Telius. Would you like to join us? Maybe you could bring your mentor's daughter as well, since she's close to their age."

He leaned back, smiling faintly at her. "She doesn't live in Valcine."

From his tone, she knew that the subject was closed. He had already told her too much. Taldra decided not to ask about the little girl again, not even her name, unless Geln started talking about her first. It usually bothered Taldra: the way he concealed so much of his life, as if he wanted to hide something terrible. But now she realized that she should respect his reasons for that. He owed them nothing.

"Then just you?"

"Gratitude, and it would heavy honor me, but I have to attend to some business, related to my friend's death."

Taldra bowed her head as she stepped back from him. "Of course. Glory, then."

"Glory."

As Taldra left, she sensed a profound longing and sadness in Geln that had perhaps always followed him, and she wondered why she had always feared him in the back of her mind: Geln, her loyal assistant who had saved Telius. But she still couldn't abolish that fear, even as she saw the weight of his loss on his scarred face.

CHAPTER 9

❀

As Telius grew, he learned from Alom, but spent little time with most of the other villagers. So Alom watched with approval one morning, when several small children pulled open the door to Alom's straw home and asked if Telius could go play in the forest with them.

"I can't," the seven-year-old replied, to Alom's disappointment. Motioning at a scroll on the table, Telius added, "I have too much reading."

"The reading can wait," Alom insisted, before telling the children, "Telius would love to go. You can take our hiliates."

"Alom," Telius objected, "I haven't finished my reading."

The children eventually gave up and left, as always, and Alom feared they would eventually quit trying at all. He gestured for Telius to sit down at the table with him, gently rolling the scroll up and pushing it away before Telius could grab it and start reading. "Telius, you don't spend enough time with other children. Why didn't you go play with them?"

"You told me to read that scroll."

"I didn't say to finish it at this very moment. Stop acting like you're already grown. You're just as bad as Zaysha!"

Telius's eyes narrowed, and his little nose scrunched up. "You think Zaysha is bad?"

"Not as in evil, but she's bad to herself by not making friends. Being a priest isn't just about studies or transcription or settling disputes. You should like the people you claim to serve."

"I do like people, Alom. You've taught me to like everyone."

"Then spend time with people. Don't detach yourself from them. You need friends."

"But when the doorway re-opens and my parents come for me, I'll lose those friends, just like I'll lose you."

In his time with Telius, Alom had never seen the boy's belief in his parents waiver, despite the fact that they never came back. Alom and Telius understood that Taldra, Hachen, and Geln couldn't really control the doorway and had wrongly assumed that it would keep opening in the initial pattern. But they also prayed constantly that, somehow, the doorway would open again. The sadness in Telius grew with each instance that he and Alom went to the secret cave at the set time, only to find nothing there. Aside from Alom's poor attempts at drawing Taldra and Hachen or describing them, Telius didn't even know their faces.

Alom touched the gentle, contemplative boy on his shoulder. "Telius, your parents wanted me to make sure you're happy, and that you live a normal life. That includes friendship with other children."

Telius relented. "If that's what you want."

"I was hoping it's what you want. I've never seen two children as lost in books as you and Zaysha. At least be friends with her, so you can both learn about friendship. When you leave, she'll have to be friend and servant to an entire village, and you'll have to make friends in a strange new place. You'll also have to adjust to not being an only child, in whatever way your parents find to work around the law against brothers and sisters."

"Yes, Alom."

Telius didn't say what Alom knew he was thinking: he wanted Alom to go with him to the future. But Alom couldn't leave his people, even though he both longed for and dreaded the day that

Hachen and Taldra returned. He hugged Telius and said, "Forgiveness if I suggested you and Zaysha are bad. You're both good people, and I couldn't be more proud of you."

"I wonder where they are, what they're doing."

"So do I."

As the years passed, Telius became close friends with Zaysha, and with most of the other Daliian children his age. But he spoke less and less often of his parents, and Alom sometimes feared mentioning them, because of the sadness inside Telius. Even when they would slip away to the cave, it seemed like a ritual rather than a mission, and Telius avoided talking about why they stood, waiting. Always waiting. Over time, Alom saw Telius's belief in his parents begin to fade, and he wondered if anything but their arrival could stop Telius from completely abandoning his life in the future.

Taldra never again spoke of Geln's mentor, or her daughter. The years continued to slip past, and Geln became a trusted friend. At times, Taldra even forgot her fear of his lingering gaze, and he even seemed to avoid staring at her.

One night, Taldra arrived home late, after her weekly debate with Dr. Tquil on the wallscreen. Hachen had prepared supper, and the kitchen lights were on their dimmest setting. His long, braided hair fell to one side of his handsome face.

"Did we forget to pay the Power Holders?" she asked, jokingly. "I can barely see."

He smiled. "I thought it would be charming, and maybe somewhat romantic."

"Until a certain twelve-year-old comes in here and warns that you're going to cause an accident. And is that docle bread I smell? He'll also warn us that I'm close to my regulation weight."

"You look perfect to me. And is that anger at our child related to your anger at a certain expert on children?"

She kissed her spouse, breathing in his cologne. Hachen rarely wore cologne, so its presence confirmed that he saw this night as a special break for them. They certainly needed one. "You smell good."

"Gratitude."

"And I'm not angry at Argen. I was only joking. Is he in his room?"

"No, Lyjia said he could stay the night there. He and Kryldon are finishing their gravity project for school. Geln helped them with it when he was here earlier."

"The boys adore Geln. I don't know what we'll do if his transfer happens." She often referred to Argen and Kryldon as "the boys," in the same way that she imagined referring to Argen and Telius as "the boys." Lyjia's son was certainly a good friend for Argen, but Taldra wished that she could tell Argen he had something even better than a friend: a twin brother.

Hachen pulled a steaming dish of docle bread from the baker. "I suppose we'll find out what they'll do."

Taldra felt a sudden mixture of joy and apprehension. Unlike Argen, she had never fully learned to love Geln, but she certainly depended on him and saw him as a friend. To the side, he was their link to the doorway energies, even if they never discussed that subject anymore. "Is that why Geln was here today?"

"Yes. He was heavy cryptic about his new assignment. It sounds much more classified than anything involving Project Life Unit."

She watched him slice the docle bread before adding vegetable gravy to it. Besides his many other attributes, Hachen always was an excellent cook.

In fact, his skills left Taldra struggling to maintain regulation weight—or, at least, she gave herself that explanation for her occasionally fluctuating weight. She usually gained the most weight during the time, the peak, the doorway moment that never happened. She would sit around eating gredga chips, or anything else that could occupy her, while Hachen continued with his insane pacing. Unlike cooking, science, or healing, the pacing was not one of his better attributes.

Taldra tried to sound confident: "We'll manage without him. Life basically runs herself these days. I just wish we could test her out somewhere else."

"One day."

He held her close, and she managed not to say what she was thinking. It would only upset both of them, the way it always upset them when the subject arose. But maybe "somewhere else" would bring Life the right core energies for opening a doorway and bringing Telius back to them.

❀   ❀   ❀

After work the next day, Taldra and Hachen came home to speak with Argen about some good news that Geln had given them before leaving. They quickly walked up the spiral staircase and into Argen's bedroom, which they rarely visited. Aside from leaving his favorite boots in the middle of the floor, he had left all three of his ceiling trunks de-activated after pulling out the contents and tossing them around the room, covering up his holo-projectors, his bed, and even his mirrors.

Hachen breathed in deeply, and looked ready to unleash a torrent of obscenities.

Taldra touched his firm chest and said, "It isn't the end of the world."

"It just smells like it," Hachen replied.

"Hachen! Taldra! What brings you to my corner?" Argen walked in, wearing his exercise clothes and carrying his hand machine.

"We heard that several people were lost in here," said Taldra.

After looking around at the wreckage, Argen briefly bowed his head and said, "Forgiveness." But then he perked back up. "I couldn't find a video chip that we needed for our gravity project. I'll have it cleaned up before supper."

Hachen touched both of Argen's shoulders. "We also heard that you and Kryldon won highest ranking at the pressure tournament. Why didn't you tell us it was today?"

"You were both so busy with work that I didn't want to bother you about it. The gravity project went well, too."

Taldra felt like she had somehow failed Argen, though he wasn't any sort of disaster. His room was, but he wasn't. She told him, "We would also like to have seen that. Argen, I'll admit that we were busy with our monthly reports two nights ago, but we finished them in plenty of time, and even took some time off yesterday. And, anyway, we would rather be late on a report than miss something that's important for you. If nothing else, I could have presented our report to the SSC while Hachen went to the tournament."

"Your mother's right," said Hachen. "She doesn't need me beside her all the time, looking handsome."

"Though you do that so well," Taldra said, before kissing Hachen on the cheek.

Argen waved his hands then held his stomach and grimaced. "Forgiveness! Wrong bedroom for that! I think the virus is failing me!"

"You wait until you fall in love," said Hachen, nodding slightly. "You'll be just as bad, if not worse."

"I hope not. To the side, I was going to tell you about winning. I just wanted to tell you in person, instead of wallscreening it. How did you find out?"

"Geln was there," said Taldra.

"He was? I didn't see him."

"I'm not sure why he didn't tell you. Maybe it was too hard for him. Geln's always kept his emotions hidden."

"Didn't tell me what?"

Taldra looked to Hachen, who sat down on Argen's messy bed with him. Hachen said, "Geln's accepted a transfer position within the SSC. It's fully hidden. We won't have contact with him anymore. We just learned that today was his last day with us."

Argen looked understandably hurt and stunned. "You mean he's gone, just like that?"

"Yes. It's going to be hard for all of us. But I know that he has good reason, or he wouldn't leave like this."

Argen turned away, and Taldra could hear the pain in his voice. "I don't want to hear his reasons, not if he can't tell me himself."

Hachen placed his hand on the top of Argen's short hair. "We're going to spend much more time with you, Argen. We promise. And we'll tell you as soon as we hear something from Geln."

Argen grew silent, and they soon left him to his privacy. No matter how much they tried, they never seemed to live up to the promise that Hachen made that day.

CHAPTER 10

Enduring the cold, Telius and Zaysha walked near the edges of a small lake that fed into the Lisuadian River. Though he cared about the other children, he felt closest to Zaysha, since she was apprentice and adopted daughter of the secondary priests in his village. They studied together, usually under the tutelage of Alom or one of Zaysha's adoptive parents.

Zaysha's fur-covered outfit revealed only her slanted eyes and part of her tiny gray nose. She was slightly older than Telius and always seemed a bit resentful that he was first in line to replace Alom; still, they were close friends who rarely argued. Taunting each other was another matter.

"I am certain that you wouldn't try to stand on the lake," she told him.

"Because I'm not crumbled," he replied, pulling his furs closer against his trembling body. Though he knew nothing of the pain of illness, he could feel the pain of a Valchondrian winter. "Would you try it?"

She shook her head. "No, but I'm not as sturdy as you."

He smiled. Unlike most of the other villagers, Zaysha had never been generous with compliments. "Do you think I'm sturdy?"

"To extremes. But forgiveness for my suggestion. It was crumbled, like you said."

"Maybe, but I feel like acting crumbled sometimes." With that statement, he strutted out onto the ice. "Come on, Zaysha! We can walk on the lake!" After he walked three body-lengths, the ice began to crack.

Zaysha screamed, "Telius, come back! I was joking."

Telius tried to steady his bundled feet, but he could feel them slipping beneath him as the ice made a terrible crashing sound. When he fell down, he fell through that ice.

At first, he thrashed about, trying to grab the edges of the opening in the ice. But then his body grew still, frozen by the burning sensation that covered his skin as the icy water quickly seeped through his coverings. Just as he started to sink, he felt a branch pushing against his face. He grabbed onto it and pulled himself up from the water, shivering as he lost consciousness.

Argen didn't take the news of Geln's departure well, especially since it came without warning and without any final words. He carried the burden of his anger and disappointment with him to school the next day. It compounded the hurt caused by the teasing he often received in the outer play areas.

One of the other boys, older and larger than Argen, taunted him as the other children gathered around him. "Dr. Tquil says that your mother is deviant, and a biological error."

Feeling his face darken, Argen replied, "That must be the 'family love' Tquil is always promoting during his video chip tours."

The boy pointed angrily at him. "Dr. Tquil is a true patriot, unlike Dr. Lorfeltez, with her anti-glory views and her rusted experiments. Does she let you play inside that triangle house she built?"

"Life Unit isn't just a house, and there's nothing anti-glory about my mother."

"She isn't maintained. Someone needs to maintain her."

Argen balled up his fists as his anger grew. "And will you be that someone?"

"Me? No. I'll do my maintaining on your crumbled face!"

The boy swung back his fist, only to have it pulled further back by Kryldon, who had suddenly pushed through the growing crowd of children. Kryldon's abrupt, unexpected gesture caught the boy off balance, causing him to fall backward. After he managed to stand back up, he ran away, amid a roar of laughter. The crowd of children dispersed, leaving only Argen and Kryldon.

Kryldon's rippling muscles and deepening voice suggested a young boy's leanings toward manhood. Argen's handsome black friend was maturing much more quickly than he was, and becoming much more confident.

"Gratitude," said Argen. "But you can't assault everyone who teases me. The Maintainers will lock you away for sure."

"I didn't assault him. I just stopped him from assaulting you. And the Maintainers can go to the vaporizers, for all I like!" Kryldon's voice revealed an anger and a passion that Argen had never seen in him before. He really was changing! "The Maintainers speak as badly about my mother as they do yours, just because she's pro-colony."

Argen's head jerked around as he scanned the buildings for Maintainer cameras. He pulled his friend close and whispered into his ear. "We can't heavy hazard speak here. They monitor the schools even more than the government buildings. We can speak freely in the walkways, after school."

Telius sat in a darkened hut, cradling the body of a dying man, trying to speak words of comfort to him. After Telius finished praying over him, he left him to be comforted by the man who had shared his life with him. They were both in their seventies, but they had been strong, robust hunters until the winter plague hit.

Outside, Telius found himself in the safe arms of Alom, who had been administering to a large family in the next hut. "This winter plague is the worst I've ever seen," said Alom. "We must be strong for our people."

"That really isn't much of a problem for me," said Telius. He could hear the anger in his own voice, though he couldn't decide where to direct that anger, or how to justify it. "I'm immune to the winter plague, to forest sickness, to facial blemishes, and to everything else. I'm a freak!"

Alom stroked Telius's long hair. "You're not a freak. The people of your time all carried a gift. You should be thankful for it."

"I would be thankful if I could pass that gift along to the people who really need it. How many villagers must we burn this winter, while I go on feeling no burden?"

"You feel burdens, Telius, more than any fourteen-year-old should feel. I've never seen anyone love humanity like you. And there is the other burden you feel."

Telius held up his hands. "Please don't speak to me about my parents and their promises. I'm in no mood for it."

Alom backed away but then pointed toward the next two huts. "Another time then. We have more people to visit."

Unable to sleep that night, Telius returned to copying scrolls, a project that he and Zaysha—his friend and fellow apprentice priest—had been dividing. Some of the scrolls in this particular book bored him, even though he loved the overall book. Frustrated, he caught himself changing some of the words, or just not always double-checking that he copied them correctly. In some cases, he even adapted parts of the story-line in the very book that he had treasured as a small child.

At his urgings, Alom had read it to him countless times, but he kept asking to hear the same book recited. Waving his pudgy hands, he would smile and chant its title: *Degranon.*

CHAPTER 11

✿

*T*aldra sat in the wallscreen room, using voice activation to sift through the messages on the collector. Several of them were ads from the Power Holders and the Wall System Conglomerate. One was a bill from the Maintainers for a podium speech permit, even though they had outlawed podium speech a year after her arrest! And the final message informed her that Argen's tendency to credit bend had caused them several penalties at the credit bank, including two penalties that the bank seemed to create especially for Argen.

"That boy," said Taldra, to the air. She spoke so endlessly to Life Unit that it no longer seemed odd to her if she spoke aloud with no one else in the room. "And to think we have two of them."

"Two of what?" asked Argen.

She hadn't noticed him bouncing in, carrying a stack of video chip boxes. His hair looked even shorter than usual, and the long collar of his shirt was all folded up.

"We have two more credit bends from you, Mall Walker." She touched the back of his head, feeling the bristly surface, before fixing his collar. "Did you just get another haircut?"

He motioned at his face and smiled. "Yes! Do I look handsome?"

"Handsome? Always! But you know how your father feels about short hair."

"Oh, Taldra!" He flung out his hands in the dismissive motion that Kryldon used so constantly. "For pro-colony people, you and Hachen are heavy traditional."

"Colonization was a Valchondrian tradition," said Taldra, trying not to sound like she was debating Dr. Tquil. "And the colonists are Valchondrians."

"I think we've had this discussion two or twenty times." He laughed and flashed his dimples at her. Even as a rather tall fifteen-year-old, he still looked like an innocent and charming little boy when he put those dimples to use. "Are you forgetting that I'm pro-colony?"

"No."

"Or that Hachen refilled my credit box from his?"

She raised her eyebrows. "I actually didn't know that, and you probably shouldn't have told me. Argen, you have to be more responsible with your credit. Your father and I might seem extremely wealthy, but the taxes and the bills on this house are amazing, not to mention setting aside your university funds."

He sat down beside her on the couch. "Forgiveness, Taldra. I'll be more careful. It's just hard being different. I want to look current."

She touched him on the shoulder. "How are you different? You're just a normal boy."

"Whose mother is attacked on the wallscreen every few minutes. To the side, normal boys don't live in actual houses in Valcine, and the parents of normal boys don't work inside gigantic triangles. And their friends don't leave them for no reason at all! Why did Geln forget us? Why did he forget me?" His manly frame suddenly seemed even more boyish than when he flashed his dimples. Any attempts at holding back his tears quickly failed.

She held him closely, stroking his hair. In the time since Geln's departure, they had rarely mentioned him, rarely considered how much Argen missed him. "Forgiveness. I never realized how hard all of this is for you. But Geln does a lot of secretive work for the SSC.

He always has. We didn't know where he was much of the time. As your father said when it happened, I'm sure Geln has good reasons for leaving the way he did. And we have good reasons for our work."

He pushed away from her. "I know you do. I believe in your reasons. So do Kryldon, and Dr. Hudza, and a lot of other people. But they're nothing compared to how many people hate us. Why do they hate us?"

Taldra also began crying. "I don't know, Argen. I wish I did."

"Just, please, don't ever leave me the way your parents left you, and the way Geln left us. Please don't."

Argen's words cut into Taldra's heart so deeply that she couldn't even speak. Instead, she replied by holding him so tightly that she feared he couldn't breathe. Finally, she stopped crying long enough to say, "Argen, you will always have a family. I will see to that. More than any of my other goals, I will see that you always have a family. And your father and I would never, never disown you."

The following day, Dr. Hudza had just dropped off Kryldon to stay the night. He ran up the stairs to Argen's room, leaving her and Hachen in the wallscreen room. Hachen was just about to offer her some glacier water when he noticed a collector message about Taldra. He clicked on the wallscreen control for it to play the message. He and Lyjia looked at the news report, which showed Taldra answering some questions during a press conference.

A question about colonization, carefully phrased to avoid the word "colonization," sent Taldra railing about "the failures of the SSC."

"'The failures of the SSC,'" Hachen repeated, stretching his fingers outward.

Looking toward the door, Lyjia stated flatly, "You know Taldra. She says what she thinks."

"I know, and I treasure her courage. But she's going to get our project shut down one day, offending the SSC and the Maintainers with her danger speak. And I agree with all she's saying, but I wish I could get her to tone it down when she's on the wallscreen."

"Have you talked to her about this?" Lyjia's halting tone suggested that she really wanted no part in such a debate between Taldra and Hachen.

Hachen rolled his eyes. "I've tried. She won't listen. She'll just pretend that nothing's wrong."

Lyjia gave him a reassuring smile. "Maybe nothing is wrong. But you knew what you were getting into when you agreed to be married with her."

"And I've never regretted that." He spread his hands outward as she walked closer to the door. "But I see your aim. Forgiveness if I made you uncomfortable."

She touched the door control. "I don't mind. B'zl probably feels the same way about me sometimes, but he's too kind to tell me. Glory, Hachen, and gratitude for letting Kryldon spend so much time here."

"Our pleasure," he said, as she walked out the opening door. He didn't say "Glory." He despised that term, as much as Taldra despised it; in fact, they both despised anything said or done without sincerity. He stood there thinking what a remarkable woman he had become married with, and he felt ashamed for his comments against her.

❧   ❧   ❧

Telius walked along the banks of the Lisuadian River until he found the cluster of boulders that concealed the opening of the doorway cave. The return to the doorway cave brought back his previous frustrations. How could he walk through a doorway that didn't exist? Why hadn't his parents caused that doorway to reappear? Would his brother accept him?

At least he usually had Alom to accompany him, but several people had needed Alom to settle a dispute. The villagers relied on Alom and Telius. Telius wondered what would happen if his parents actually did appear. Would he just tell Alom to manage on his own? Telius liked his life in the village, and he wasn't sure he wanted to jump forward to some strange future where parents abandoned their children. He didn't want change.

The cave hadn't changed. The presence of vrix in the stalagmites still gave enough light to illuminate the inside, but not so much that it glowed into the water. Alom and the occasional hunter were the only other people that Telius ever saw near the thick of the Lisuadian Forest, so it surprised him when he heard someone at the mouth of the cave speak his name.

"Zaysha?" He recognized his colleague and friend, but couldn't believe she was there. Alom found the cave by accident, and he told none of the villagers but Telius. With the constant demands on him, Alom liked keeping a place of solitude, and Telius usually left him to that solitude.

Zaysha's slanted eyes squinted as they adjusted to the eerie light of the cave. Her fur-skin boots were wet from the splashing of the river onto the boulders. Her hair was braided and twisted against the left side of her head, making her look more grown-up than Telius had noticed before. With her unique and astonishing beauty, she reminded him of no one else he had ever seen.

She asked, "Are you so surprised, Telius? We only had one secret between us. Didn't you think I would be curious about it? Didn't you think that someone who studies with you and spends time with you almost every day would notice that you always leave Dalii, for one reason or another, on the last week of every fifth month?"

He felt surprised, and guilty. He never meant to deceive anyone, but Geln had warned Alom about supposed dangers of exposing his differences and his origin. Telius thought that Alom put too much trust into that Geln person, who sounded a bit strange. As she approached him, Telius asked, "How long have you known?"

"Almost two years. But after I followed you and Alom here and saw how sad you both looked, I decided to respect your decision for not telling me. You always have some rationale for everything. When we used to play games together, you would modify any rules that you didn't think of as practical, even if they made the game harder for you. You've always been so funny, even when you're serious. Everyone likes you. You'll be a good leader." He could see how her discomfort was making her ramble, and he could see how guilty she felt for invading the secret cave.

"Or you will," he added, touching her on the shoulder.

She shook her head and looked away. "The people don't accept me like they do you."

"What makes you say that? You know the teachings better than me, and you care deeply about all the villagers."

"But I'm not one of them."

Those words hurt Telius, but he also liked them. As cruel as it seemed, he needed for someone else to feel as isolated as he felt. And, of all people, he wanted Zaysha to share his feelings. He knew that, if his parents didn't return by the time he reached manhood, he wanted her to propose marriage with him. He wasn't sure that he was in love with her, or what it meant to be in love, but he could tell that she would make a good spouse for him. "Why don't you think you're one of them, one of us?"

"Because my skin, like my mother's skin, is yellow. I've told you how she came from beyond the mountains, after a volcano destroyed her village. Her people had a different skin color from you, and from Alom."

"How could skin color matter?" asked Telius, sincerely astounded by her claim. He had never realized that she was a different color than him, or that she felt so isolated. "No one cares about that."

"You can say that, but you aren't yellow, and you can't help but notice that I am."

"Actually, I can help. I mean, I know that your eyes and your eyebrows are more curved than those of red-skinned people, but you look the same as a red-skinned person to me. I don't see colors."

She placed both hands on her hips, while slightly moving those hips. It seemed oddly provocative to Telius, though probably not in the way Zaysha intended. "Of course you don't," she replied, with overstated sarcasm.

"I don't. I've never told anyone but Alom this, but I can only see in black, white, or gray. Alom says that some people can't distinguish their colors properly, but I'm the only person I know of who can't see colors at all."

"So, you're not actually perfect?"

"I never said I was."

"You never had to. You don't get sick, even when the people around you are dying."

He wanted desperately to tell her the truth, but he respected Alom's guidance on the matter. "Zaysha, I wish I could give you all the details. But please understand that I'm also different, in good ways and bad ways. I have to keep coming here at the same time. It's a part of my life. And, yes, it does make me very sad."

Her eyes revealed a deep empathy. "Forgiveness for the intrusion. I won't follow you here into the cave again. But I will always be waiting for you when you return. I'll always be your friend." She kissed him on the cheek and left.

Telius trembled with a mixture of feelings that assaulted him like never before. He just wanted to be a part of Dalii, and he wished Alom never would have told him about his other life. But what if the doorway opened? Sometimes, the vrix glow in the cave increased, as if the embers were about to start.

But they never started.

❦   ❦   ❦

From the control room, Taldra watched her spouse leaning against battery seven, his chest heaving in exasperation. He had taken a similar pose the night before, while watching her on the wallscreen, representing the SSC in a panel while speaking a little too vocally about the very pro-colony views that could easily cause the SSC or the Maintainers to shut down Life Unit.

She eventually gave up on any change in the readings and distracted herself by connecting to their house's wallscreen. The collector had a message from the Supreme Science Council. The speaker looked like someone barely out of university: a very proper young man with tight clothes, long hair, and a condescending, nasal voice.

"Dr. Lorfeltez, you might not know me, since you can't be bothered to meet with all your coworkers before making your media appearances, but I'm with the Executive Reorganization Committee of the Supreme Science Council, and it's my unfortunate duty to inform you that you now only have one job with the SSC. Despite certain…reservations…about Project Life Unit, you will continue with that work, as one of our researchers.

"However, as we've begun reexamining our resources, we no longer feel that someone of your viewpoints should represent the SSC on the wallscreen. However, you're welcome to continue your wallscreen appearances with Dr. Tquil, as you clearly state those…views…as your own. This decision is only about giving more employment opportunities to others and should not be seen as a failure on your part, even if we were disappointed by your performance at times, such as your recent wallscreen appearance. Gratitude, and glory."

The message ended, and Taldra switched her screen back to monitoring battery seven. Again, she watched her spouse, who had begun pacing around the battery room. As always, she would soon walk in there and hold him. Then they would both begin crying. This time, she had something extra to cry about, as if not seeing her son weren't upsetting enough by itself.

"Great timing, SSC," she whispered.

CHAPTER 12

Jase-Dawn stopped and looked at the blue glass of the acknowledgment panel before placing her hand on it and allowing it to scan her fingerprints. She glanced down the shadowy hallway of the circular building that housed the university she attended, as well as the office she was about to enter, the office of Minister Geln, the military leader who had been away on a strange mission for most of her life. Fortunately, most Ministers in the Fourth Circle were only figure-heads, run by the priests and the economic leaders, so no one really noticed his absence very often. But Jase-Dawn noticed it, preferred it. Unlike her mother, who had considered him her greatest trainee, Jase-Dawn never liked him.

She was far too familiar with his cruelty to want to step onto his electric walk-help again, after it transmitted a fire virus into her boots the last time and nearly incinerated her. Still, she placed her feet on it, one boot at a time, while waiting for her acknowledgment, knowing it was too wide to walk around, and that she couldn't reach his office any other way. She tapped the back heel of her left boot against the metal grating of the walk-help, as if testing for traps. The digital watch in the corner of her right contact lens said 7 S; the graduation ceremony started at 7:45 Solar! She had already put on her blue and black university uniform (even the braided headband that got lost in her shock of frizzy black hair) for fear he would delay her until after the time for the chief instructor to hand out the micro-chips.

A rumbling stirred under her feet, even more than the usual moan of a walk-help activating. Geln's door withdrew into the ceiling as the acknowledgment signal buzzed and the walk-help jerked for-ward, almost tossing Jase-Dawn backwards.

A giant robot claw grabbed at the air just in front of her throat as a second claw knocked her down and pulled her toward the closet where Geln stored his so-called "security devices." Minister Geln, a tall, heavy-set man who had recently gone bald except for a patch of hair around his ears and a separate patch just above his brow, chewed one of his fingernails as he watched her struggle.

Jase-Dawn grabbed the claw that had toppled her onto the water-padded carpeting. The second claw ate into the first claw's wires, freeing Jase-Dawn as the machinery shut down. As Geln rose from behind his dethua desk, the buzzing completely ceased, and Jase-Dawn stood up. The walls and ceiling were also made of dethua, a soundproof material made from a plant the colonists had taken with them from Valchondria. Despite dethua's advantages, Jase-Dawn still found it repulsive: a swirl of various green shades with a reputation for absorbing paint jobs. The military seemed to like it mostly because no one could paint anti-war graffiti on it. The warmonger-ing artwork adorning Geln's walls did little to compensate for the dethua's ugliness. She stopped looking around the room when he finally spoke.

"You made a poor choice," he said, sitting back as he pointed to the chair attached to the front of his desk. His scratchy voice reso-nated, despite sounding almost devoid of Degran inflections. "You might have been electrocuted if I had not cut the power so quickly."

"You are merciful." She accepted the seat, glad that he had spoken, giving her the clearance to speak. She knew all the formalities of the Degran military, though none of them interested her, and though she held no sincere respect for this man who helped to protect the circle that her ancestors had called home since the colonization of planet Degranon. "But, sir, it was my only course of action. My weapon was taken from me at the elevator checkpoint."

"As your mother taught me, there are always alternatives," he said, without offering any. "The important thing is your ability to destroy your enemy."

"But I'm not a soldier, sir." She strained to keep the "sir" from sounding sarcastic. Her parents had taught her awe and reverence for Degranon, but she held neither for Geln, especially not after her parents and her sisters died in the very civil wars that spawned people like him, people who lived only for the next battle. His patchwork robe, a mixture of outrageous colors and patterns, affected her tastes as negatively as his personality affected her mood. Even his new name bothered her; he had taken the rather odd chosen name of "Gazer," without even becoming married! Fortunately, she wasn't in a position where she would feel obligated to use his chosen name.

"You always say that you're not a soldier." He smiled, the same fake smile he always used when he appeared on her wallscreen collector, filling his supposed obligation of checking in on his mentor's only surviving daughter. "However, you continue to show the aggressiveness and resourcefulness of a Degran warrior. I suppose I should be impressed."

"Gratitude, sir. May I ask why you requested my presence? I'm supposed to be at my graduation."

"Here's your diploma." He gave her a tiny gray computer chip, encased in a monogrammed glass container.

"Minister Geln, why does this say 'Valcine University'? That isn't the name of my school. I don't think there's even a school by that name in our circle."

"No. It's a school on Valchondria, which is where you'll soon be. I trust that you understood your briefing about Valchondria?"

"Yes, I understood it, but my teaching position." Jase-Dawn leaned forward, then stood up. "I requested it. The education minister approved it and accepted my gratitude credits."

"Jase-Dawn, sit down and calm down. You have a mission to fulfill that will prepare you for your teaching job, and, of course, all teaching positions can be revoked if any minister sees the applicant as inappropriate or simply needed elsewhere."

"I completed my military service when I was fifteen, just like any other Degran."

"Yes, but your performance there and in school proved that you would be more than adequate for this new opportunity. Now be seated. I don't like to be stood over."

She sat down and waited for him to speak again.

He continued, "If I had given this mission to any of your peers, you would have been jealous. But, to be honest, none of your peers share your knowledge and enthusiasm for history and science."

"Sir, may I speak bluntly?"

"You always do," said Geln, emphasizing the word "always" a little too much.

She accepted that as a yes. "My education is complete, yet I know little about the home planet. You call me competent in history, but the history of Degranon begins on Valchondria."

"Loyalty to Valchondria is avoided by avoiding the subject," said Geln. "If any of your teachers had made more than a passing and extremely negative reference to Valchondria, they would have been executed as a threat to Degran values. There are some understandings never mentioned at university."

"Such as the power of ignorance?" Jase-Dawn tried to remember the particulars she'd gleaned about Valchondria, the home world. It was the planet of the colonizers, and it was a planet that stressed leisure above ambition. Most importantly, it was the planet where the great kings of Degranon first reigned, but Valchondria had turned against Degranon, three thousand years in the past. Still, most of what she knew of Valchondria was gossip, since the Valchondrians allowed no communication with anyone outside their atmosphere. She'd heard that they all carried diseases, that they didn't believe in God, and that they sometimes ate their own children, but she wasn't sure how much of that she believed. "Is there a doorway to Valchondria?"

"Yes, and they are too primitive to understand such things. For much of your life, I worked with Dr. Naldod and Dr. Lorfeltez, chosen names Hachen and Taldra, two of the home world's most ambitious and most controversial scientists. I transmitted a recording to your video system that will further brief you on your mission, but basically, you are to pose as Hachen and Taldra's assistant—my replacement, except that we will take advantage of your age by calling you their student. You will soon learn not only about the only two great minds in Valchondrian science but also the secrets of ancient Degranon. We sent one of their twin sons into the past, to the time of the last great king." He paused for a moment before asking, "Are you interested now?"

She assumed he had already seen the interest in her eyes, but all of this sounded too incredible, too easy, like walking into a history book. "Does it matter whether I'm interested or not?" she asked, trying to hide her growing enthusiasm.

"Only for your convenience. You'll leave in a few months. Oh, and make sure you bring some clothes with at least one green stripe. It's how Degrans recognize each other on the home world."

"Won't we stand out by not being mutants?"

He cocked his head. "Mutants?"

"From the radiation sickness. The Valchondrians are all mutated and hideous."

Geln leaned back, laughing. "You really shouldn't believe what you read in the history books."

The statement somehow offended her more than anything else he had just said and done. "But I'm a history teacher. And I love books."

"Well, burn all your books. The Valchondrians certainly have."

She shuddered even more from that statement, but her imagination continued to race, as she considered the fascinating possibilities of her mission.

CHAPTER 13

The giant video screen in the dusty old wallscreen studio formed the words one at a time, treating Taldra and her constant rival, Dr. Tquil, like slow readers. Taldra slowly came to hate these meetings, these debates, because she knew no one watched them. Dr. Tquil always tried to trick her into saying something that would bring her some form of embarrassment, and then the gossip masters would discuss it on their programs for a week or two. Next, her parents would call and ask why she said such things, adding that she should be more responsible with her choice of words when she appeared on a show that could reach all eight billion Valchondrians. However, Taldra knew that no one but the gossip masters would really miss *Lalololalo's Celebrity Show* to see one of Valchondria's last pro-colony scientists argue with an obnoxious psychologist.

"Do you know how to speed this thing up?" Taldra asked Tquil. "It seems to run more slowly every time we meet."

"I am not a computer technician," he replied, tossing a hand outward and nearly touching one of the stars on the shoulder of Taldra's new pullover.

Like most of her pullovers, its material depicted stars and planets. As with many other Valchondrian women who wore pullovers, she had gained some weight. In fact, during the seventeen years since the birth of the twins, she had constantly lost and gained weight, sometimes coming dangerously close to surpassing her height/weight ratio. Tquil had once remarked that she dressed like a teenager—Tquil in his 8000c suit with the diamond buttons.

Tquil added, "You should have checked the equipment before the debate. I think it's archaic enough to fit into your field. But I'm not surprised that nothing here works. Most of the people at this network are heavy hazard hiliates." He jerked his round head back to cover the wireless microphone on his one-side collar, apparently realizing his response had gone over the air. No one else was in the room—just them and the ancient machinery—but they could hear their words echo on an unpersoned monitor.

The green glow of the letters reflected patterns of light onto Tquil's forehead, making him look like some strange lifeform, like the alien beasts Taldra heard about in anti-colony propaganda videos. As always, Taldra wished it were not illegal for gifted people to tell anyone about the colors they saw, or even that they could see in color. Just as she thought of a legally-permitted response to his insult, the computer vocalized the question that had slowly formed on its screen: "Is there anything outside Valchondria?"

"Yes," replied Taldra. "There are Valchondrian colonies in outer space. Our ancestors also found life on other planets and left it undisturbed."

"Colonies is not the proper word," said Tquil. He squeezed his belt buckle as he talked, as if he were about to snap his credit box from it. "We should say experiments. Failed experiments. The colonists reverted to primitive behavior, hungering for the savagery of our earliest ancestors. Between the religious cults, the race wars, and all the attacks from other species, we can only assume that they're all dead."

"We wouldn't have to settle with assumptions if we allowed contact outside Valchondria."

"The glory of Valchondria is within," said Tquil. It was one of the many phrases Taldra had heard all her life; even more than the rest of

Valchondria, Tquil seemed to think in clichés. "If we are to lie to the public and tell them there is anything better, or even anything equal, then we are the ones who destroy their patriotism; we are the ones who tarnish the glory of the only true civilization. It is time we abandon those radical notions about something greater out there." He scratched his pointed nose.

"It is time we move forward," said Taldra, though she could remember having the same conversation before. Sometimes she thought she dreamed actions and conversations that later happened in reality, but she eventually realized that actual events and conversations repeated more often than anyone wanted to admit, like a video chip stuck on Repeat. "We're rotting in the soil of our past. When is the last time we had a major scientific discovery?"

"You mean besides the giant tomb you call Life Unit?"

"Life Unit is not a tomb. Where do you get such bizarre ideas?"

"It looks like one of the tombs of…never mind. Consider this: you are in your fifties, and—"

Taldra knew he made such mistakes on purpose, but she still corrected him: "Forties."

"You are in your forties, and yet you still look like you're around twenty-five. Do you not like the virus that flows through our blood, eating away cancer and all other impurities? Valchondria gave the virus to us. Can anything outside Valchondria offer eternal life?"

"I'd hardly call the virus a recent invention. To the side, the concept of the adjective 'eternal' suggests beliefs that can't be promoted anywhere but on or beneath the walkways, as you would be quick to remind me if I were so reckless as to use that word."

"I wasn't being literal. You're obviously not familiar with the concept of hyperbole." Tquil's lower lip twitched a little.

"Time has past on our final question," said the computer, in its halting monotone. "Are there any final comments?"

Taldra thought about how her father had suddenly started aging, despite the virus. Even in the quick glimpses she caught during his collector messages, he certainly didn't look twenty-five any more. In fact, he looked much older than she thought he would look without the virus. Her mother had also looked worse in their last few taped rebukes of Taldra. Of course, she never saw them in person, and they would never even grant her an actual conversation over the wallscreen.

Neither Taldra nor Tquil said anything else, so the lights shut down as the computer-operated transmission ended. Taldra knew Tquil had something to say. He always did.

"How many more of these debates must we endure?" he asked, slapping his knee, just left of the green stripe that his pants always included. Taldra's eyes followed his hand as it pulled away from that strange action. Everything about Tquil seemed incredibly strange to her. And why the green stripes? Geln also loved green stripes, usually on his credit box strap or on his shirt. Was there some trend among colorsighted people? And, if so, were Geln and Tquil both color-sighted? It sounded like an interesting notion, but Taldra really wanted neither of those two in her group.

"I lost count of how many of the debates we've already endured." She looked past him at the dust-covered computer terminals that towered over them like robot sentries. "I might cancel the others."

"Why? I hear you lost your little media job with the SSC, though I didn't hear if it was because of your radical ideas or your girth. Really, Dr. Lorfeltez, what could take up your time?"

"A project, a spouse, and a teenage son." She hated his smug demeanor; she hated when she found herself answering his rude questions; and, most of all, she hated her determination to keep him from learning about her problems at home. What did it matter if he knew? Why would he want to know? But she constructed her answers to conceal the simple fact that her family was suddenly coming apart. "One of my assistants—you remember Dr. Geln—he resigned a while back. It's been a challenge for my spouse and I to keep Project Life Unit going without Geln's help."

"Project Life Unit," said Tquil, again shaking his head. "Don't you care about our project any more? Even if it was the gossip masters who suggested putting us on the same show, you're the one who wanted to get Valchondria's youth excited about reforms, about political involvement."

"I still do, but no one watches the show. And please stop sending me your video chip samples. I don't have time to sit in front of the wallscreen all day."

"You should take time, as a parent, if you love your child. My new chips are focused on teens Argen's age."

"Glory," said Taldra. The salutation meant nothing to her; it merely served as a way to end a conversation, which she felt would be safer than the more appealing choice of punching Tquil in the face for his implication that she didn't love her son. Besides, punching Tquil sounded more like something Hachen would do. Earlier in the year, at the annual Maintainers Appreciation Party, Hachen began fighting with some fellow for making snide comments about Taldra's political views. Of course, the Maintainers broke that one up quickly.

"Glory," said Tquil. "Tell your family I won't keep you away from them any more."

He touched her shoulder; she jerked away. Taldra left Valcine Signal Complex as quickly as she could walk without running.

CHAPTER 14

Kryldon and Argen had been best friends since attending pre-school computer training together, just as their mothers had been friends during school. Few secrets remained between them. Entering their late teens and Valcine University, they shared a dissatisfaction with their stagnant world. During their visits to the filthy but unmonitored haven under the walkways, one of them would repeat something that one of their parents had said at home, such as "Nothing on Valchondria changes but the fashions," and the private debate would begin. They discussed many topics that no one dared bring up at the university, such as what happened to rape victims and invalids, why most Valchondrians were poor, whether the virus really improved living quality or helped elderly people, and how often credit bank malfunctions destroyed people's lives.

They even discussed a man who kept avoiding Argen, a man who would turn and walk the other way whenever Argen saw him in the dusty corridors of Valcine University. Kryldon blocked the man's path one day so Argen could grab his shoulder.

"Don't you know who I am?" Argen asked. "I'm your grandson."

The man pushed Argen away, saying, "I don't have a child, so I couldn't have a grandchild."

"I'm your grandson," said Argen, unable to believe that someone could reject his own child and his own grandchild, whatever the reason. But everyone hated Taldra, so they had to hate her son as well.

That scene kept repeating in Argen's mind, distracting him from Kryldon's current surprise.

"Thinking about your grandfather again?" asked Kryldon, as the elevator brought them to the basement of Valcine Plaza, the floor that included Leader's quarters. Whoever led this underground group Kryldon had fallen into obviously enjoyed some government contacts. After all, this same building contained the homes and meeting places of the Supreme Science Council. Argen still couldn't believe that the guards even let them into the elevator, but it sped down to the lower decks, its restricted access lights flashing across its dome ceiling.

The elevator stopped.

"Argen?" asked Kryldon, as the round metal booth opened. Argen's friend looked skeletal with his hair cut nearly to nothing and his weight at what his healer called "dangerously low." Argen had asked about his appearance several times, but Kryldon would just say he liked his "new look," instead of admitting the loss of his muscular build.

"I wish I could stop thinking about that old hiliate." They stepped out into the wide, dimly lit basement, seeing no windows, no banners, not even the advertisements Argen would expect to find on nearly every wall of every building in Valcine. Instead, a few hundred chairs encircled a large, portable platform.

"Then stop. Can you believe how big this place is? It's great!" They passed dozens of familiar and unfamiliar youth—many of them as slender as Kryldon—then sat near the middle of the row of chairs closest to the podium.

"Kryldon, big isn't always great. We got into big trouble last week. Was that great? No, I don't think it was, and gratitude for asking." Though he never acknowledged it, Argen had barely convinced himself to come. Kryldon had offered only sketchy details, as if he feared Argen wouldn't come if he knew more. The fact that Kryldon usually gave more details than anyone could possibly want only added to Argen's nervousness. What was this place, and what was happening to Kryldon?

"Well, this is different from childish pranks. This is something that mature, responsible citizens attend."

"Yes, I see some mature, responsible citizens walking in the door. I wasn't even aware they'd been released from their cells in Urloan Control."

"See? That's just my aim. They now have a channel for their rebellious tendencies."

"They found a lucrative channel at a credit bank. And have you noticed the virtual lack of adults here?"

"We have nothing against adults. We just think that youth have been less poisoned by the Maintainers. They have cleaner minds, and they can take a stand for truth. We believe in them."

"We?" Argen grimaced. "When did you go plural? And when did you start involving yourself in people's minds? You should really find a boyfriend, or a hobby, or something other than this basement scene. It's really crumbled."

"It isn't crumbled. Don't re-filter me."

"Then don't fling religion at me. The priests use the same heavy hazard phrases you were just using. You know you can get arrested for pushing religion outside the walkways."

"This isn't about religion. It's about truth. Those who don't believe every word Gazer says simply haven't read the truth."

Argen couldn't believe what he was hearing! "Read? Where did you find books?"

"Be quiet. Gazer is about to begin."

"Begin what? Gazing? I've never heard such a weird-sounding name."

"Stop it, Argen." Kryldon effected a slow, assertive tone, as if talking to a baby. Argen met this tone with a threatening glance, unaccustomed to his friend speaking to him that way. Kryldon leaned closer to Argen and whispered, "You said you wouldn't embarrass me tonight. Now just watch who appears on the stage."

Argen watched, ignoring the strange chant that had begun, watching the man in the multi-patterned robe walk out. Though the shock of whom he saw made it difficult for him to speak, Argen managed to state the obvious: "Kryldon, that's Dr. Geln."

"He took Gazer as his chosen name."

"I didn't know he had become married. Why didn't you tell me that Geln was going to be here?"

"You wouldn't have believed me," said Kryldon, tapping Argen's knee with his fist, as if sharing some elaborate joke. "Just listen. You'll be glad you came."

Gazer stood before the crowded mass of teens with his hands stretched to them in greeting, a king before his subjects. Everyone grew silent as his hands dropped.

"Glory, my friends," he said, his voice sounding more confident than Argen had ever heard it. Geln had always seemed nervous or upset around Taldra and Hachen. Suddenly, everyone seemed different to Argen, like a dream that borrowed from reality but then distorted it. "There are many here that I have not met, but I will gladly spend time with each of you after presenting the truth to you. My name is Gazer. Tonight I will speak to you about the evil ones. It seems that our activities look too much like progress: something the evil ones fear. A group of Maintainers found some of our confidence pills and took them to Urloan Control, the place where they make plans to destroy all progress, all truth, all creativity. They claim what they do is for the benefit of all Valchondrians, as if they care about anyone but themselves. And do they tell us what eventually happens to the items they confiscate? No. I will tell you: they divide it among themselves. And do you know why the evil ones don't want us to have confidence pills?"

Gazer stared into the audience, slowly increasing the targets of his attention, but his eyes stopped on Argen. A smile came to Gazer's square face. "Yes, I see the answers in your eyes. You are enlightened like me. The evil ones want to take away anything that can help us believe we can change our world, and they don't want us to have any secrets or any communion. What do the evil ones say?"

"No brothers, no sisters, no friends," most of the crowd, including Kryldon, said in unison. Besides feeling increasingly uncomfortable, Argen felt insulted by the way Gazer talked to them, the same parent-to-baby tone that Kryldon had just used in their conversation.

"The evil ones, they know the confidence pills deserve their name." Gazer held up a large plastic canister.

"This is largely weird," whispered Argen, but Kryldon didn't seem to hear him.

"Can we surrender to the evil ones?" asked Gazer. "Can we let them continue to inhibit our lives and our growth? How long will it be until they drag you into one of their hospitals and kill you in the name of Valchondria? We know the elderly are reported dead if they have to visit a hospital more than three times in a year. We know what happens to them. We are not fooled." Sweat poured from Gazer's forehead, though the room grew colder than Argen could stand. "Tomorrow night, Gazer's friend, Dr. Tquil, will teach us how not to be manipulated by the evil ones. I want you all to be here. And bring a friend. Now line up if you want a confidence pill."

The chanting resumed, and Argen managed to discern the words: "Gazer hates the evil ones. Gazer is my friend."

"I'm going up," said Kryldon. His habit of leaning forward, elbows on knees and hands on face, had obscured his eyes to Argen, but now he faced Argen with a blank gaze, as if staring into nothing.

"So am I," said Argen, his voice decisive. "I'd like to talk to Geln, or Gazer, or whoever he is."

"Don't say anything stupid." The blank gaze faded into an emotion: annoyance. "This is serious."

"Note: I am a mature, responsible citizen. Get in line for your confidence pill. I hope you aren't going to take it, but it's probably a placebo anyway."

"What's a placebo?" Kryldon's voice squeaked on the word.

"By glory, you're so naïve! A placebo is a fake pill to cure illnesses and chemical problems that no longer exist. Depressed people take them, and they feel better."

"This is real, Argen. You'll know. To the side, you have to take it in front of Gazer. He doesn't want us to get into any trouble by leaving with them in our possession."

"How noble of him." Argen breathed in deeply as they drew closer to Gazer, who climbed down from the stage and began giving the pills to his docile followers. The teens lined up as if taking part in some sort of religious ceremony. It bothered Argen that Kryldon seemed undisturbed by the strange silence that now filled the room, in place of the former chanting. Total quiet existed in few places on the crowded world of Valchondria, and Argen certainly didn't expect to find it among a group of teenagers. When Argen finally stood facing the author of this calm chaos, Geln looked no different than the day he suddenly left them and Life Unit, with no previous announcement.

"Argen," said Gazer, looking at him as if he were a present still in its holo-casing.

"Glory, Dr. Geln," said Argen, as naturally as the circumstances would allow. Despite their friendship, Geln had never tried to contact Argen after his departure, never left a collector message.

"I knew you would come to me one day," said Gazer, smiling like a used hovercraft salesman.

"You never transmitted an invitation."

"Don't, Argen," warned Kryldon, who had already swallowed his pill. But Argen wanted answers, not more confusion.

Gazer continued, "Argen, we stand at the threshold of a new era, ready to bask in a world of glory."

"I'm sure my grandparents heard the same rhetoric when they were my age—when they received the virus. But does the glory we speak so obsessively and blandly about really exist on Valchondria? You've got your rallies and your vid-ad slogans, but can you change the fact that we live in a world where geniuses waste their time watching the wallscreen, a world that treats visionaries like my parents as some sort of threat, a world where parents disown their child for being different? I've breathed enough exhaust for one day, Geln."

"My chosen name is Gazer." The next boy tried to push Argen aside, but Gazer waved his hand between them. "Don't discourage our friend's boldness, true believer. He is as brave as his mother and as subversively skeptical as his father. Argen and I are a special breed."

"Who are you?" demanded Argen. "Who are you, really?"

"Your friend. I'll stand beside you and encourage your dreams. You can dream, can't you Argen?"

"Of course. What—?"

"Allow me to enhance those dreams. Allow me to help you dream in color." Gazer turned the canister sideways, making a tiny capsule fall through the hole in the top, onto his fleshy palm. "This is not an intoxicant. It won't limit your thinking. Instead, it will break you free from the influences of the evil ones. Your mind will merge with the possibilities it has imagined. The virus was only the beginning; the confidence pills interact with the virus, helping you reach your true potential."

"I don't believe in you, or your pills."

"Then what is the harm of taking one?" Gazer offered him the pill, dropped it into his trembling palm. He moved it around with the fingertips of his other hand, grasped it, put it in his mouth, and swallowed it.

"I don't feel any different." He shrugged his shoulders.

"You will," said Gazer, as the next boy tried again to push Argen away, this time succeeding by the sheer inertia of all the teenagers pressing behind him.

"Gazer is your friend," said Kryldon, after finding Argen in the crowd that seemed to keep getting tighter, more restrictive, more ominous. Like Dr. Geln, Kryldon seemed to become someone unknown, someone secret, like the mysterious person Taldra and Hachen talked about when they thought Argen couldn't hear them. In the midst of the sweaty crowd that suffocated him, pushed against him, Argen felt excluded, cut off, separated.

❧   ❧   ❧

Later, Argen and Kryldon sat together under the walkways, against a moldy wall of a building's basement level. The cold night wind blew trash down the long corridors of gray stone walls, keeping the hover-fumes from ever becoming dense and noticeable. Occasionally, walkway people would shuffle about nearby, paying no attention to the two boys whose clothing looked much newer than theirs.

Walkway people knew normal people when they saw them, just as normal people knew walkway people when they saw them. It reflected the class structure of Valchondria. Like his parents, Argen despised that structure, but they lived at the top of it, not knowing how to change it. Argen wondered if the fact that he saw walkway people at the rally meant that he could now work with them and help them.

Still, Argen's mind drifted back to other matters. "Kryldon, are you certain that this is the best way for change? Recognize, we've gone completely undermall with a gang of anti-techs, walkway people, and ex-inmates."

Kryldon tilted his head. "Don't be so maintained! We're also criminals by common thought, simply because our thoughts aren't common."

"Such a clever boy!" Argen slapped Kryldon's chest. "But we could get hurt, or arrested. Can you endure that?"

"With you? Yes." Kryldon's gray eyes peered into Argen's. When he touched Argen's shoulder, he left his hand there. "Argen, I have...feelings for you."

Argen shrugged his shoulders, and Kryldon's hand fell away. "I know. We're best friends."

Kryldon looked away. "Yes, we are. But that wasn't my aim."

The thought had never occurred to Argen, until that moment. "Oh. But I'm not same-gendered, or even both-gendered. And, to the side, we're both too young to discuss our romantic feelings."

"You're sounding maintained again! But I didn't know if you were. I mean, we've never talked about it, except when my parents bragged about the fact that I am. I just hoped...."

"Forgiveness. If I were, I would want to be with you...when we're older. It must be great being same-gendered. Someone always wants you to uncle them or safe-friend their daughter. And you don't have people lecturing you about zero population. You're born into the ideal group."

Kryldon chuckled. "There is one thing that's odd about me that you wouldn't like. And I think it's somehow related to being same-gendered."

"Really? What's that?"

"Sometimes, when I hear fast-paced music during a wallscreen vid, I feel like dancing, in a big crowd of people."

"Dancing? Like old people used to do?"

Kryldon laughed, tossing his head back. "I know, it's rusted!"

"All the way through!" Argen also laughed a little, but then became serious. "Gratitude for being honest with me."

"Gratitude for listening." Kryldon fidgeted about, obviously looking for words that might not be legally permitted but that expressed his feelings. After watching a family of rodents run by them, he finally spoke again. "Argen, I want a world where all people can be honest, and where a few people don't control everyone else. The Maintainers talk about 'compassionate control,' but it's still control. We have to work for reform, and all the traditional venues have failed in that effort. So, yes, I can endure anything to bring back the glory.

"When our mothers spoke at that rally, they were starting something that we must bring to a new level. We weren't a part of their lives yet, but we were a part of their ambitions. We're intertwined with their goals of a better Valchondria. I believe in the things Gazer tells us, because they're things that I already thought, and things that could help us fulfill what our mothers and our fathers dream of."

Argen took all that in, and it made sense, to a certain limit. "But the confidence pills: I'm not sure how safe they are."

"Gazer is a true patriot, and patriots always think of children first. He wouldn't endanger us. He's helping us, Argen."

"I recognize that," said Argen, with little sincerity. He stood up and watched a bearded, gray-haired walkway person who stumbled around and slapped himself while mumbling insanely. From two levels above them, hovercrafts buzzed and shook the vine-covered walkways, making their rusted beams sway ever so slightly. The stench of hover-fumes and walkway tossings filled Argen's lungs as he breathed in deeply and unsteadily.

The confidence pill worked for a while, but that feeling of confidence now became a feeling that he couldn't quite breathe properly, a feeling that his heart and his life were moving too quickly. He wanted to slow down, but he also wanted that moment of confidence again.

The walkway person shuffled past them, a little more steadily, but with a tear streaming into his beard.

CHAPTER 15

Taldra sat at the kitchen table while her spouse paced the gray-carpeted floor. She wondered if he could see the big red stain she had tried to scrub away the night before, or if he knew she had spilled that glass of meda squeezings while he slept peacefully. He kept stepping across the stain. Was it a different shade of gray to him?

Her eyes followed him back and forth, as if his pacing could somehow satisfy her own need to somehow act out frustration. The deterioration of their family had begun when the doorway's collapse left Telius in the past. That deterioration increased a little every time the date came and went for the doorway to re-open, always with no results. Hachen and Taldra would guard the doorway throughout the expected times, but they never saw the slightest sparkle where the multi-colored lights had once swirled around inside Life Unit.

Then came the day when, with very little warning, Geln deserted them. They never heard from their loyal, awkward, and discomforting comrade again. Taldra secretly rejoiced in his departure, but it meant more pressure on her and Hachen. To make matters even worse, the SSC suddenly and unexpectedly deleted her position as one of their media representatives, a position that most of the SSC claimed she never deserved in the first place. Then came the stories about Taldra on the wallscreen every day. Story after story expressed the rage of people who branded her an enemy of Valchondria, a disrupter.

All of those problems, though they still plagued Taldra, seemed less relevant than their problems with Argen, the son they had chosen to raise. She tried to protect him from the subtle hostilities of their world, tried to arm him with the ability to think for himself and make rational choices. She tried, but he never seemed to listen, or even to acknowledge her efforts. He would just say something like "I see your aim, Taldra," then wander away somewhere with Kryldon.

"Argen seems so distant," she said, after Hachen finally stopped pacing and sat down beside her at the table.

"He's seventeen," replied Hachen, as if that reminder could somehow settle every problem in the universe. Taldra had expected a more logical response to the dilemma, or at least some hint of a new revelation. After all, Hachen's pacing or finger tapping usually reflected his inward contemplation, his active mind. "Telius is probably going through the same phase. I don't understand it, but Dr. Tquil says the worst things for a seventeen-year-old are criticism and pressure."

"I am not concerned with Dr. Tquil, aside from how I can best avoid him. I am concerned with our child." She didn't mean to sound angry, but she could hear the anger in her voice as she spoke.

Their arguments had become increasingly frequent over the past several months, especially after she lost her secondary job. The grant money for Life Unit never went as far as intended, but she wanted to continue their work. Still, their financial situation hardly threatened to destroy them; they still owned and paid weekly taxes on a two-story house in Valchondria's crowded capitol. She didn't know why they argued. In fact, she usually forgot what they argued about, long before each argument ended with one of them storming out of the room. But the fights continued, like a moon locked into its orbit.

Taldra added, "I think Argen is involved with that cultic little group, the Youth For Valchondrian Reform."

"He discusses politics with a close circle of friends, as it is. We've always wanted him to become a political activist. We need pro-colony representatives."

The abrupt silence only contributed to the tension as Argen stumbled through the wallscreen room, into the kitchen. Taldra could smell the alcohol he would always claim not to drink. Hachen's eyes pleaded with Taldra to suppress her comments. Her hands clenched her arms, as if she feared what they might do.

"Glory, Argen," said Hachen. "There's a message from Kryldon on the collector."

Taldra said nothing until Argen left the room, but she noticed his lack of courtesy. He didn't even acknowledge their presence until Hachen mentioned Kryldon's name, and then he stumbled back into the video room without a word.

"He's drunk," said Taldra.

"Yes, I noticed."

"What should we do? I've already paid two 1000c fines for his public drunkenness and legally un-permitted language."

"We can start by talking to him about what he's going through."

"Fine. Maybe we can discuss the fact that three members of what you call his 'close circle of friends' were caught breaking into Urloan Control today and then saying 'Gazer knows the true glory.' I want to know who this Gazer is I keep hearing about, and what he's done to our child."

"We'll find out," said Hachen, wiping the tear that hid in the corner of her left eye. "We'll find out."

"And what if he's drunk one night with a girl? What if they do something, and she becomes pregnant?"

"He knows the laws. He wouldn't risk chemical castration."

"I just wish he were same-gendered, like Kryldon. I'd feel safer."

"Well, we could have changed his genetic structure, while we were breaking the other reproduction rules. He'd be—"

Argen stumbled back into the kitchen, grabbed a package of gredga chips from the top circular shelf, dropped them on the floor. He muttered something to himself, as if alone.

"Are you all right?" asked Hachen. Taldra was glad her spouse spoke first, since she felt unable to speak. Because of his temper, Hachen always told Taldra that she was stronger and more emotionally controlled than he had ever been. Right now, she felt so weak and uncontrollable that she just sat there, sorting through euphemisms and verbal patterns that she had seen on the child-rearing video chips she so hated. She thought of all of them, especially the ones from Dr. Tquil, as thorough mind surges in legally permitted language. Still, she couldn't keep them out of her mind, especially in such desperate moments. Why couldn't raising a child be as simple as programming a computer?

"Yes, Hachen, I'm adequate," said Argen, his voice gentle but loud, like his father's. He resembled his father in many ways, both in looks and personality, but Taldra couldn't imagine Hachen ever acting so irresponsibly. "I'm sorry I was out late, but I was looking through the library for the colonization documents, for this friend of ours."

Taldra wanted to ask which friend. Gazer?

"I wasn't aware that you had other friends," said Hachen, as Argen sat down with them.

"I never said I didn't." He gave them the rolled eyes, a non-verbal pattern he learned at an early age, before he could even recite the Pledge of Legally Permitted Language. "As I was trying to tell you, I was looking for the vids, but they aren't there."

"That's good," said Taldra. "It means someone must be watching them. If you're interested, I have copies of most of the ones I used for my video chip."

Argen sat down at the table and leaned forward. "*Other Valchondrias* isn't in the library either, or in the stores. The SSC agreed to let the Maintainers remove it from libraries, with all other pro-colony materials, because children have access to libraries. Haven't you played the news bulletins on the collector?"

"Not since the one about the break-in at Urloan Control," said Taldra, unable to remain silent any longer. "Did you hear about that? It sounds like those Youth For Valchondrian Reform are becoming quite a problem."

His face twitched a little before he regained his defensive countenance. "This is a problem. The Maintainers have put a hundred-year renewal on the law that says to leave Valchondria or attempt outside contact is to deny its glory. Any attempts to do so will result in heavy fines. They've also discussed outlawing any pro-colony speech, writing, and video, even if it avoids the word 'colony.' They want to reclassify anything like that as danger speak and anti-glory. There's even a push to make the word 'space' illegal."

"How?" Hachen stood up and slammed his fist against a plastic wall. "How can they think of this overcrowded junk heap as paradise?"

"We can speak with Leader," said Taldra, in her calming tone. She feared what Hachen might do in his anger, and she came to resent that anger when she realized that Argen inherited it. "Recognize all the funding he has approved for Life Unit. There must be an explanation."

"If we don't hasten, we won't be able to argue our case, because the words we need won't be legally permitted. It's maddening! Why have language if you can't talk, or a brain if you can't think? I speak clearly, Taldra: one day I'll shout every word of profanity, danger speak, anti-glory, and heavy hazard at the people who've imprisoned our minds. I'll shout those words, not because I want to disrupt, but because we've drained the life from the few words we still dare to speak. I want new words, Taldra. I want new hope. I want our work to continue."

She slapped her own body, just above her heart. "And you think I don't? But I really don't know how much power Leader still holds."

Hachen had to regain his breath before speaking. They had seen Leader's powers fade as both the SSC and the Maintainers became more powerful, especially the Maintainers. "At least he'll listen, which is more than we receive from the SSC." The extra redness in his face faded to its usual lighter red as he regained his composure and put on his mask of serenity. "Forgiveness if I suggested you don't care about our work. You've done more for the cause than anyone has. Argen, your mother and I will speak with Leader, but I want you to tell me something first."

"Yes, Hachen?" Argen started to stand up, but sat back down, apparently to keep from falling. Despite this new crisis, Taldra's eyes still followed her son's clumsy actions. Red lines surrounded his irises like scars on his eyes, which were surrounded by puffy black skin on his otherwise red face.

"Who is Gazer?" asked Hachen.

A look of surprise swept over Argen's face before turning into a contrived smile. "I don't know, but, honestly, I don't know who Telius is either."

Taldra first took offense in the sarcasm of Argen's statement, then in his casual lie about not knowing who Gazer was, but nothing prepared her to hear Argen speak his twin's name. It shocked and delighted her, and it made her feel guilty for withholding a secret from him: Argen was the only Valchondrian teenager with a sibling.

"I've always wanted to say the whispered name, to repeat it with you," said Argen, his voice filled with accusation and envy. "You take such pleasure in saying it to each other. Sometimes you even cry when you say the name. Who is this Telius person that he makes the two of you so proud and so sentimental? He sure isn't me."

"Lessen your tone," Hachen demanded, though he looked more dumbfounded than angered by his son's outburst.

For them, such honesty with their child had become foreign, a concept they only heard about on the wallscreen. Taldra knew Hachen could offer no logical response that wouldn't sound completely hypocritical. What should he say? That they wanted him to stay away from outlaws but that they had broken one of the highest Valchondrian laws? Instead, he said nothing.

"Argen deserves to know," said Taldra, clasping her son's short black hair between her fingers. She could feel his body trembling, trembling as hard as her own body trembled when she had nightmares about someone hurting him or Telius. "We were wrong not to tell you, Argen. We…just wanted to protect you."

"From what?"

Taldra read the sudden drop in Argen's tone as a connection. He seemed to realize her concern.

"We'll explain all about Telius when we return," said Hachen. "But I must speak with Leader now. Geln won't return calls from me or Taldra, but I don't think he'll refuse you. Call him and ask him to meet me at Valcine Plaza immediately. Taldra, I don't think you should go, considering—"

"Considering that I'm anti-glory and the enemy of all civilization," said Taldra, with more resentment than her flippant remarks usually revealed. She had enough problems without their whimpering leader crawling before those power mongers, who, for no apparent reason, called themselves scientists or Maintainers. The scientists never invented anything. And what sort of title was "Maintainer"? She wanted to call them "eroders" or "reducers." What was there to maintain, even if they did live up to their title? And why simply maintain? Why not progress?

"I'll meet you back here later," she said, before standing up and kissing her spouse. That was the only time they'd kissed lately: when going away from each other. "I'm going to the university to get the master copy of *Other Valchondrias*…before it conveniently goes the way of books."

As Hachen left, Taldra realized that they had already abandoned Argen to his confusion, already forgotten about their inquiry over Gazer. She decided she should tell Argen something, anything, about

Telius, but then she noticed that Argen had passed out at the table. She would have to be the one to call Dr. Geln.

❧   ❧   ❧

"Are you healthy?" asked Geln, as his image appeared on her wallscreen. After not seeing him since his sudden departure, it surprised her that they still had the correct wallscreen address for him. His hairline had receded even more, but one thing had not changed: his eyes still revealed something she didn't want to see. And why did he always inquire about her health, as if she might die at any moment?

"I'm fine, Geln. But we need your help, your persuasive voice. Could you meet Hachen at Valcine Plaza?"

"Now? I'm occupied. How is Argen?"

"Argen is very contented right now. Please, Geln. It's an emergency. All our work could be lost."

"Oh, surely. But you owe me for all my tolerance. Glory."

Taldra could feel the chill leave her back and see the tiny bumps leave her arms as Geln's image faded. She had never told Hachen how much Geln had frightened her at times, or how much she resented the night he came into their home. She even resented Hachen for inviting him.

Geln often seemed like a friend to her. But sometimes, his tiny eyes bore into her soul, making her feel like she had somehow betrayed him, and that he wanted to punish her for that betrayal. At the same time, those eyes revealed his love for her, and not just the love of friendship.

CHAPTER 16

❀

*A*rgen called his mother's name from the kitchen as he opened his eyes. He wasn't sure how long he slept, but he could still feel the effects of mixing confidence pills and meda squeezings. The veins in his forehead kept beating against his skin, as if attempting an escape. He tried to remember how he and Kryldon had gotten the squeezings this time, but his recent memories all blurred together. That happened to him a lot, starting the night he took his first confidence pill. He did remember telling Kryldon that he felt no different after taking his first confidence pill.

And now....

Now he had said the secret name. Instead of feeling like he was a part of the secret, like he finally found a way of relating to his parents, he felt ashamed for having said it. What right did he have to expose their secrets? What had they done to hurt him? They were only concerned, and understandably so. He couldn't walk straight, talk clearly, think at all. And when his father mentioned Gazer's name, Argen had almost repeated one of the slogans Gazer taught him: "Gazer is my friend."

What gave Gazer such power over his followers that they opened their mouths only to speak his words, that they never even questioned those words, that they treated those words as above questioning? Why had they merely replaced the Maintainers with another who also maintained them? Sometimes Argen imagined himself writing Gazer's simplistic slogans on his clothes, on his walls, on the back of his parents' hovercraft, or something else absurd like that, so he could see them as often as he heard them, so he could reassure himself and everyone else of their validity.

"Taldra?" Argen called. "Where are you? Is Hachen back?" He stood up and wandered into the video room. "Taldra?"

Instead of finding her, he found the collector's blinking light. A message from Leader said that Life Unit might lose its funding. Argen wouldn't allow it.

He ran up the spiral staircase, tripping twice, eventually reaching his room. A switch on his wall released one of the magnetized storage cases from the ceiling, slowly lowering it to the floor. Argen tossed out chip case after chip case until he found the one that contained the laser pistol Gazer had given him. He removed the compact gray cylinder from the plastic container.

From another case he retrieved an undermall version of a confidence pill, though he couldn't remember how many he had already taken. Despite Gazer's efforts at monitoring their distribution, the confidence pills quickly made their way into the drug undermall.

While trying to design a plan, Argen swallowed the round pill. It felt like a rock in his dry throat; he almost spat it up but managed to force it back down. He thought of possibly acknowledging Leader's broadcast and asking how the discussion with Gazer was going, but he knew Leader could do nothing if the Supreme Science Council had made their decision. From there it went to the Maintainers, who listened to no one, stood above everyone.

Argen wanted to protect his parents' work. He had failed them so many times in the past: the drinking, the vandalism, the legally unpermitted language. "Why did I do those things?" he asked himself. "And why have I trusted Gazer so much, but not my own parents?" Argen had attended every YFVR meeting for the past two months, learned every slogan, implemented every recruitment technique, learned the official argument for every issue, taken every confidence pill Gazer offered.

What about what Hachen and Taldra offered? He stood up, but fell against a plastic wall. The room seemed to move beneath his feet, turning sideways. The lights on the walls and ceiling seemed to flash off and on.

As soon as his balance steadied enough for him to walk, Argen ran out the house, between the crowded buildings, down the hot and dusty walkways beneath the buzzing noises of the hoverlanes that entangled vine-covered buildings. Though nearly bumping into several walkway people who were holding out their credit boxes and begging for credits, he refused to let anyone slow him down. Soon, he reached the tiny, waist-high fence that surrounded Life Unit, designating it as government property.

Because of the constant crowding in Valcine, no crowd needed to gather for a commotion. Argen, waving the laser pistol about, already had an audience.

Everyone is listening, and everyone is afraid, he told himself. *They're afraid because they've done wrong. They are the evil ones.*

He braced his feet against the fence, ready for whatever might happen, wondering what might happen. He hated Life Unit for taking all of his parents' time, but now he wanted to save it. He wanted to keep their dreams alive.

Several Maintainers tore through the crowd, carrying the sleep rifles that they used for youth-related disturbances, but Hachen made it through before them. Gazer appeared in the crowd for an instant, then disappeared into the confusion. Hachen pushed quickly toward Argen before becoming a blur. Argen's face dripped with the sweat that burned his eyes as he aimed the laser pistol at everyone and no one. The hover-fumes loomed even worse than usual, filling his lungs, making him groggy; he just wanted to sleep. No, he couldn't sleep; he needed to save Life Unit.

"Argen, what are you doing?" demanded Hachen. His face became focused as he walked toward his son.

"They...they...." Argen could barely organize his thoughts enough to speak. Hachen looked angry. *No, he isn't supposed to be angry at me; he's supposed to be proud of me for saving Life Unit. Why can't he ever be proud of me?* "Hachen, they're going to destroy Life Unit."

"That won't happen. We're just going to have to make more thorough status reports, to justify the funding. Now give me the laser pistol before you hurt someone."

"Move away from the boy, Dr. Naldod," said one of the Maintainers, pointing his sleep rifle at them. Argen noticed the thick black stripe down the front of his gray body suit. A captain. *Good.* If he gained enough attention to pull a Top Maintainer from Urloan Control, then his actions would make the news immediately. *The evil ones have to see...have to see...have....* Argen watched the world smear then turn black.

"Discard your weapon, Argen," said the captain.

As his vision returned, Argen thought he recognized the voice, but he wasn't sure. It might have been the one who arrested him when he painted Gazer's name over a wallscreen at the mall. The rifle aimed at him meant nothing. With the strength that the confidence pills gave him, he could fight the effects of the sleep bullets. He wouldn't let the evil ones hold power over him.

But Hachen. Why doesn't Hachen understand? Life Unit means progress, according to Hachen. And Hachen wants progress, so we have to protect Life Unit. What is Hachen doing? Why is he trying to grab the laser pistol?

"Hachen? Why?" Argen yanked back on the laser pistol, causing it to fall. As it hit the ground, a beam of light shot upward, burning into his father's shirt. "No!"

❦   ❦   ❦

Returning home from Valcine University, Taldra saw the crowd that had gathered near Life Unit. After disengaging her craft from hoverlane mode, she piloted it to her reserved parking area, jumped out, and ran into the crowd. Somehow, she knew it involved Argen. She sensed it in the worst way, knowing it without possibly knowing or wanting to know.

And there he was, being dragged away by the Maintainers, his head bouncing around.

"Let him go!" she screamed.

Several Maintainers rushed to her side. One of them, a bearded black man with a thin face, touched her shoulder, but with a firmness that felt more like restraint than greeting. "Dr. Lorfeltez, we'll need to find you a counselor. There's tragic news."

She pointed at him. "I don't want a counselor. I want my son." It suddenly occurred to her that Hachen should have returned and would probably have noticed the commotion. "Why didn't you contact me, or my spouse?"

The Maintainer shook his head, looking sincerely hurt by what he needed to tell her. "Dr. Lorfeltez, we can't release your son, because he just shot Dr. Naldod. I didn't want to tell you this way." His hand remained on her shoulder.

She pushed his hand away. Her mind rushed with thoughts and feelings she couldn't comprehend or express. "Are you rusted all the way through? Argen doesn't have a gun."

He held his hands in front of her. "Dr. Lorfeltez, please, we don't understand what happened either." One of his hands again rested on her shoulder.

Before she knew what or why or anything else, Taldra landed a forceful punch squarely on the Maintainer's nose. As the other Maintainers grabbed her arms, she shouted legally un-permitted curses and called out for Hachen and Argen.

CHAPTER 17

❀

Shadows climbed every wall within Life Unit as Taldra forced her body more tightly into the darkest corner of the utility room. Her eyes stayed on the open doorway that could lead her through the control room, into the battery room. She knew Telius might be in there, and in danger, but she had no weapons, and she couldn't activate the alarm or hit a Maintainer button without Life Unit announcing her presence.

She heard Gazer's voice; somehow, she recognized it, even though she had never heard it before. It tore through her skin like broken glass. The Youth For Valchondrian Reform followed close behind him. Taldra repeatedly swallowed each legally un-permitted curse she wanted to make at Gazer for destroying their lives, for destroying Argen. She stayed in that position as he drew closer, as she awoke from her dream.

The Maintainers had left her in Valcine Regal Hospital, strapped to a bed. She hated that hospital, because it made her think about the day that she had first lost Telius. It made her think about Hachen's death, instead of the lives the healers saved there. She stared at the open doorway for what seemed an eternity before someone walked through it. She hoped it would be her parents, but it was a Maintainer with a thin, slanted stripe across her uniform. A lieutenant.

"Where is my son?" asked Taldra.

"In a mirror prison, at Urloan Control," said the Maintainer, a tall black woman with her hair pulled to one side, into a braid that hung over her face from under her headband. She looked strangely familiar, but Taldra kept imagining her hair differently for some reason.

"'Prison'?" The word was painful to repeat. Taldra tried not to envision her child in one of Urloan's mirror chambers, haunted by the shame of his image.

"Yes, Dr. Lorfeltez. You know the sentence for killing a member of the SSC: Argen may see no one but himself for the rest of his life."

"But it was an accident. There were witnesses. I—" Taldra stopped and stared at the tall woman's beautiful face, and remembered a shock of hair springing from her headband. "Don't I know you?"

"Not in a good way. I'm the one who arrested you, during that riot in Valcine Plaza. Somehow, that makes you my case."

Not sure how to respond to that last comment, Taldra returned to the more urgent concern about her son. "Why was the trial held without me?"

"Your psychological state is obvious by the straps around your body. There was already doubt about your witness qualifications anyway. After all, you approve of radical viewpoints, and, forgiveness for my language, space exploration. Beyond that, you allowed your under-aged son to become intoxicated."

"All of that is totally unrelated to my rights as a witness. Argen might have had a few drinks that night, but—"

The Maintainer interrupted: "Argen's heart is pumping a strange drug through his bloodstream that interacts with the virus; we're not sure exactly what results from that interaction, except that he went into convulsions after a day without the drug. Several canisters of the same drug have been confiscated from the Youth For Valchondrian Reform. The walkway term for them is 'confidence pills.' And, yes, Argen had a few drinks that night, quite a few. We know that he's in the Youth, and I have pictures of him talking to your former assistant. Am I showing my aim?"

"No, you aren't. Argen has never taken drugs, and I don't see what is so shocking about him being seen with someone he's known all his life."

"And someone you thought you knew. But my investigation has led to an interesting discovery about your Dr. Geln. I only regret reaching the hospital after Geln left your spouse's body here."

The Maintainer walked to the other side of the tiny room. Taldra strained her neck while attempting to look across to the Maintainer, but the restraint belts kept her from moving her back. "Please tell me. Please be done with this."

"I de-programmed one of the Youth For Valchondrian Reform. There wasn't much left of her mind, but she was able to tell me that your former assistant, Dr. Geln, is the terrorist known as 'Gazer.' He's revived the Degran cult and plans to turn Valchondria into a new Degranon."

It made a bizarre sort of sense to Taldra, who had always feared that Geln was hiding something evil. "Who else knows this?"

"Everyone will when I finish my report. I'll go straight to captain for this, and I'll get a million credits for wallscreen interviews—not that I want to exploit your spouse's death in any way. But Maintainer salaries aren't what they used to be, unless you're a Top Maintainer. And now I have a family to think about."

Taldra pulled at her restraints. "You mean no one else knows what's going on? You haven't made a report?"

"Not yet. I was hoping you'd have some helpful information."

"My spouse is dead, my son is in prison, and I'm tied up like an animal. Does that help?"

"Now, there's no need to project hostility, Dr. Lorfeltez. That doesn't help anyone. Bringing Gazer to justice might affect your son's case, if he'll witness against Gazer's anti-glory. When you think of something truthfully helpful, call me at Urloan Control. My given name is Sydra." She walked closer, almost close enough to touch

Taldra's hand. "To the side, I hear Leader has made some special arrangements for you."

"Will I be able to go home soon?"

"Yes, but that isn't all. You'll be allowed to remarry, and to have another child. Congratulations." Sydra smiled in a way that suggested she could not have said anything nicer.

"I already have chi—. I already have a child. Do you have a child, Sydra?"

"My spouse and I are adopting a walkway boy. Gratitude for asking."

"Don't let anyone take him from you. He's your child."

She smiled again, and her voice sounded pleasant, as if they were old friends. "I must go now. Glory."

"Don't leave, Sydra." Taldra knew she spoke loudly enough, but feared her emotions had muffled the words. She had never felt so alone before. Even this stranger who insulted her needed to stay, but Sydra was leaving, touching the door button on the wall. Someone needed to stay.

Sydra finished her daily check of the central computers in Urloan Control. All the Maintainers appreciated her gift with technology, but they never seemed to appreciate her in any other way. Why else would they give her the Lorfeltez assignment, of all things? All the Maintainers considered Lorfeltez completely rusted. But they didn't realize how closely Dr. Lorfeltez fit into the largest, most dangerous case in Maintainer history: the Degranon case. Sydra had found it all, even the identity of....

"Gazer."

He strolled around the rows of computer panels, boxing her into a corner.

Waving a laser pistol at her, he said, "You're probably wondering where the other Maintainers are. Some of them had a sudden but insistent drowsiness; it will dissipate after they wake up. But some of them simply turned aside."

Sydra instinctively reached for her laser pistol, but then remembered setting it on her desk. The Top Maintainers never allowed weapons in the upper levels of Urloan Control. Apparently, the Top Maintainers never expected the leader of the Degran cult to slip past the most advanced security systems in all of Valchondria. "What is your aim? What did you do to them?"

He grinned, boyishly. "Nothing. Not that I never tried. But they kept confiscating the confidence pills, and eventually, some of them sampled the product. And then they wanted more, and then they were mine. Everyone wonders who maintains the Maintainers. Well, I do."

"Maybe some of us, but not me."

"I suppose not. You tried to hurt me, Lt. Sydra. No one hurts me." Gazer drew his laser pistol from inside the flap of his shirt and waved it at the computer interface panel. "There is too much wiring in this room. If your fire system went off-line…." He shot the monitor box on the ceiling, melting it. Instead of fire-killing foam, three drops of burning plastic dripped down, nearly burning Sydra. The stench of burning plastic filled her nostrils as her heart beat painfully fast. "If your fire system went off-line, as it has, and an accident happened, as it will, the fire could spread quickly within this tiny enclosed area, without alerting whichever Maintainers are out saving the world at the moment. Your unfortunate death will be a message: a warning, if you will."

Sydra backed slowly against the wall, then edged closer to a Maintainer button.

"I know what you're thinking," he said, pointing the pistol at her. "They're just a signal away, ready to protect you from the bad man and anything else that might disrupt their vision of Valchondria. Or maybe not."

He shot the button, and sparks flew from it, forcing Sydra to draw her arms up and duck away from the ensuing fire. He told her, "Now you're going to find out what happens to people who try to hurt me." Pulling down on the skin beneath his right eye, he added, "The man who gave me those two scars is dead now. I vowed that no one else would ever draw a single drop of blood from me or hurt me in any way without being duly punished. And now, I'm here to maintain you."

Sydra, no longer feeling powerful or fearless, crouched into a corner as he fired at her.

❦   ❦   ❦

Taldra woke the next day to see the restraint-straps gone, but she still felt their pressure, still saw their indentations on her skin. A healer sat in the chair beside her bed, chewing his fingernails.

"How do you feel?" he asked, in a tone that suggested boredom, as if he grew tired of asking everyone that same question day after day.

"Physically: like I need to walk around. Mentally: don't ask."

Upon seeing her failed attempt to sit up, the healer looked at her with her mother's look of disapproval: that overstated expression of raised eyebrows and sucked-in lips. "I thought I should tell you here, in case the news causes a relapse of your breakdown."

"Tell me what? That Leader is really the host of *Catch Those Credits*?" Taldra realized that he was too banal and maintained to understand the sarcasm. "Forgiveness. What is it?"

"There was a fire at Urloan Control. But don't worry, it didn't spread to the prison. The Maintainers' computers and file rooms were damaged, and there was a casualty, your only visitor."

"Sydra?"

"Several gossip masters have asked to talk to you about Maintainer Sydra's visit. Would you grant an interview? It would more than pay for your hospital bill, and it might get us some media coverage for our non-cosmetic work."

Taldra spoke forcefully: "I'll pay the bill. Just don't let the gossip masters near me."

The maternal look again. "I won't. Also, a Dr. Hudza left a message for you via my collector, that her son has moved out and severed contact with them, and that she and her spouse are going undermall, for reasons she can't explain, so she said that you won't hear from her for a long time, if ever. From the sound of it, you probably shouldn't have contact with her anyway. She'll just mix your mind up even worse than it already is. Now get some sleep. You'll go home tomorrow."

"Healer, wait."

Alone again. Why wouldn't anyone stay? Why didn't her parents at least check on her? How was she going to live without her family?

❦   ❦   ❦

How was he going to live without his brother?

That single thought had kept occurring to young Geln as he returned home to his parents, on his final leave before beginning his mission to Valchondria. To his knowledge, he would be the youngest Degran ever sent on such a mission. Still, the young constantly fought the evil ones. Parents would keep their children home from school to burn effigies of the evil ones, or even to throw rocks at their embassy complex. Those were small children: boys with no signs of manhood, girls with no signs of womanhood. That was how desperate they had become to defeat the evil ones.

But this mission. It would change everything. It would unite the ten circles of Degranon, and transform the home world. When Geln's mentor entrusted him with that duty, Geln saw it as nothing less than a sacred calling from God, and himself as nothing less than a warrior for God.

Still, the thing he planned for that day was neither holy nor sacred. And he carried it out. When his parents retired to bed, Geln told his mother that she had a collector message that sounded urgent.

Geln's father never missed sleep, so Geln knew he would remain in bed, even as Geln approached, holding a knife behind his back.

The scars that Geln put on his father's face went so much deeper than his own scars.

So much deeper.

When his mother returned to the room, she became hysterical, pointing, threatening, and accusing—even striking him. He had no choice but to silence her.

He kept telling himself that through the years.

He had no choice.

CHAPTER 18

❀

Wearing one of his favorite robes, Leader stood quietly in his morning lounge, lightly scratching the dry, wrinkled skin on his slender face while looking around the room as if to relearn his surroundings. It was like any morning lounge among the Valchondrian upper class: designed to make people think of nature, but betraying how out of touch the Valchondrians were with nature. The artificial trees and the artificial waterfall near the far wall of the immense room might have looked beautiful before, but they suddenly became distasteful for this particular Valchondrian because, before the introduction of the virus, he could have seen them in color. More and more often, he hated things for the colors they hid from him.

Over his lifetime, much Valchondrian artwork had been destroyed and many Valchondrian songs forgotten, because most people could only see in black and white and could not hear certain musical tones that were once frequent in their songs. Not seeing or hearing all of it, they lost interest. He sometimes heard that young people didn't even listen to music anymore, that they saw it as dull, unrelated to their young lives.

If only they could hear the songs of my youth, as I heard them in my youth, he thought. *But when I hear those songs today, even I can't hear the lost frequencies. My mind used to fill them in, but not anymore.*

Before the virus, he could have experienced the blueness of the water and the orangeness of the trees. Now his old eyes could barely distinguish objects from their shadows.

"Leader?" asked the formal-sounding woman who stood behind him as he leaned down and cupped water in his frail hands.

"They don't write songs like I used to hear," he said, without turning around.

"I've heard some fairly good battle themes in the past few years, but I'd prefer something romantic," she replied. "We're too preoccupied with fighting. It's a waste of talent." He found it odd that she didn't end her sentence with "sir." The SSC and the Maintainers always dwelled on such condescending reverence, mocking him with the hollowness of his office. Even Gazer would observe those tokens of respect, though Leader knew Gazer could turn on him at any moment rather than go through with his promise to restore the position of Leader to being more than merely a figurehead.

Leader turned to see a beautiful black woman in a black body suit similar to those he had worn years ago, when he worked as an over-ocean pilot. In those days, he dreamed of how his determination and his parents' wealth would one day make him one of the most powerful people in the world. Now, he felt increasingly less powerful, but he kept hoping Gazer could change that, and that Gazer could help him make Valchondria something greater.

Before Gazer, Leader stood alone in his struggle, isolated, a relic of past governments. He felt like those rare white-skinned or yellow-skinned people he read about, thanks to one of the books in his secret library. They eventually left for the colonies, because everyone called them "freaks" and threw things at them. He realized that now they could live peacefully on Valchondria, since no one could tell white or yellow skin from red skin, which was always one of the accepted skin colors.

"You are Jase-Dawn?" he asked the woman, looking into her wide eyes, wondering what color they were.

"Yes. Gazer said I will require access to Life Unit."

"I trust Gazer won't crash this operation? I feel he's partially responsible for what happened to Dr. Lorfeltez's family, for Hachen's death."

"You'll have to talk to Gazer about that, but I won't be involved in anyone's death. Now if you can contact Dr. Lorfeltez…."

"Shouldn't you first learn more about our customs? Gazer said this is your first visit through the spatial doorway."

"I wouldn't be here if I didn't feel adequately prepared. If you're referring to my failure to address you as a superior, it was only because there's no one else here. I'm sure your ego won't die of malnutrition. To the side, it's best that you know my lack of respect for anyone who would betray his own people."

"You're far too young to understand. Please sit down."

They reclined on the padded lounge chairs beside the artificial waterfall. Leader touched the hologram control on the arm of his chair. The response took longer than he expected, but eventually came in the form of Taldra's voice emitting from the tiny speaker on the chair's other arm.

"Dr. Lorfeltez, your image isn't coming through," he said into the black panel beside the speaker. Then the image of her face and upper body hovered in the air just in front of Leader; he tried not to notice that she looked slightly close to exceeding regulation weight for her height. From the lines in her eyes, she also looked like she'd been crying. In fact, Leader noticed her hands leaving those eyes as the holographic image appeared. Her hair had grown long and thick, flowing past her shoulders.

"I'm sorry, sir," said Taldra. "I forgot to activate the image."

"Is everything adequate? You look upset."

"Yes, Leader. Everything is fine. I think I've cleared up all the computer malfunctions I discovered during inspection. They weren't really malfunctions. We programmed Life Unit to be completely reliable, to survive any situation, so its programming was resisting the shutdown required for full inspection."

"I trust you've been sleeping occasionally between all this work." He often caught himself sounding fatherly toward her, even if he could no longer father a child. Though he had once tested definite for the possibility of siring a healthy child, the virus had left him sterile—a side effect that no one ever discussed, a side effect that had caused his spouse to leave him for another man.

A healer had once told Leader that it happened to less than one per cent of Valchondria's population. When Leader asked the healer how she'd obtained that statistic, she gave the same response the SSC, the Maintainers, the media, or even the Degrans would have given: "highly reliable sources." No one ever questioned numbers; that would require mathematics, which would require thinking.

"Do I sleep? Yes, constantly." Taldra laughed the last word out, as if desperate to make some amusing remark. Seeing her smile made Leader wonder what joy she could still have. Taldra's frown returned quickly. "I have to run some diagnostics, then I'll be done for today."

Leader noticed Jase-Dawn thumping the arms of her chair, reminding him of why he called. "Next time, you won't be working alone."

"What is your aim, sir?" asked Taldra, her eyes revealing at least a spark of interest.

"I have your student here with me."

"Student? As in…student?"

"That's the basic concept."

She shook her head. "I have no teaching abilities, sir. Why me?"

"Don't worry. Jase-Dawn has incredible learning abilities, and she graduated from Valcine University this year with a degree in machine dependency. She'll live with you, and she'll work with you every day. Valchondria needs more scientists like you, Taldra, and I want to see that we get them."

Taldra pushed her bangs back from her face. "Leader, I—"

"Taldra, I realize this might cause you some confusion, but we must think of what's best for Valchondria, and for Project Life Unit. Glory."

"That's true, sir. I just wasn't expecting this honor. I—" She paused, looked down, sighed. "Glory." Her beautiful image faded into nothing.

Jase-Dawn cocked her head slightly. "Dr. Lorfeltez's files show that this is the first time in her life that she's ever lived alone, and that she's given to clinging. Yet she seems hesitant about accepting an apprentice."

"As I said before, you're far too young to understand some things. She'll accept you more readily now than she would have before she lost her family. It really doesn't surprise me that Gazer would exploit someone in a time of mourning or loss; that seems to be the most popular recruitment tool for his Youth group. Just, please, try not to get Taldra killed."

"I'm not a murderer." Jase-Dawn stood up, facing the waterfall, watching the water splashing onto an area of the metal floor that was covered with rust spots. "Posing as an aspiring scientist won't be hard. Aside from Life Unit, most of our science dwarfs yours, so I can seem to invent some of the items I learned about in first level. I certainly won't have any trouble impressing her with my knowledge of the basics. When this is over, I can go back to my life on Degranon and become a teacher. That's all I care about."

As she left, Leader realized just how well Taldra and Jase-Dawn would probably get along, but he still tasted his betrayal of Taldra, his violation of her home. It tasted like bile on his tongue.

CHAPTER 19

❀

*T*aldra thought about Leader's sudden use of her chosen name. No one had used it since the last time she had seen Hachen and Argen, three long months earlier. Still, she felt somewhat flattered that Leader held her in such high regard as to use her chosen name and to give her a student. She liked the idea of having someone Argen's age in her home again. She had known enough loss and rejection: her people, her parents, her family. Any hint of acceptance seemed appealing now.

She pushed her swivel chair away from Life Unit's wallscreen, and leaned her head back. "Life Unit, have you detected any of the doorway energies yet?" she asked, loudly. Her eyes moved to the glass cylinder that housed battery seven. She had waited for the doorway within the shell to open, but nothing had happened.

"Negative," Life replied. "My arms have reached into the safest depths, so I'll need to re-direct."

After activating a camera inside battery seven, she stared at the image it transmitted to her wallscreen, hoping to see multi-colored sparks arise. She couldn't bring Hachen back from the dead, and she couldn't bring Argen back from his life sentence at Urloan Control, but she could bring Telius back. During the past two weeks, she had seen spikes in the batteries that reminded her of the doorway; that hadn't happened since the last time the doorway opened. It would open again: she felt sure of that. But the spikes never reached their former patterns.

She had already found a good cosmetic healer; Life Unit's newly enhanced attachments to Valcine Plaza's computers would take care of his new identity. She only needed to bring him back to his own era, so he could become someone new.

"The doorway time has passed," said Life Unit.

"I know," said Taldra. "I'm going home. Activate security systems."

Telius watched and waited in the dim cave Alom had taken him to so many times before. They had always managed to create some excuse to leave the village. This time, however, Alom was in the middle of an all-day marriage ceremony for two of the women in their village. As the adopted apprentice of the village priest, Telius belonged at the ceremony, but he had learned long ago how to feign illness and then sneak away from behind Alom's hut.

It seemed especially ironic that he would use that particular excuse when attempting to contact his parents, since they had given him the virus that protected him from illness. Sometimes, he felt healthy to the point of deformity, the point of exclusion. All of his friends experienced the various childhood afflictions, and the entire village sometimes fell to winter plagues. But he remained freakishly resistant to every sickness.

How could he understand them when he was so different from them, so far removed from their suffering? His training as priest already put him at risk of self-righteousness. The virus distanced him even further from his peers. He felt like the woman in a story he'd read, who would climb onto a branch that extended over a river, criticizing the fish for never climbing trees. One day, she fell in and drowned, while the fish criticized her for never learning to swim.

Like that woman in relation to the fish, he seemed too different from the villagers to judge them in any way.

And the villagers asked him such disturbing or even absurd questions. "How have you managed to avoid facial blemishes? Can you believe that feeling in the back of your eyes from this winter's plague? How can you wear such thin clothes during the winter?" The questions all became tiresome, especially considering that he had to lie to answer them. He, the person they saw as the future spiritual leader of their village, the person who constantly spoke about virtues, was a liar and a fraud, thanks to his parents.

The question he hated most was "Why don't your parents ever visit you?" It was normal for parents to give up custody of their child for the sake of an apprenticeship, but not for them to never visit, even if they supposedly lived "past the third mountain range." He always evaded questions about his parents, because he still wanted answers for himself. Why didn't they ever visit? Why didn't they come back for him, like they said they would? Why did they leave him there, always hoping that this time they would return?

"Liars!" he screamed. "Liars! You're never coming back for me. You've got Argen. You chose him as your only son. You don't want me. You never wanted me."

He had made the accusations countless times before, but he could no longer convince himself that they weren't true. Alom would offer assurances. He would remind Telius that Taldra had cried when she agreed to let him take one of the children she would soon bear. Alom would also remind Telius how Taldra and Hachen risked everything to send him back through time, how they went against all the injustice of the future in order to save his life. It all sounded so noble and idealistic, like the laws Alom taught him, but it wouldn't change the fact that he always stood there waiting for something that never happened.

No sparks rose from the ground. No rays of sunlight appeared in a circle. No one magically appeared.

Telius adjusted the skin-tight straps that tapered across the firm but slender muscles of his chest, shoulders, and back. He re-tucked his pullover shirt into the belt where his straps intertwined, the belt that held his hunting dagger. Then he paced around, deeply breathing the cave's stale air, breathing the pollen of nocturnal plants that always made Alom sneeze. With all his stall tactics exhausted, he wondered how long he'd been there, and if he would ever return.

Something on his shoulder…a man's hand.

"Father?" he asked aloud, but turned to see the man who had taken his father's place for the past seventeen years, the man he always wanted to call "Father."

"Forgiveness. It's just me." Alom had aged considerably over Telius's lifetime, but he still stood tall and proud. As he dropped his hand from Telius's shoulder, his eyes revealed empathy; he knew how much it hurt Telius to come there and wait for nothing.

"What happened to the wedding?"

"I managed to delay it on a technicality. They've barely started courting. You know how female couples can be."

Telius smiled a little, enough to show his dimples. He knew that always stopped Alom from worrying—just seeing dimples. "I don't know much of anything about relationships, Alom, considering that I've never had one."

"And what if you fell in love with some girl? How would you take her back to your world? How would you explain her to it, or it to her?" Alom started sniffling from the pollen in the cave.

"Oh, truthfully, Alom. That could only happen if my parents returned, and we both know that won't happen."

Alom dismissed Telius's claim with a motion of his hand. "Your parents love you."

"Then where are they?"

"I don't know." Alom's voice suddenly became contemplative as he made a suggestion: "Maybe it's time we go to North Edge."

Telius rolled his eyes. "Please, Alom, not more legends."

"How can you be such a skeptic when you yourself are such a miracle? You are growing up in a time long before your own birth, which your leaders wanted to stop. Isn't that a bit unbelievable?"

"When you phrase it that way." Something about Alom's voice always calmed Telius down, comforted him.

"I've heard all my life that God sends visions to those who visit North Edge."

"We'll freeze to death. Even I can't withstand extreme cold."

"Yes, I remember that time you fell through the ice. Your skin looked blue for days. If not for Zaysha pushing that branch against you, we wouldn't be debating North Edge, or anything else."

Telius smiled—a real smile this time—and held up his hands. "I believe I've admitted two or twenty times that it was reckless and childish, but I was still a little boy."

"So you were. But now you're a man, a man who needs to find his past."

"Find my past, in the future? The whole concept is annoying!"

Alom twirled the fingers of his left hand. "Not as annoying as your failed attempts at wit and your refusal to listen. We'll find your parents, even if it means going to the edge of Valchondria."

"Which is what we're doing," said Telius, in a tone of resignation.

Alom sneezed. "Exactly."

Taldra went home and fell asleep on the couch in her video room, but the door buzzer woke her. Her eyes opened and scanned the impeccably clean room full of couches, video equipment, solar system charts, and video chips. Her body showed no intention of moving. To add to her total lack of energy, her legs protested with a sharp pain in the calves that tore through the grogginess in her mind. She had stood, working, for almost two days with little more than a loaf of docle bread and an occasional relief room break. Since her arms remained cooperative, she pulled herself along the side of the couch until she found the remote control and activated the door search on her wallscreen.

The speaker's steady beep meant the visitor had no weapon. The image of a skeletal system then a muscular system faded into that of the girl Leader called Taldra's student; he had wallscreened her an image just after first telling her about the arrangement he'd made. Wearing a black body suit with a single green stripe beside her credit box, Jase-Dawn carried a small trunk with one hand and a transparent case of video chips with the other.

"Again with the green stripe," Taldra whispered. "I wonder if she's colorsighted. And I wonder what she's been viewing."

Taldra used the remote to magnify a section of the screen and browse over the video titles. *Please, nothing from Dr. Tquil,* she thought. The first one was Dr. Hudza's video, *Our Galaxy*; Taldra had upset the SSC by endorsing it. They never banned it, though, because Dr. Hudza was clever enough to discuss other worlds without ever mentioning colonization or using the newly banned word "space." *Smart lady,* thought Taldra, wondering why she hadn't heard from Dr. Hudza since that strange message about going undermall. The other titles were *The Science of Fabric, The Hidden Dangers of Free Thought, Existence, Tranquil Conformity, Valchondrian to the Core,* and *The Necessities of Teen Alliances.*

That last video featured a caption in large letters: "With a closing word from Dr. Tquil." *Oh, well,* thought Taldra, *infamous people are doomed to keep hearing each other's names.* Taldra had finally stopped her wallscreened meetings with Dr. Tquil, but he still manipulated debates with her through his appearances on the gossip shows.

The door buzzed again. Taldra wasn't ready for this, but Jase-Dawn stood outside on the walkway, struggling not to drop her trunk or her video chips as she touched the chip case against the buzzer.

"Come in," said Taldra, after pressing her remote's button for the door and turning around to greet her student. She tried not to make any unpleasant faces as she walked up to Jase-Dawn, but her legs hadn't cramped up so much since the year exercise enjoyed a brief popularity.

"Glory. I'm Jase-Dawn, your new student." She set her things down just inside the door. Shocked-out hair, brown eyes, perfect figure: Taldra wondered what Telius might think of this young lady.

"My first student." Taldra's voice reflected her approval.

"I didn't realize that until today. And I thought I'd learned all about you from the screen."

"Someone of your intelligence should know better than to rely on the screen for information." Already she'd sounded cross. Taldra asked herself, *how do I talk to this person? How can I relate to another human being when everyone sees me as threatening or menacing? Why do I come across as some sort of monster?*

Jase-Dawn admitted, "That's true. The wallscreen tends to be unreliable." She looked around the room at all the video equipment, her eyes stopping on the long black grid above the wallscreen. "A door search. Those are efficient devices."

"It's a necessary precaution. I'm sure you're aware that I have a few enemies. Some of them are violent."

"I know. And that's such ignorance. I think your views are a bit progressive for our time; that unsettles people."

"I've seen the word 'progressive' attached to my name almost as many times as 'dangerous' and 'anti-glory.'" Taldra wanted to kick herself for obviously making Jase-Dawn feel so terrible; she could see the embarrassment in Jase-Dawn's eyes.

"Forgiveness. I had no aim to—"

Taldra waved her hands outward. "I need the forgiveness. I shouldn't re-filter you that way. There's nothing offensive against using reason, at least not in this house." She retreated into being the scientist; it seemed safe.

"I'll remember that," said Jase-Dawn, her slender shoulders relaxing a little.

Taldra smiled, relieved at finally saying something that Jase-Dawn could take positively. "I just bought some jarred water. It's from a melted glacier. Would you like some?"

"Yes! I haven't had glacier water in a year! But could you show me to my room first? I'd like to get this junk out of your wallscreen room."

"Of course. It's right up the stairs. And there are plenty of magnetic clamps on your ceiling." Taldra picked up Jase-Dawn's trunk, pretending not to notice the weight of its contents or the returning pain in her calves.

Jase-Dawn stopped at the top of the spiral staircase and walked into the first bedroom, Argen's bedroom. Taldra had forgotten to close the door. She noticed Jase-Dawn's surprise at seeing a teenager's boots against the far wall, as well as several holograms of female wallscreen celebrities. Jase-Dawn's image reflected in Argen's mirror.

"Not there," said Taldra.

"Oh," said Jase-Dawn, stepping backward into the hall.

"I don't use that room." Taldra pressed a button in the hall; the door slid shut as she stared at the room's contents. Argen had always loved those boots; he wore them to school almost every day. It surprised Taldra that he didn't have them on the day of the accident, but nothing about that day made sense to her. "I must have left the door open after I cleaned this morning."

"You do your own cleaning?"

"Yes. My spouse and I always knew just how we wanted everything, and you can't get robots or even clean-ups to give you your exact touch."

Jase-Dawn nodded in agreement. "I would like to have met your spouse. He designed some of the computer programs we still use at Valcine Uni."

"More than you realize. To the side, have you met my father, Dr. Norn?"

"No. I don't believe so."

"I figured you would have. He manages the video chip archives."

"Oh, Dr. Norn." Jase-Dawn looked angry with herself. "He's always let us use his chosen name."

Taldra laughed. "I guess the saying's true that people change a lot as they get older."

"Does he visit often?"

"No. We haven't spoken in a long time. But we won't discuss parents. I don't know why I mentioned him. Just thinking about him lately, I suppose." Taldra wondered, *but do my parents ever think of me?*

Taldra opened the door to the guest bedroom. No one had ever stayed there, except for that time Geln had worked late into the night and Hachen had suggested he just sleep there instead of driving home half-awake. Taldra felt a chill as she thought of Geln sleeping in her house: Geln who always seemed to want to touch her, Geln who destroyed her son's life and caused her spouse's death, Geln who may have killed Sydra.

She had tried reporting Sydra's story to the Maintainers, but they only laughed. "Degranon?" one of them asked, his voice annoyingly squeaky. "You're even crazier than the wallscreen says you are. And don't think we won't be watching you, because we will."

Even Leader had seemed skeptical about her charges against Geln, but he said that he would urge the Maintainers to investigate. He later told her that the Maintainers found Geln's former apartment deserted. When Taldra contacted SSC Personnel about Geln, they said that he had left his job and given no forwarding wallscreen address.

Jase-Dawn set her luggage down in the guest bedroom. "I think I'll like it here, Dr. Lorfeltez."

"Taldra."

Even as she tried to make Jase-Dawn feel comfortable and at home there, Taldra wondered how much danger they would both face from Geln, and from his followers. Taldra feared loneliness, but she also feared what could happen to anyone near her. If her life followed any pattern at all, the people close to her all drifted away from her, or something tore them away from her.

Part of her wanted to warn Jase-Dawn to leave immediately, to become apprentice to a scientist that everyone considered more socially acceptable. But another part of her immediately saw something she desperately needed: a friend.

CHAPTER 20

❁

"*A* rgen."

A familiar voice. All the voices seemed familiar. They echoed in his mind. But they spoke too quickly, and all at the same time. What were they saying? Why was he here?

Argen didn't want to open his eyes; he would just see his image reflected in the walls, ceiling, and floor of his cell. He had tried to count his reflections once, but the attempt proved even more frustrating than the monotony of sitting there and staring at the image of a murderer. That was why he was there: he murdered someone. But who?

His memory completely faded several times. Still, he remembered names: Kryldon, Hachen, Taldra, Telius, Argen…. Argen—that was his name. Someone was talking to him. The voice came from outside his cell, not inside his mind.

"I'm Argen," he finally said, in response to the voice.

"Argen is my friend," said the voice.

"Gazer." Gazer and friend—those words belonged together.

"Yes, Argen, it's Gazer, your friend."

"Let me out. I can't see you." Though keeping his eyes closed, he could tell the light was on in his cell. The light reflected off the mirrors, creating a glare he still saw with his eyes shut.

"If I try, your cell will explode, and the mirrors will impale you. Your mother was afraid I would try to get you out."

"My mother," said Argen. "Taldra. Why hasn't Taldra come for me? Why doesn't she want me to get out of here?"

"Because she hates you. Your only friends are Gazer and those who follow me."

"Gazer is…. Why didn't you come before?"

"I did. Don't you remember?"

"I can't remember anything." Argen rubbed his forehead. "Has my father come?"

"No, Argen. Remember? The evil ones killed your father and then blamed you for it. But we're going to get you out soon. Then we're going to use Life Unit to destroy the evil ones."

Discerning one of the phrases he heard in his mind, Argen spoke it: "I hate the evil ones."

"We all do, Argen. All right-minded people hate the evil ones." The voice outside grew louder, more clear. "Did you know the evil ones have your brother?"

"No brothers, no sisters, no friends. That is what the evil ones say."

"Which of the evil ones?" demanded Gazer. "Is it the guards I just bribed with confidence pills? Is it your parents?"

"My parents are evil?" He didn't want to believe anything bad about Hachen and Taldra, but the voices kept telling him about the evil ones. Most of the voices were Gazer, and most of them repeated his phrases. One of the voices was Geln. No, Geln was Gazer. Argen wanted to escape—not only from Urloan Control but also from his own mind.

"Your parents never told you that you have a brother. He lives inside Life Unit. They told me that they love your brother and hate you."

"I have a brother?"

"Yes, but he's been corrupted by the philosophies of the evil ones. He's been deceived. They've turned him into one of them. His name is Telius."

"Telius," said Argen. The name, the secret name his parents had spoken in private. He remembered that. "Telius is my brother?"

"Not anymore. Now he's evil. No brothers—"

"No sisters, no friends." Argen opened his eyes, pretending that the images he saw were of his brother.

"I'll be back soon, or I'll send someone else to get you. We'll use Telius against the evil ones. Taldra broke the rules she expects others to follow. Telius is proof of that. Glory."

That was something else he was supposed to repeat. "Glory."

With a loud clang, Argen's gray food tray appeared at the bottom of his tiny cell, through the slot that disrupted one of the mirrors. He liked the tray because it wasn't reflective, but he didn't want what was on the tray. The confidence pills would only confuse him more. He had noticed how they made him lose parts of his memory and how they made it hard for him to think, though they seemed to help everyone else. He had noticed all of that, yet continued to use them, deciding the side effects were temporary. They made him stronger and helped him see through the deceptions of the evil ones. If they weren't good, Gazer wouldn't give them to him. Gazer was his friend.

Gazer knew the name, the hidden name: Telius. Taldra and Hachen hid it because it was evil.

Lyjia remembered trusting her son. He was unusually smart, unusually athletic, unusually everything. He was perfect in every way. Or at least he seemed perfect.

Then the meetings started, the drinking started, and the weight loss started. For days at a time, he would barely talk to her or his father at all. Then Argen had gone crumbled, embarking on a rampage that left Hachen dead and Taldra near the brink of insanity.

Seeing those horrible, violent images of her old friend Taldra on the wallscreen made Lyjia walk up and turn it off. She never turned it back on after that.

B'zl, Lyjia's ever-comforting spouse, understood, and added, "We need each other, not the wallscreen." But even faithful B'zl couldn't convince her that their son wasn't somehow turning against them, that his odd mood swings were nothing more than teenage hormones.

Eventually, Kryldon stopped coming home at all, long before he finally returned for his clothes and his vid chips. Lyjia and B'zl knew very little about his situation. But they knew that it involved the Youth For Valchondrian Reform, and that he made frequent contact with the fanatic known as "Gazer." They knew that much from comparing information with Taldra and Hachen. They also knew that Argen and Kryldon had always spent a lot of time beneath the walkways to the west of Valcine University, near the amorphous edge of the undermall.

She had constantly warned them about the dangers of walkway people and undermall traders, but she also knew that the boys came to this strange, shadowy place so they could speak freely and express themselves freely, somewhere other than the confines of their homes. So it seemed like a healthy extension of their education, a chance for the boys to deliberate and grow intellectually in ways that legally permitted language would never allow.

But this place pulled him into a dangerous cult that exploited his desires for a better world. That cult destroyed his best friend, and his best friend's family. Lyjia determined not to let it destroy Kryldon. She and B'zl lived as walkway people for several weeks, discretely following any congregations of teenagers they saw.

This time, they thought for certain they had seen Kryldon in the large group of teens that walked around, handing out vid chips to the other teens they found in the undermall, especially the walkway ones and the drug takers.

At least one helpful thing came from Lyjia's wallscreen, before she turned it off forever. In learning about the Youth and their tactics, the gossip masters had reported that the Youth often pulled rejected or unpopular people into their ranks with an overwhelming sense of acceptance, validation, and warmth. While thinking of that wallscreen special report, Lyjia stood in a darkened basement doorway, witnessing the very same process, realizing that the Youth probably lured Kryldon and Argen in the same way. From there, the boys quickly fell into Gazer's heavy hazard mindlock.

A frail, dirty girl, barely more than fifteen, accepted one of the vid chips into her tiny hands as the Youth began touching her shoulders, encircling her, giving all their attention to her: listening to her and talking to her. Yes, acceptance, validation, and warmth. This poor walkway girl obviously needed those things.

But didn't Kryldon receive acceptance, validation, and warmth from his parents? Didn't they love him? Didn't they allow him, and constantly encourage him, to be himself? She couldn't understand why he would look to these opportunists for something he could find at home.

The same went for Argen: his parents loved him with no reservation. They even sometimes said that they wished they had two of him. Why would Argen give that up, for this, and then find himself in the mirror prison? And why wasn't that horrible series of events enough to scare Kryldon away from the Youth? What would it take, his own imprisonment?

"No, I can't think that," Lyjia whispered to herself, wishing she had B'zl's hand to hold at that moment. She saw a rather tall man among the Youth, turned the other way, but it didn't look like B'zl.

He had gone around the block, hoping that the Youth's path would take them to him, and take Kryldon to him. Lyjia had stayed behind, in case Kryldon tried to sneak away when spotting his father. Above her, a fog bank circled around the dead vines of the crumbling building's base, denying her the view of the Youth as they began to move along. The stifling air intensified the lingering smell of hover-fumes as the other buildings seemed to move closer together, trapping her.

The hover-fumes began to affect her breathing, and she wondered how people could stand to live in such an environment. Rubbing her eyes only made them burn worse, but she couldn't help it. When she moved her fingers out of the way, her eyes focused on a darker image.

Dr. Geln stood before her, a loose-fitting black body suit hanging from his hulking frame, a devious smile folding his thick lips outward and away from each other. His right hand reached out to touch her shoulder.

"Dr. Hudza," he said, casually, as she jerked from his touch. "I would never expect to see you here."

She tried to sound composed and unafraid. "Dr. Geln. You were with the YFVR?"

He tilted his head coyly and chuckled, as if she asked the most ridiculous question imaginable. "Now, why would you think such a thing?"

Despite her alarm, she managed to force her voice through her mouth. In fact, her voice seemed louder to her than usual. "I saw you, from a distance. I didn't recognize you then. But it was you. You're involved with this somehow. You know what happened to my son."

He swung one of his huge hands about. "Nothing happened to Kryldon. I've helped him grow in ways you never could. I know what's best for Valchondria's children."

A horrible realization pierced into the very marrow of Lyjia's bones. "You…you're Gazer, aren't you?"

He sighed in response, and she continued.

"All of those times you took Argen and Kryldon to the pressure tournaments or the mall, you were influencing them with your plans for turning them against Valchondria, against their families." Her finger pointed at him, and her voice challenged him, but she feared his massive presence, and she could feel that fear in her throat.

In her throat.

His thick fingers, pressing.

Her head pressed against the mold-encrusted wall, the eroded brick's sharp edges tore into the skin on her back, where the collar of her shirt dipped down. The leaves and the stems of the vines scratched at her neck, but that caused a minor annoyance in comparison to Gazer's hand and the brick.

She felt the blood dripping from her cut skin as he pressed harder.

"I'm saving them," Gazer insisted, his breath hot on her face, his beady eyes glaring at her. "I wish you and your spouse wouldn't have interfered. You both showed so much promise. Pity."

His grip grew even tighter.

Strangely forgetting the man whose hand slowly pushed the life from her body and the brick that slowly released the blood from her neck, Hudza thought of the first time that she and B-zl saw their beautiful son in his pressure tournament suit, how he had smiled and looked suddenly like a young man.

Then her thoughts faded as a final rush of hover-fumes filled her nostrils.

CHAPTER 21

❀

The arctic winds dried Telius's eyes, scraping against them like sharp fingernails. The cold numbed his bundled-up body. His legs became heavy, and his feet felt trampled on—not that Alom ever walked closely enough to step on his feet. Alom stayed several body-lengths ahead of him and never spoke, like a silent ghost leading Telius through a dream. Telius wondered how long Alom would try to hide his declining health by simply not talking. Most of the time, Telius could see nothing of Alom but what little bit of his body the lantern illuminated. Though the dethua sap in the indented center of the lightweight svey-stone carving could burn for another two weeks, and though Alom had taken an extra bota of dethua sap, the lanterns gave off much less light than an actual fire. Even with more light, Alom and Telius could not have seen much of each other's faces, because of the fur hoods that hung forward over those faces.

The snow-covered mountains had seemed to continue for a week, but Telius couldn't really distinguish time in the perpetual darkness of North Edge. His lantern kept getting heavier, but he dared not put it in the svey-stone case inside his backpack, because he couldn't see well enough without it.

He just wished their hiliates could have traversed the mountains, but they had sent both hiliates back home early in the trip. As they entered the increasingly cold climate, the shells of the giant crusta-

ceans had started cracking and peeling at the segments of their elon-
gated bodies. Fortunately, any hiliate could find its village, no matter
how far away it traveled, so Telius knew his faithful pet and carrier
would be waiting for him at home.

A high-pitched howl engulfed the mountains: the combined howl
of several animals, their individual tones barely distinguishable.
Telius felt like a trespasser; he had never heard such a noise. It traveled like the wind, swirled around the wind's own howl, chased them
across the icy mountain.

Two shiny eyes appeared near Telius, hovering in the darkness. He
couldn't judge height on the slopes, but he could judge distance, or
the lack thereof. The creature advanced, growling.

"Alom, what is that?"

"Hold your light to it," said Alom, stopping where he was.

Telius lifted the lantern in his right hand and saw the canine creature, which nearly reached his ankle in height, with its eyes on the
tips of its pointed ears. The creature, apparently frightened by the
direct light of the lantern, dashed away as Alom burst into laughter.

"That thing might have devoured you, if you gave it two or twenty
years," said Alom. His laughter quickly turned into coughing.

"What was it?" Telius saw nothing funny about being frightened,
but he still couldn't help laughing with Alom. It just bothered him
that the laughter revealed Alom's winter plague. However, he knew
to say nothing about it. Alom couldn't stand becoming the subject of
any fuss or worry; he always wanted to take on everyone else's problems, never admitting his own.

"I don't know. Something like a lerthern, but smaller, and with
eyes. Everything is different here. It's all strange." Alom emphasized
the word "strange," but not the way Telius had always heard him
emphasize it—as something to avoid. Instead, his enunciation of the
word sounded like that of a favorite food or place, or like the name of
a friend.

"You sound fascinated. Are you turning into an explorer?" While asking that question, Telius thought he heard footsteps, but he worried about seeming paranoid, especially after his recent humiliation.

"Maybe." Alom smiled. "Have you noticed it's getting lighter?"

"Yes, but I'm not sure I can see better." The snow and ice reflected the few rays of sunlight that shone through the clouds, creating patches of blinding light within the darkness, light that somehow isolated itself into tiny cubes without affecting the darkness around it. Telius knew that this coexistence of light and dark simply resulted from a trick of the eyes, an illusion caused by the cold, or Alom would have said something about it. Still, he longed for regular daylight.

As the howling grew louder and the sun grew brighter, Telius wondered what other creatures might lurk in the snow. Alom walked beside him now, his skin turning increasingly pale, his face shivering. Telius stopped to rewind the extra furs around his boots and retie them with the stretchable vine that bound all the furs to his body. He thought he felt something tugging on his backpack, but realized it was only slipping down his back because of his bent-over position.

This sudden development of apprehension annoyed him, but he couldn't help feeling like something could happen at any moment—something wonderful or terrible. The constant idea of not knowing had always upset Telius: not knowing if his family were still alive, not knowing if they wanted to see him, not knowing if the doorway still worked, not knowing if he should just start a new family with Zaysha. He tried not to think of his family at all, sure that they had forgotten him. Now all that mattered to Telius was this absurd journey where Alom could help him look at supposed visions.

What if he saw his family in the visions? What then? Would those visions only show him something he could never have?

The mountain kept growing steeper with each step, eventually forcing them to put their lanterns in their backpacks, to keep their hands free. The light fully replaced the darkness for a time, but a developing snowstorm kept Telius from seeing past Alom, as they climbed both with their feet and with their gloved hands.

Tiny snow lizards leapt from rock to rock, some of them taking larger bounds than others, as black spiders the size of lertherns crawled out from under the rocks in search of food. The spiders all seemed to watch Telius, and he kept worrying he would accidentally grab one. He hated spiders! Occasionally, one would jump up to catch a snow lizard, then scurry beneath the snow with it. In his mixture of amusement and worry over the spiders, he barely noticed Alom passing him again.

Some of the snow made its way between the folds of fur at Telius's wrist, melting on his already cold palms. This new surge of coldness made Telius open the hands that gripped the rocks. Without that extra security, his footing also slipped. Unable to manage another grip in time, he tumbled until he reached an area with a less severe angle.

Uninjured, he returned to his task, hoping to find Alom again. As he climbed, he felt his hands growing numb from the moisture that penetrated both his gloves. His arms caught the rocky surface, and he pulled himself up to where he faced only the clear sky and the sun. With the snowstorm gone, he could finally see, though his eyes burned with dryness.

They had reached an icy plateau so expansive that nothing else seemed to exist. Alom walked cautiously across the ice before stopping to look down. Telius called out to Alom, his voice echoing.

"Now we know why it's called North Edge," Alom shouted back, without turning around. "Walk carefully. There's not much rock or loose snow for footing."

Telius approached slowly, because his feet slid sideways as he walked, and he knew that one quick step could bring him to the frozen ground. Of course, he kept thinking about that day he fell through the ice.

Though the snow stopped falling, the swirling wind threw an occasional flake into Telius's already sore eyes. When he finally reached Alom's side, after dozens of tiny and deliberate steps made with stiff muscles, he learned why he could no longer see the other mountains: he stood on a cliff at what seemed to be the highest point of Valchondria, above mountains and even clouds. Sometimes, the plateau trembled slightly beneath Telius's feet, but Alom never even acknowledged the barely noticeable shaking.

The clouds rose, even with the two men, then higher. Below the clouds, directly in front of Telius and Alom, a black triangle materialized and expanded. Alom pointed to the object, though it had already captured Telius's attention. They could see inside the triangle as it became brighter and turned into a sort of window.

Through that window, they saw people, unaware of observers, fighting a battle with strange weapons that shot fire. A gray fog engulfed the battle as the triangle grew dark again before producing another vision. This time, they saw a room where strange, star-like lights flashed on the wall. A man sat on a chair, crying. As he began to turn around, a woman walked up to him and held him against her bosom. She was also crying.

"Hachen," said Alom. "And Taldra. Telius, those are your parents. They're looking for you."

Telius nibbled at his chapped lips. "My—? How?"

"I don't know. But that's Life Unit, the place where I met them when I stepped through the doorway."

Telius reached out, wanting to embrace them, but they were too far away. Alom grabbed him and pulled him back. "Don't get so close to the edge, boy. It's a long drop to the next mountain."

When they looked back up, they saw yet another vision: inside the triangle, fire shot up everywhere as countless people looked into the triangle with wonder. This time, the people on the other side seemed aware of their onlookers. An older man near the front of the crowd held a wounded man in his arms. It was Telius, or Argen; his strange, loosely fitting clothes looked burned. And he looked dead. The triangle shrank again then ascended into the clouds.

"What does it mean?" asked Telius.

"It's a sign from God," said Alom, his raspy voice fading to almost nothing. "Your family needs you, and they're trying to find you."

"But the dead man? Was it me, or my twin brother?"

"That I can't say, but maybe you can prevent that death. Will you return to the cave next time? Will you keep trying, until you succeed?"

"After this? Yes, I think they want me to come home." The ground shook again, but not so hard that it kept Telius from noticing the low growl behind his back. "Not one of those little...." As he turned, he saw another of the canines, but this one stood at an equal height with him. As it slowly drew closer, drool dripped from its massive fangs, the sun glistened on its black pelt, and its claws scraped into the ice.

Telius reached through his furs for the knife on his belt, but it had frozen into its sheath, encased in ice. Fortunately, Alom had stored his knife in his backpack. He retrieved it then stood between Telius and the creature. Its eyes fixed on them both as it closed its mouth and stopped growling.

"Give me the knife and back up," said Telius.

"We're not in a position where backing up would be a good idea."

"Well, back aside. Just give me the knife."

"How far would you say we are from the edge?"

The creature turned its head to one side and began growling again.

"Almost two body-lengths," said Telius.

"Good. Move!" As the creature pounced forward, Alom drove the knife through its left eye/ear and fell sideways. Instead of jumping out of the way, Telius dropped to his back, kicking his legs up, trying to kick the beast over the edge when it pounced on him.

Even off balance, the creature's weight proved overwhelming for Telius. Instead of falling off the edge, it merely jerked sideways, regained its balance, then retreated, bellowing in agony.

Alom helped Telius up.

"A warning would've been nice," said Telius, pain shooting through his back.

"True. I think we should go home now. Maybe it was at least hurt enough that it won't try to follow us. We probably just came too close to its lair."

As always, Telius wanted to share his mentor's optimism, but he couldn't. In the distance, he heard the creatures howling again.

CHAPTER 22

✿

*J*ase-Dawn met with Gazer in Leader's morning lounge, a room she had been enjoying until Gazer's arrival. Leader had programmed the elevator to allow her, the other Degrans, and the YFVR to any floor. No one else could come there. She wished Gazer couldn't come there. She had loved the past few days away from her overbearing superior.

"You look comfortable," said Gazer, as he approached her from behind the lounge chair by the waterfall. He sat down on the one beside it, stretching his fingers outward. "Tell me, do you think your placement with Taldra has been a success?"

"It has." She looked at the splashes of multiple blue and green shades on his baggy suit, thinking how the Valchondrians would laugh at him if they could see in color. "Do you have any news from Degranon?"

"The civil wars continue, but the true patriots will win out. You don't have to worry about such matters. Just worry about your mission. I want to know all the latest about Taldra, the details I can't get from the wallscreen."

"She's as brilliant and noble as you said. In fact, what I've seen of the home world is no better or worse than our world. Why did you insist on sending me here? What is this obsession with Taldra?" Jase-Dawn realized the tone and the boldness of her question too late.

"The obsession is with claiming what is ours." His raised eyebrows wrinkled his long forehead, and Jase-Dawn could hear his attempt to mask the anger in his voice. "We must strike in the hour of Valchondria's weakness, before they see what the virus is doing to them."

"Forgiveness for questioning you, but I just worry that I'm trapped in the middle of some emotional complication." He seemed wounded, frightened. Jase-Dawn couldn't help but enjoy that. He embodied all the worst qualities of her parents: the qualities that kept war alive on Degranon.

"I will speak of this matter one time, but never again. I was, years ago, somewhat infatuated with Taldra, but I knew that those feelings could complicate my mission, so I subdued them."

Jase-Dawn found herself actually feeling sympathy for him and decided to change the subject. She had never even considered the possibility of Gazer falling in love, but he was human, even if he often acted otherwise. "I notice the Valchondrians seem to look for any reason to disown Taldra, and I'm afraid she won't be received much better in the newborn world."

Gazer frowned on one side of his square face. "She brings it on herself. She should be content with simply performing her function, while the government freely performs its functions. *The Book of Degranon* says 'Many people began to oppose the great ones, but soon met their deaths.'"

"Yes," said Jase-Dawn. "I've had that verse quoted at me every time I've ever dared to use my brain."

"Being a teacher will let you use your mind, and foster the minds of countless children."

"And help them think for themselves?"

"Of course, as long as their thoughts are consistent with the truth."

"Whose truth?" Jase-Dawn knew she was approaching blasphemy. No Degran ever questioned *The Book of Degranon*.

"The book's truth, of course. That's the only truth." Gazer made no further comment, but he stood up when he saw Dr. Tquil step from the elevator and approach them.

"Jase-Dawn, you look lovely with your hair trimmed so short on the left," said Tquil, his voice evoking images of the salespeople Jase-Dawn had encountered the previous day, on a sporadic shopping binge with Taldra. She abhorred Valchondrian materialism, but she had to fit in, and she enjoyed seeing Taldra look happy for a change. Tquil added, "You make a perfect Valchondrian."

Jase-Dawn wondered if he meant that as an insult; after all, Tquil seemed capable of little else.

"You were to speak to my Youth this morning about being people of integrity," said Gazer, his eyes accusing Tquil of failure. Degran men perfected the exchange of threatening glances at an early age. Jase-Dawn saw it as an absurd game, and as nothing to intimidate her.

"I was...detained," said Tquil, his rare smile revealing uneven teeth. "I have an identity to uphold."

"If you're so concerned with your mission, why haven't you been giving all your video chip profits to the cause? It isn't as if you actually wrote any of those chips. We plagiarized them off those annoying moralists in the Tenth Circle of Degranon. But we were supposed to use the money, and the influence, for our mission, not for your pleasure."

"You're wrong, Gazer. What use would I have for Valchondrian credit?"

"You might spend it on the retreat you purchased in the North Edge project, or on that married Maintainer who has been sharing your nights. That isn't what Control had in mind when she sent you here to infiltrate the Maintainers."

"I don't—"

"I think you do." Gazer drew his laser pistol from the side pocket of his baggy shirt and shot Tquil in the heart, the blast flinging him into the waterfall. The water splashed Gazer and Jase-Dawn as his lifeless body sank into the bottom of the fake rocks.

"No mistakes, Jase-Dawn," said Gazer, turning to her. "Be careful what you say and do."

"I realize the sentence for treason has always been death, but this is hardly a court," said Jase-Dawn, looking at the body, watching the waterfall splash from it. "This demonstration wasn't needed."

"Perhaps not."

Shaking the water from her arm, she stood up and walked away, but he called her name before she could enter the elevator. Projecting his voice like when he addressed the Youth, he told her, "But if it were needed, you might one day be saved by the power of your memory."

The elevator door slid shut, freeing her from the sight of him.

❧   ❧   ❧

Gazer pulled Tquil's body from the waterfall and dragged it to the incinerator in a side room. It was closer to Degran tradition than bringing him to those barbaric devices that the Valchondrians called "vaporizers," where an atomic jolt turned their bodies into energy while shooting them into Valchondria's soil. The idea of placing a human body in the ground seemed hideous, even after all the atrocities that Gazer witnessed on Degranon. A Degran's body always went into the air and sky, if not outer space.

Since none of their cremation technology existed on Valchondria, Gazer resorted to pushing the body into that waste machine, but leaving the door open so that Tquil's ashes could escape into the air. Maybe one of the Youth could have done it, but Gazer didn't really want the Youth to see this unfortunate part of his work: the killing.

But when people fail to follow the book, don't they deserve to die? Gazer often asked himself that question. As he watched Alom's ashes floating in the putrid smoke, he asked it again.

CHAPTER 23

✿

Taldra walked into the battery room as if it were a dangerous walkway, filled with alcohol-addicted walkway people. Her eyes searched for movement. She knew this feeling from her dreams: though she was the only person allowed to enter Life Unit, she felt like someone followed her. Despite her near-obsession with cleanliness, dust covered the control panels and the battery chambers. Her sense of duty soon overtook her paranoia, and she addressed Life Unit's voice-activated computer about the matter.

"Dr. Lorfeltez," it said. "Voice recognized. Chosen name: Taldra. You are Life Unit's creator."

"I thought I programmed you to recognize me as your co-creator."

"The one you called 'Geln' never acknowledged his parenthood of me, and is no longer a part of me."

"You're forgetting about my spouse."

"Dr. Naldod no longer exists. Therefore, he cannot create. Creation is a constant. You continue to create me; Dr. Naldod does not."

"Life Unit, I think I overstated the new security measures. My chosen name is sufficient acknowledgment. But you should understand that past actions are not undone, and that they can be perpetual. Did you die with Dr. Naldod?"

"Life Unit cannot die." Her voice rung out emphatically. "My programming does not allow for that variance. I must continue functioning."

"Life Unit is dying of rust, and she didn't answer my question."

"I still exist." A flurry of activity on the computer panels filled the momentary silence. "Much of your logic requires human intuition. Life Unit is not human. You claim in the video chip you fed me that the world's past creativity has been lost to its complacency, yet you say Dr. Naldod, who cannot help but be complacent, is still creating."

Taldra cringed at the way Life Unit phrased Hachen's death. "Work on your euphemisms for being dead, and make a note to reconcile the contradictions in this discussion. I'm not as smart as you are, and I'm certainly not as efficient. I hope the custodial robot I purchased will match your dust-collecting rate. It will obey your commands. Survey your interior, then have it remove any traces of dirt or rust."

"Dirt can harm Life Unit, but it enters every time you use the entrance. I am searching. There is a food substance on the bottom of your left boot."

As Taldra investigated her boot, she thought she saw a shadow moving across the room.

"Why did I not detect the other person?" asked Life Unit.

"I don't know. Seal the battery room."

"Taldra!"

It wasn't Life's voice, but Life responded by swiftly dropping the huge metal door that led to the battery room. The clanking of metal echoed with Taldra's name as Jase-Dawn jumped forward to avoid being crushed.

"Jase-Dawn?" asked Taldra. Had she overheard? "Why are you here? Life Unit is non-access."

Catching her breath and glancing at the door that had nearly crushed her, Jase-Dawn said, "Leader gave me access. I blocked Life

Unit's sensors and auto-announcers. Leader was upset when he learned that I wasn't involved in all of your work."

"You don't want to be involved with this part. People will hate you."

"If I were concerned with my popularity, I would have requested a different teacher."

Despite her discomfort, Taldra almost laughed at that statement. "I suppose I shouldn't refuse help with my main project. If I'm not careful, the SSC might turn Life Unit into a wallscreen parlor."

"I was not designed for that purpose," said Life Unit.

"I wasn't talking to you, Life."

Jase-Dawn smiled in amazement, her brown eyes lighting up. "The voice simulation is perfect!"

"It makes working alone more bearable."

"You don't have to work alone anymore."

Taldra smiled, but then spoke her thoughts aloud. "I want whatever technology or virus you used to override Life's code. If I'm not safe here, then I can't continue my work."

Handing over her credit box, Jase-Dawn said, "It's a holographic technology, transmitted from Valcine Center, that duplicates your fingerprints and sends a false signal about your genetic structure. It also overrides auto-announcers, making them think they have already made the announcement."

"How undermall!" Taldra exclaimed, not sure whether to be insulted or impressed. She closely examined the credit box, but it looked like any other. "And Leader sanctioned this? Leader sent the signal?"

"I tapped into his wallscreen and put the signal on a timer. As a member of the SSC, your genetic structure was stored there. I wanted you to be aware of this flaw in your security system. There is an energy trace that Life Unit could detect, if programmed to watch for it."

Taldra handed the credit box back to Jase-Dawn, asking her to remove the holographic technology from it. She wanted to believe Jase-Dawn's explanation for using that technology. After all, Jase-Dawn was helping her, and making her safer. Taldra wanted safety.

❀   ❀   ❀

The safety of North Edge's light quickly faded as Alom and Telius began their journey back home. After climbing down just a short ways, they stopped to strike together their shards of vrix stone. Soon, the sparks fell into the dethua sap of their lanterns, re-igniting them. Flipping the lantern handles back up and gripping those handles tightly, they began climbing down again, never acknowledging the distant howl.

But Alom concealed another fear as well. He feared that this winter plague would kill him, leaving Telius again without parents. Despite the added risk of this journey to his health, he needed to help Telius find answers and see how much his true parents loved him. They loved Telius as much as he did, and he wanted to make sure that Telius went back to them when he could.

He owed them that. They had given him a precious child for the last years of his life: a son to make him proud. Telius's enthusiasm at learning all he could from Alom also made him feel incredibly needed, in a deeper and more rewarding way than the other villagers made him feel needed. He could not imagine that his own child would have made him feel more complete, if his beautiful spouse had not left the world so soon.

But the pain in his chest differed from the loss he felt of his spouse. It also differed from the hurt and frustration of knowing about the unborn child she was carrying when she died, or the fact that he could never even stay composed enough to mention that child to Telius or anyone else. It even differed from realizing he would not be able to provide guidance for his noble apprentice much longer.

It was the winter plague, gnawing at his body, just as real as the creature that he knew still followed them.

❧   ❧   ❧

Taldra waited for Jase-Dawn to leave before telling Life Unit not to mention doorways or Telius while Jase-Dawn was inside. But how could she keep it a secret if she found Telius? Taldra wanted to tell her about Telius. She wanted to say, "This is one of my children." She couldn't share that secret with anyone else, but she almost trusted Jase-Dawn. Finally, she had someone in her hollow, plastic home: a young adult looking to her for guidance.

But could she give the right guidance? What about what happened to Argen? She kept thinking that she failed him, that she should have told him about Telius, that she should have done something more to keep him away from drugs and alcohol, that she could have been a better mother if not for her work. But that work stood to benefit her family, and everyone else.

Leaving an almost repugnant metallic stench, the square robot skittered across the floor, then up the batteries, walls, and ceiling, held by its magnetized wheels against Life Unit's interior. It left a foam residue, which slowly faded to reveal Life's newly shined walls. It sputtered, whirled, beeped, and hummed, but even the best models tended to make so much noise that Taldra feared they might explode. The SSC had surprised her by releasing the funds for such an expensive custodial robot, one valued at twice the credits of the units from the wallscreen's one-day ads. Unlike any of those over-hyped models from the one-day ads, this robot actually cleaned up every mess it found.

She asked herself, *why does the SSC bother keeping Life Unit alive if they have no use for it? It's only a relic to them, and I'm part of that relic.* She knew part of the answer: certain SSC members needed a funding project to justify their positions and keep getting them voted back into office. But she knew that something else motivated the SSC's funding, something that would probably upset her.

Taldra's work seemed futile at times, but she had nothing else, and no other hope of finding Telius. She somehow knew inside that he was alive and safe, but she needed to see him. The closed doorway kept her from him as completely as the closed gates of Urloan Control's prison area kept her from Argen.

Taldra decided not to go home and answer all the questions her protégé would have, not while she kept entertaining thoughts of telling Jase-Dawn everything. That time would come, but it would have to wait until Telius's arrival. She went to Life's tiny leisure room and reclined on the couch she and Hachen had taken turns sleeping on during the doorway times. She could think of Hachen these days; it hurt less, comforted more.

Sleep came quickly, as she thought Hachen's shift would soon pass.

* * *

Just as Telius and Alom made their way down the precipice, to a wide plateau, three of the tiny canines circled Telius, then Alom. They stood close by, yapping and howling.

"Three this time!" Telius exclaimed, disgusted. Most of the animals he had encountered in the Lisuadian Forest had been peaceful. If the forest animals weren't as friendly as hiliates or lertherns, they at least avoided people. But these North Edge creatures seemed to look for people.

Then something occurred to Telius, just before Alom voiced the same idea.

Motioning at the yapping trio that barely fell into the light of his lantern, Alom asked, "Do you think the small ones help the big one find prey, then it kills the prey and shares it with them?"

Clenching his fists, Telius added, "And we're the prey? Yes, that's exactly what I was thinking. I was also thinking that we should leave." Another of the small creatures darted by Telius, then several more. He grunted, then asked, "What if we fed them?"

"They'd have more incentive to follow us."

"What if we just killed them, or chased them away?"

Watching more of them racing down the precipice, Alom replied, "I think they'd keep coming."

The creatures, still growing in number, began growling, circling around both men in waves. Annoyed, and wanting to step on them all, Telius said, "I know these things resemble lertherns, which are the best pets in all of Valchondria, but I can't imagine anyone having something so tiny and noisy as a pet. They're obnoxious!" Telius noticed Alom taking off his backpack and retrieving his bota of dethua sap. "Refilling your lantern already?"

"It isn't for my lantern," Alom said, as he pulled the rubbery lid away from the bota. "It's for our old friend. We can—" Alom suddenly stopped speaking or moving.

Telius looked just past Alom to see a single glowing eye, reflecting the light from their lanterns. With his attention focused on the eyes of the smaller creatures, he had failed to notice the much larger remaining eye of their attacker.

Just as the creature drew into the light, silently brushing against Alom and sniffing his scalp, Alom poured the bota out on its good eye. The creature knocked him aside with a swipe from one of its massive front paws, and he landed outside his lantern's light.

Telius realized Alom's plan and charged the creature, smashing his lantern against its head. The fire spread across its upper body, leaving it illuminated even as it lunged from the light of Alom's lantern. It roared in pain, running around, rolling in the snow.

As the snow doused some of the flame, more of it re-ignited, thanks to the dethua sap that clung to its gray fur. It shook its massive head around, burying it in the snow, even as the flames shot down its back. Finally, it lost its balance and collapsed.

Even though its legs continued to flail about, the smaller canines turned on it, covering it and tearing away at its burning fur until the only light Telius saw was the light of Alom's lantern. The sound of their yapping gave way to a hideous collective growl as they ripped the dying beast apart. It cried out: a pathetic, desperate cry that made Telius suddenly pity it.

Alom called to Telius, telling him to hurry. They shared Alom's lantern as they quickly descended to the next plateau, and the next. Soon they reached a less mountainous area, but the deep snow still forced them to take slow, difficult steps as they moved southward. The few stars in the sky were enough to guide them back to Dalii.

Telius could see beneath Alom's hood again, thanks to their close proximity. Alom's skin looked chapped and icy, his eyes filled with lines and surrounded by matter. The winter plague consumed him. When he placed his arms around Telius's shoulder, his apprentice accepted the weight and helped him walk across the ice, across the mountains, and back to the village, but Telius kept wondering if he could still refer to that village as "home."

CHAPTER 24

*A*rgen's eyes opened. It still happened involuntarily when he awoke, but he quickly closed them when he saw his reflections and the reflections of his reflections. He could hear two guards outside.

"Welcome to Urloan Control," said one of the guards.

Urloan Control is Valcine's maximum-security prison, thought Argen, *and the headquarters of the Maintainers. They took me here.* Argen tried to bring the images in his mind together, tried to assign meanings or names to them, but words and pictures kept drifting away from each other, repelling each other. He had started forgetting again. Reality existed somewhere outside his room, but he could only see himself. He was his only reality.

"Who's in the judgment cell?" asked the other guard.

The judgment cell? Is that what the Maintainers call my mirror prison? It's a sick judgment. Argen felt to see if they had put anything in his food tray, his hands smearing the cold glass with the oil from his skin, sliding across the inner surface of his world. He had smeared the glass by the food tray slot enough times that it at least gave a distorted image, a blurred one, a sort of variety, but his hands always dried out before he could do much damage. All too often, a mist would rise from the floor and clean the mirrors, undoing his work.

He found nothing in his food tray and decided that it must not be time for one of his meals; he could never tell, except that he was often hungry, always desperate for a break in the monotony of his existence.

Sometimes, they left the food tray there, apparently forgetting about it; he only wished he could pull it loose from the slot, use it to smash the mirrors. He didn't care if he cut himself; he just wanted to smash them all. Sometimes, he bruised his fists at every angle, trying to shatter at least one mirror, but he never even caused a crack.

"Argen's in that one," replied the voice of the more familiar guard.

"The boy who killed a scientist? Isn't he Dr. Lorfeltez's son?"

"That he is. The man he killed was his father—or maybe he wasn't, with some of the things I've heard about Lorfeltez."

"She's certainly a disrupter. I don't believe everything I hear on the gossip shows, but there must be some truth to all the things they say about Dr. Lorfeltez, or all the rumors would have died out eventually. I've been hearing bad things about her since I was a boy." They grew quiet for a while, then he asked, "Does Argen ever get time out of that cage?"

They walked down the hall, becoming less audible. Argen looked at the mirrors, hoping to see their silhouettes, knowing that he couldn't. He wanted to hear the answer. He could only leave to go to the relief room beneath his cell, when the sliding hatch opened, allowing him to climb down. But he faced just as many mirrors there, as well as a time limit and a frequency limit.

He liked the shower, the water splashing from his body; it almost felt like standing on a rooftop in the rain. With no computer interface panel, he couldn't raise the temperature above its usual lukewarm state, but he still liked standing under the nozzle, activating the sensor with his presence, feeling and hearing the water.

He also liked finding enough space to walk around a little more; his cell only gave him the room to walk one body-length. During his long walks with Kryldon, they talked about everything, even heavy hazard thoughts. He missed those walks, and his best friend.

He had rarely exercised for his health; few Valchondrians worried about such matters, since going liquid could bring their weight down, if needed. However, Kryldon had convinced him to take up exercise during their preparation for the pressure tournament. Now, it seemed like a good way to pass the time. In the judgment cell, Argen often alternated between pacing, push-ups, and sit-ups, all out of sheer boredom. Still, he liked the way it made his arms and chest look and feel; he thought his developing muscles looked even better than the implants that he would be able to credit box if he were older—older and not locked away in his torture room.

Unlike his body, his face never changed. He remembered now that, after his sentencing, a healer gave him an injection that would stop all of his hair from growing. The Maintainers wanted him to always see himself the same way: the same murderous criminal.

Footsteps. He heard the two voices again, as well as another voice, one that reached into his memory, trying to attach itself to a name. Argen had heard the guard's name before, from a guard who had just had her job deleted. He knew their names, assigned those names to their voices, imagined how their faces might look. Sometimes, he would silently join in their conversations, pretending he was a part of their lives. But now he couldn't remember the names he used for them.

"He's not even allowed visitors," said the voice of the familiar guard. "But I let your mentor through sometimes. He gives me these."

Argen knew what "these" meant: confidence pills. Maybe Gazer would bring him some more. He began to remember when he first started taking the confidence pills, when he first joined the Youth and attended the nightly rallies. Almost every phrase of every sentence that they repeated in unison contained Gazer's name or "the evil ones," the title Gazer had given those who disagreed with him in any way about anything. The Youth spoke with awe when using phrases with Gazer's name, but they spoke with disdain when using phrases about the evil ones. Argen could barely manage to say, "Gazer hates the evil ones," not because he didn't believe it, but because of the conflictive emotional forces of the two names. But he learned to say it again and again. Soon he could repeat all the phrases without thinking, without even hearing himself.

"Gazer hates the evil ones!" shouted Argen. "Why must I repeat these things? Is there nothing else? No Taldra, no Hachen, no Telius, no Kryldon? Kryldon?"

He heard the guards talking to Kryldon and another Youth. Kryldon was there! Argen heard Kryldon's laughter as he watched the sealant of his cell melt down the inside, separating the tiny mirrors. They dropped to the floor and shattered as the cell's framework retreated into the ceiling, shattered without hurting him at all. The Maintainers had sealed the prison around him; now it came apart around him. He could see Kryldon and the other Youth, and the rest of the room. He could see!

Kryldon helped him to his feet, said his name, and embraced him, then stepped back. The other Youth stared blankly at them, her eyes glazed over with too many confidence pills.

"Kryldon," said Argen, as he tried to compose his thoughts well enough for coherent speech. He couldn't remember the last time he'd talked to someone. The guards never talked to him, except to call out his time limits for the relief room. Gazer had talked to him one time, had warned him of something. Now he remembered.

"Kryldon, the cell might explode. The evil ones set it up."

"Gazer took care of everything. Gazer…is our friend."

Though busy trying to adjust to the dimmer lighting outside his cell and to the sudden onslaught of images, he still noticed the disbelief in Kryldon's statement, the forced, stilted tone. Kryldon knocked Argen to the floor, and several shards of broken mirror shot into his arm on impact. A blast from a laser pistol shot over Argen. A Maintainer. The other Youth shot the Maintainer in the head, burning his face.

Kryldon had saved Argen by pushing him over. Argen looked beside himself, pulled his friend's lifeless body closer, touched the burn mark on his chest, found no heartbeat.

"No brothers, no sisters, no friends," said Argen, still trying to find a pulse or a heartbeat. "That is what the evil ones say. Gazer hates the evil ones. I hate the evil ones."

"We have to get out of here, before the other Maintainers get back from the distraction we've set up," said the tall young woman, one Argen had seen at many of the rallies. He loved this one's face, the distinctly feminine strength he could somehow see in her eyes and forehead. He could tell she was a friend, but Gazer said there were no friends. Gazer even said that he was their friend, even though there were no friends. It made no sense anymore. Nothing made sense anymore.

She helped him carry Kryldon's body. Two Maintainers walked down the hall, making eye contact but pretending not to see, marching like robots.

There is no meaning, thought Argen, as they bolted for the roof. *I want a meaning. Gazer is my friend. What does that mean? Kryldon is my friend. Kryldon is dead. Who will repeat that? I killed my father, and I caused my friend to be killed. I belonged in that prison, if I belonged anywhere at all.*

"Glory, Argen," said Gazer, when they reached the hovercraft on the roof's landing area. He barely seemed to notice them as he started his engine. Gazer had an over-sized hovercraft, the kind often driven by members of the Wall System Conglomerate or the Power Holders. Even with the two other Youth who were already in the back area of the vehicle, Argen and the girl found plenty of room for themselves and for Kryldon's body.

As Gazer piloted them through the twisting hoverlanes to Valcine Plaza, he finally began talking. "What happened to our friend Kryldon?"

Argen didn't reply, but he swallowed the confidence pill one of the other Youth handed to him.

The girl replied, "The evil ones." The appropriate response.

Why did Gazer even ask? He knew what he would hear. He created all the answers, yet kept asking the questions. Why? What made him want other people to repeat his thoughts to him? If he believed so strongly in freedom, why didn't he encourage people to think for themselves? Wasn't that a part of freedom? No, people needed freedom from wrong-minded ideas; Argen remembered that now, or remembered memorizing some such declaration during his first-level education. He wasn't sure if he had ever believed it, even then.

"Kryldon was Gazer's friend," said Gazer.

"Kryldon was my friend," Argen added. He pressed his trembling face against the back window of the hovercraft, watching the crowded-together buildings, old and crumbling, with vines eating into their walls and their windows, killing them. *Everything kills. Everything dies.*

"You know, Argen, Kryldon will go straight to the Highest World for dying as a martyr for good," Gazer told him. Gazer rarely used such long sentences when talking to Argen, so it caught Argen's attention.

"I want him here." Argen pulled the shards of glass from his bloodied arm, dropped them on the floor of the hovercraft. He thought his arm should hurt, but he only felt the pain of losing Kryldon. The confidence pill took care of any other pain. It just couldn't make his loss go away.

CHAPTER 25

Taldra and Jase-Dawn had worked late on Life Unit. As the day turned into night, they compared charts, holographic simulations, and equations. Jase-Dawn's research abilities and understanding—coupled with the fact that she actually found mathematics fascinating and would work on a problem even after Taldra gave up—showed that they could easily shorten her apprenticeship time. But Taldra couldn't force herself to say that, to give that compliment, not when it meant losing her only friend, leaving the house empty again.

Still, she kept worrying about Jase-Dawn's safety, especially with Gazer still loose, and especially with all the hatred stirred up against Taldra by the gossip masters. "Conspiracy!" they shouted. "Deadly agenda! Highly reliable sources say that ninety percent of all Valchondrians see Dr. Lorfeltez as anti-glory and would not want her teaching science to their children." Sometimes, Taldra wanted to unplug every wallscreen on the planet, and to erase her own work as part of the media, her own former promotion of the SSC. She wanted no connection with the shouting voices on her wall.

"Life will have to double check our figures," said Jase-Dawn, catching her breath the way she always did when she wanted Taldra to notice how long they'd been working. She rolled her eyes enough to activate the chronometer in her right eye. "But we can get that from her in the morning. Could we hover to a food module? We've been here since 7 solar, and it's almost 7 lunar."

Adjusting her center earring, Taldra said, "Hover on over there, and get me something too. Something small, though, and without gredga chips; I'm still trying to drop back to perfect weight. I'll meet you at home later. I just want to look at a couple more things. My report's due in three days. It has to be impressive. The more facts and figures, the better. And I'll have Life generate some charts. You know how the SSC's funding committee loves charts."

"Taldra, you need food and sleep. We've worked together a while now, and I'd like to think I'm your friend."

The word embraced Taldra, and she smiled. "Of course you are."

"Then as your friend, I have to say, you work too many hours without rest. I don't see how you've continued this way for so long."

Taldra playfully slapped Jase-Dawn's arm: something she had seen Hachen do to Argen countless times. It had always made her feel that Argen saw Hachen's love, even if he never followed Hachen's advice. She wanted Jase-Dawn to see her love; she wanted Jase-Dawn to be her daughter. "Continuing this way is called 'determination.' You'll understand when you've been involved with something for many years. Now move your feet that way. I'll meet you back at the house."

"When?"

"Soon."

Jase-Dawn sighed. "You're somewhat stubborn," she said, as she walked out the control room.

"Somewhat," Taldra replied, as the metal door slid down. She liked how Jase-Dawn would just walk away, never saying "Glory" first. She despised that word. With eight billion Valchondrians saying it several times a day, it no longer meant anything at all.

"Jase-Dawn has left," said Life Unit. "The doorway has activated itself."

Taldra jumped up from her chair. *Doorway?* "Life Unit, repeat your last announcement." Life didn't respond. "Life Unit?"

❧   ❧   ❧

Telius helped Alom walk to the doorway cave. Though the virus caused Telius to recover quickly from their journey to North Edge, Alom had spent two weeks in bed with the winter plague, and he still couldn't walk long distances alone. They stopped at the mouth of the cave when they saw sparks flying out of it.

"The doorway," said Alom, answering the question in Telius's eyes. "Go in."

Telius walked through the sparks to find a cyclone of lights inside. Despite the brightness, none of it hurt his skin or his eyes. The shades of gray broke apart and began splashing against each other, like the waters of colliding rivers. A middle-aged and slightly pudgy black man stepped from the center of that cyclone, wearing baggy clothes made of some thin fabric.

"Father?" asked Telius, though he looked nothing like the man in the visions. Alom entered the cave and stood beside Telius. The man from the lights stumbled a bit then regained his balance while Telius grabbed Alom's shoulder. "Alom, is that—?"

"It's good to see you again, Geln," said Alom, before Telius could finish the question. "As I promised, I took care of him, but you can see that."

No, thought Telius. *Why didn't they come? Why would they only send their apprentice, as if this were some trivial errand that would only waste their valuable time?* "You're Geln, the man who helps my parents?"

"Yes, but call me Gazer; it's my chosen name." His eyes looked Telius up and down. "You're completely grown, and if it weren't for your hair being longer, I couldn't tell you from your brother." He sniffed the air. "I don't remember it smelling so bad in here. Please tell me you've learned good hygiene. One only wants certain aspects of primitivism."

"Of what?" asked Telius. "Where were you? Where are my parents, and my brother?"

"You'll see them when you walk through with me, but I have to talk to you about something first. I know I should wait and ask later, but I can't wait. I just can't. What have you learned about Degranon?"

"Everything."

"Everything?" Gazer smiled madly.

"Everything. I've heard it recited several times, and I've personally written down a copy. It took more scrolls than I thought I could ever make."

"No, not scrolls. I mean the place. Have you been there? Have you met the last great king?"

"What?"

Alom laughed, watching the sparks dart off the walls inside the cave. "Only in his nightmares." Alom's laughter again turned into coughing.

❦   ❦   ❦

Taldra pounded against the metal door that led from the control room to the battery room, then she pressed the door button again. She couldn't remember closing the door; she had turned away from the battery room during her conversation with Jase-Dawn, so maybe Jase-Dawn closed it. "Life Unit, open the door. Open the door! Why don't you answer? Why don't you acknowledge my voice?"

"The doorway is becoming unstable," said Life Unit. "My sensors have been compromised. Someone else is here, but I don't know who."

"Let me in the battery room!" screamed Taldra, pressing her body against the door. The doorway glowed so vibrantly that she couldn't see anything but a solid blanket of light through the windows that led to the battery room. "Let me in. I need to see my son! Telius!"

❀   ❀   ❀

Gazer advanced toward Alom, their faces nearly touching. "What is your aim? Why do you laugh at me, old man?"

"Forgiveness, Geln, but you refer to a children's story as if it were real."

Geln's voice brimmed with moral outrage. "Degranon is real! I've read about it all my life, just as people have read about it for thousands of years. Where I was born, everybody learns all about Degranon from their priests."

"As here, but there's no truth to it, not literal truth. It's a warning against greed, arrogance, and violence. It's all metaphor, allegory! None of the characters are actual people. They just symbolize problems that we struggle with in reality."

Gazer's beady eyes seemed to retreat even further into their sockets as he began to sweat and tremble. "No, it's nothing like that! You obviously aren't of God! Degranon was glorious and righteous! It was the kingdom of God on Valchondria!" Geln's voice grew louder with each word that he spat into Alom's face.

Telius touched Geln's shoulder with one hand, drew his dagger from its sheath with the other. "I would prefer that you step back from the village priest. It is a fatal crime to hurt him or me."

Gazer pulled a metal object the size of his palm from his robe and pointed it at a boulder near the cave's door. A beam of light shot from the object, blasting a hole through the boulder. Tiny particles of rock stung Telius's face and hands as he tried to shield himself from the explosion.

"Drop the primitive weapon," said Gazer. "My laser pistol is a bit less outdated, and I could use it against your mentor."

Telius tossed his weapon away as Gazer put his back into his robe, but while Gazer was occupied with that action, Telius tried to grab the weapon from him.

Gazer punched Telius, knocking him to the damp floor of the cave, then slammed Alom against one of the cave's walls. "You've lied to Telius. You've poisoned the minds of children. He is of no use to me now." Alom's body slid down the wall as Gazer walked into the center of the lights and disappeared.

"Alom!" screamed Telius, pulling himself up. He wanted to stop Gazer, to punish him for his fatal crime, but he could see Alom needed him.

"Telius," Alom whispered, as his apprentice leaned over him and grabbed his hand. "Go after him. Find out what happened to your family." The circle of gray lights passed through their bodies, growing ever smaller.

"I can't leave you here. You'll die." Telius squeezed Alom's hand tightly, praying that somehow he could send life back into Alom's body, that the miracle virus that protected him could somehow revive Alom. That prayer went unanswered, like so many others. The virus was his one miracle, but it only benefited himself, not the person who needed it. He wondered if he should cut himself and give his blood to Alom, but his parents had told Alom that the virus couldn't spread that way.

Alom began coughing. A mixture of blood and spit poured from the corner of his mouth. "I've been dying for the past year. There's no stopping it now. I had the honor of being your guide from the time you were born until the time you became a man. You no longer need a mentor, but you still need family. Your parents love you as much as I do; I've seen it in their eyes."

"Then they'll help you, because they know what you've done for me. They'll use their medicine, their machines, that Life Unit thing. They'll—"

Alom placed one of his huge hands over Telius's mouth. "I thought you had learned to listen. Go. Let my life end with the joy of knowing you will see your parents."

Telius jerked away, forcing himself to step into the doorway. "I love you, Alom," he said, as he walked into the fading circle of lights.

❧   ❧   ❧

Taldra kept repeating the command into her computer-interface panel until the door to the battery room finally opened, putting her face to face with her nemesis as the time doorway collapsed onto the floor, throwing sparks across the battery room.

"You just missed the doorway," he told her.

"Geln?"

He smiled, motioning for her to come in. "Please, Taldra, use my chosen name."

"When did you become married? And who was that dumb?"

"Actually, it was you. I've married you in my mind a million times as I've gazed up at the stars and thought of the worlds you wanted to visit, the worlds we could conquer together."

"I had to ask." She reached for a Maintainer button, pressed it frantically.

Gazer smiled smugly. "I've cut all transmissions."

Breathing in deeply, Taldra looked up. "Life Unit, initiate invasion policy immediately. Phantom Code 154." Though she spoke the numbers in a frenzy, she hoped Life still understood them.

Life responded this time. "Initiated. Also, the temporal doorway is reactivating."

Gazer's head jerked back as if someone punched him in the nose. "I didn't encode an override for that command."

"You didn't know about that command. It was embedded in Life Unit's phantom files. Surely you knew that I kept some measures secret, you stupid son of a hiliate!"

Smoke began pouring into the battery room from the ventilation system. A rainbow of lights bounced around the room, flinging Taldra against Gazer, who fell over. As Telius stepped from the center of the lights, Taldra grabbed his arm and pulled him out of the battery room, into the control room. "Life, seal the door."

"Sealing." The door dropped down, closing off most of the smoke.

Taldra touched her son's face, afraid this was all nothing more than another dream. "It's really you." The smoke began pouring from the control room's vents.

"What is that?" asked Telius, coughing. "It hurts my insides!"

"An organic poison. The virus will protect you, but it's still disorienting if you've never been exposed to it."

"Dr. Geln just left," said Life Unit. "However, I have not been able to rectify the programming errors he caused."

"Disable invasion policy." She yanked on Telius's hand. "We'd better go. The Maintainers will be here as soon Life recovers and that button signal goes out. This is probably our only chance to get you out of here safely."

Telius rubbed his eyes. "Mother?"

"Yes, I'm your mother. I'll explain everything on the hoverlanes. Let's just get out of here."

The sparks disappeared, separating Telius from the world he knew.

🍁   🍁   🍁

Zaysha had kept her promise by no longer following Telius to the mouth of the cave, but she waited at the edge of the forest. Something had told her that this time was somehow special to Telius. He had seemed different since his return from North Edge.

Hearing shouting inside the cave, she became worried and decided to abandon her promise. As she entered the cave, she thought she saw a flash of light, but she was more interested in what she definitely saw.

"Alom!" She found him, lying on the cave floor, near its furthest wall. Zaysha fell beside him and cradled his head. She could feel a faint attempt at energy, as if he vacillated between life and death. "Alom, what happened to you?"

"Degranon," he whispered, with great difficulty.

Zaysha held her ear nearly against his mouth, hoping to hear better. "What about Degranon?"

"Real…the ones who left…the last great king…."

"Alom, I don't see your aim. Where is Telius?"

"Gone to Degranon…."

She shook his face gently, but with no response. "Alom? Are you saying that Telius is in Degranon, that it's real? Did the Degrans do this to you? Alom? Alom!"

Tears streamed down her face as she rocked their spiritual leader in her trembling hands. The last great king was real, and he had murdered Alom. But why would Telius go back with the Degrans? That was the secret he held: he had been meeting with the Degrans, in the secret cave, and possibly elsewhere. They had done something to make him different. They had deceived him, lead him astray, blinded him to their evil!

The Degrans weren't like the people of the village she would one day lead. They were evil. She decided that, after Alom's fire ceremony, she would warn the priests of every village about the powers of Degranon.

CHAPTER 26

❀

In the strange machine where they sat down, Telius could see nothing but the glowing hoverlanes and hovercrafts, though the lanes seemed to weave around houses that were as tall as mountains. His mother had explained this mode of travel, but the twisting and weaving at such speed still frightened and nauseated him. His hiliate never ran that fast; if he'd ever tried to make it run that fast, it would have reached back with one of its front claws and yanked him to the ground.

"Why is Gazer doing this?" asked Telius, finally managing to catch his breath enough to speak.

"Because he married me in his mind, as he put it, and because he wants to revive Degranon."

"I'm not sure what married in the mind is, but he told me about his Degranon fantasy. Degranon never existed. It's just a book."

Taldra looked confused. "A book? You would still have books in your time, I suppose. But I don't know where Gazer would have found one; the Maintainers banned them after the advent of hand machines. Still, he's crumbled enough to believe what he reads in one."

These ideas seemed incomprehensible to Telius, who had spent much of his life reading. "You don't have books?"

"We used to have electronic ones, but no one read those. The wallscreen gives us all the information we need."

"The wallscreen?"

She rubbed her forehead. "You'll have to see it to understand. The wallscreen is basically the center of Valchondrian life, I'm sad to tell you. So, did you tell Gazer that you think Degranon is just a book?"

"Alom told him, and he murdered Alom for it."

Taldra shuddered. "I'm sorry. Alom was a good man. There was a kindness in his eyes that made your father trust him from the instant he stumbled through the doorway."

"I'm glad we're able to communicate fairly well. I sometimes worried that the time difference would keep us from understanding each other."

"Our worlds aren't so different." Taldra touched his hair. "We need to stop at an all-night beauty palace and get your hair cut. Young men in this time period never let their hair grow long; it's unfashionable. Your father used to have fits about how short Argen kept his hair. You'll also need modern clothes; most people don't wear animal fur."

Looking at his fur-skin shirt, Telius said, "That's fine. But I was going to say that language was constantly changing in my time. It had changed so much in the generations before my arrival that the way people first wrote and spoke became known as 'the old language.' But three thousand years have past since my time."

"I've never heard about changes in the way we speak, except for certain words being added to the banned list. There's rarely change in any aspect of Valchondrian life, other than fashion trends, and even those repeat themselves in predictable cycles. Your father and I always talked about the lack of change. He wanted change." Taldra's voice and her eyes revealed that she wanted to cry.

"Wanted? Mother, is—?"

"There was an accident." She wiped her eyes.

"What happened?"

"Your father is dead. Argen—Argen was blamed for his death. Gazer had pulled Argen into the Degran cult by giving him some sort of drug, and a weapon. When Hachen tried to take the weapon from him, something happened, but it was an accident. Hachen died on his way to the hospital. I haven't been allowed to see Argen since."

"He's in exile?"

"Exile? Yes, from all humanity."

Her brief explanation preceded the first break in their conversation. During that long moment, Telius began to feel separated from his family again, though his mother sat beside him. Some of the buildings they now approached were lit, towering above them; Telius wondered if they touched the clouds, like the mountains at North Edge. The hoverlanes intertwined, forming nets that captured the buildings. The lights shone like the reflection of a starry night in a lake. All of it inspired Telius's imagination while he tried to understand his father's death. It all seemed so unreal, so dreamlike. The hovercraft came close to one of the buildings as they wove around it, close enough to see the vines and the cracked bricks.

"Do you live in one of those structures, Mother?"

"Telius, why do you keep calling me that? My chosen name is Taldra."

"I know, but you're my mother. I shouldn't use either of your names."

"I understand. It's some primitive custom from your time. Well, until we decide what to do about you, we can't let anyone know who you are." She touched his chin. "You look old enough for a facial modification. There are plenty of modifiers in Valcine who won't check your age if I use my credit box."

Telius's face twitched. "Facial modification? That sounds painful."

"Most people say it's worth the pain, but your father and I never tried it. I liked how he looked, and he liked how I looked."

Telius spoke emphatically: "I'm not ashamed of who I am, not even if Valchondria's laws tell me that I should be ashamed. The problem is the laws, not me."

"With that attitude, anyone can figure out that you're my son." Taldra steered off the hoverlanes, onto a landing area.

"Gratitude."

Taldra laughed. "I didn't mean that as a compliment, but I'm glad you took it that way. Still, just for the next few days, while I decide whether to tell Jase-Dawn the truth, I want you to wear a healing mask. I told you about all the trouble we're in, and how we probably shouldn't involve her."

"Yes, but—"

She patted his knee. "Just for the next few days. We can buy one while you get some of that pretty hair severed at the beauty palace. You're way too young for that look."

Telius eyed her with a quizzical expression; they stayed in the hovercraft, talking a while longer. He couldn't help telling her that "People have gotten away from being individuals."

Taldra grew silent for a moment. "Maybe you're right, Telius. But please remember that there are certain things you just can't say, and certain things that you just can't question. We have a code of legally permitted language. The Maintainers designed it, claiming they know what's best for us, and that they have to protect us from linguistic terrorism."

"I've never heard of anything so absurd," said Telius, flinging his hands over his head. "How do you communicate? How do you solve problems?"

"Usually, we don't."

"It isn't like that in my time. We consider it dishonest not to speak what you think."

"Then you can say whatever you want?"

"As long as you believe it's the truth, and you say it in a respectful manner. Our laws are simple: we interact with each other in dignity and honesty. From that premise, even painful truths are bearable. Your Maintainers sound afraid of letting people think for themselves, which tells me they have something to hide."

Taldra breathed in deeply, sharply, as if someone kicked her in the stomach. "Telius, you can't talk like that outside this vehicle. You'll be arrested."

Telius rolled his eyes. "You call yourselves advanced, and you think of my time as primitive. But in the past, people weren't afraid to talk to each other, and they weren't forbidden from disagreeing with any oppressive law given to them by their leaders. People often disagreed with Alom, and he was the leader of our village."

"Well, actually, we're allowed to do that."

"There must be some condition. Do the Maintainers choose the words for you?"

Taldra shook her head. "No. It's thoroughly free expression, whatever we wish to say, as long as we're alone, in a dethua chamber. It's completely soundproof. There aren't any listening devices or recorders; it's just solid dethua. But we're at the headquarters of the Maintainers, so we seem to be talking to them. We can do that once a week."

"And that satisfies you?"

"No. But it's the best we have. I go every week. It isn't the same as podium speech, but it's all we have left. You don't know what Valchondria's become."

Telius looked away from her, ran his hand across the bottom of the window. "I'm not sure I want to know. Why don't we just find Argen and take him back to my time?"

"Because it isn't your time, and it isn't that easy. The doorway collapsed before we left, and I don't know if it will ever open again. This is your time, and we have a lot of challenges ahead of us. Valchondria needs you, Telius, and I need you."

"All right, I recognize your wisdom. Does that beauty palace sell weapons? I left my dagger in the doorway cave."

"Weapons are illegal."

"But Gazer had one; he called it a 'laser pistol.'"

Taldra breathed in deeply. "Those are especially illegal. Gazer might seem a bit pathetic, but he's a very dangerous man, and he has an army of followers in the group he's formed. They call themselves the 'Youth For Valchondrian Reform,' and all of them recruit other young people into the group."

As the doors to the hovercraft popped open, Telius said, "With a name like that, they sound harmless, even positive."

"Of course they do. That's how it works." Taldra smiled, but not a happy smile. It revealed an attempt to hide fear.

CHAPTER 27

Telius liked the tight black body suit Taldra had bought him at the beauty palace, but the healing mask felt like wet mud on his face, though it looked hard when he gazed into the thing that she called "mirror." Worse yet, the back of his neck itched from being shaved. He had never heard of people shaving their necks. However, in some of Dalii's neighboring villages, people who recently lost their spouses would completely shave one side of their heads.

The inside of Taldra's house looked much like the inside of Life Unit, though it at least didn't smell like a dung heap, as the battery room had. In fact, Telius noticed an absence of smell until Jase-Dawn walked down the stairs, wearing an intriguing perfume. Her robe, with its pictures of stars, looked almost like Taldra's. Her beautiful face also caught his attention; he knew he would never see Zaysha again, but he now realized that the future held possibilities of its own.

"Telius, this is Jase-Dawn," said Taldra. "Telius's father was an old friend of Hachen's. He'll be staying with us for a while."

"Oh." Jase-Dawn touched his shoulder. "What happened to your face?"

"I—" said Telius, looking at her hand as she pulled it from his shoulder.

"He had a late-night facial modification," said Taldra. "He's still groggy from the drugs. I'm afraid he inherited his father's over-sized cheek bones."

Jase-Dawn let go of his hand, which he used to gesture at his cheeks. "Well, I'm sure you'll like it here." Her countenance became serious as she turned away from Telius. "Taldra, there was a message on the collector about a Maintainer button being pushed in Life Unit."

"It was nothing," said Taldra. "I saw it on the wallscreen at the beauty palace and called the Maintainers. They said there wasn't any sign on the outside of an attempted intrusion, and that a power surge could have caused the button to go off. We stopped back by there, and everything was fine."

"Good. Also, your parents visited."

"My parents?" Taldra's eyes widened.

"Yes. I tried to contact you at Life Unit, but its video line wasn't working. They said they plan to move to the North Edge project in a few months, away from all the crowds, and that you can come live with them there if you...." Jase-Dawn's spinning fingers showed that she preferred not to finish the sentence.

"Regain my mind?"

"Something of that nature. They didn't stay long."

Telius could see the sadness in Taldra's eyes, a sadness that revealed why she had not mentioned her parents during their long night of conversation. He hadn't told her about all the times he had felt rejected by her, but learning that her parents had actually rejected her somehow connected them, like two orphans.

Instead of responding, Taldra told her, "Try to get your project finished today. I need to turn in my approval. Telius, you can sleep in your...in the first bedroom upstairs."

The window-like object that Taldra called "wallscreen" began flashing, and the image of a woman wearing too much make-up appeared on it. "This is a news flash from Valcine Wisdom," she said.

"Members of the Youth For Valchondrian Reform have again broken into Urloan Control. At least one Maintainer was killed in the attack. Argen, son of the controversial scientist Dr. Lorfeltez, was apparently freed by the Youth. He was serving a sentence of life mirroring for killing his father, who was also a scientist and happened to be married with Dr. Lorfeltez. As always, Dr. Lorfeltez has her video line blocked from all news agencies and gossip masters, so she is unavailable for comment. We hope to have live footage of her bedroom windows soon, in hopes of seeing if she's hiding anyone."

"My son?" asked Taldra, frantically. "I'm going to Urloan Control to see if someone will listen to me."

"Can I go with you?" asked Telius.

"No, they'd only detain you, and there would be some other complications that I'll explain later. Please stay here."

She left. The door slid shut.

Separation.

❦   ❦   ❦

As Taldra entered Urloan Control, a Maintainer pulled her aside and began waving a metal wand up and down her body. He then stopped to look at the read-out that appeared at the tip of that wand.

"Did you know you're overweight?" he asked her, in an accusatory tone.

"No," she said. "I'll go liquid for a week. Just please listen."

He shook his head. "I'm going to have to fine you."

Grunting, she handed over her credit box, steaming with resentment at the embarrassing situation and the timing of it. "Fine me then, but let me speak with the Top Maintainers. It's urgent."

"You're Dr. Lorfeltez." He attached his palm machine to her credit box and began making the transfer to the Maintainer Fund. "What do you want with us?"

"I need your help." She looked at the transfer rate on his palm machine. "And don't overcharge me. I can't be more than five percent overweight."

He smiled in a fake, condescending manner. "Twelve percent."

❧   ❧   ❧

Telius rolled around on the bed for a while before deciding to lie on the carpet, which felt much more like his fur-coat bed in Alom's house, but he still couldn't sleep. This was Argen's room. Taldra had almost said it: "In your brother's room." Telius tried to find a candle or a lantern in the hall but only saw lights. Why wasn't there a light in Argen's room?

He walked down the staircase to ask Jase-Dawn about it, but stopped when he heard her voice. She was talking into the stack of machines that Taldra called her "video system." As he understood it, someone could use the video system to send news to everyone through their wallscreen, or could talk just to one person, and talking one-on-one allowed both people to see each other. It sounded much like the visions at North Edge, and he still wanted to speak with his mother about those.

But all of that became less interesting when he realized that Jase-Dawn was speaking in the old language. Despite his limited vocabulary in the old language, he could figure out that she was talking about him. He also recognized the other voice as Gazer's, though he couldn't see the wallscreen from his angle. As he walked down the stairs, she looked up and pressed some of the buttons on the system.

"You scared me," she said, but she didn't look frightened to Telius.

"Forgiveness. I couldn't sleep. So what about the project you're supposed to finish today? What are you working on?"

"It's a line of computerized clothes that will modify themselves according to the pattern of whatever else you're wearing. It will soon lead to a line of clothing that can change density according to the temperature of one's surroundings. That would be useful for all the people who've been flocking to the Arctic regions, looking for more room."

"That would also be useful for the col—" Telius realized he was about to use a legally un-permitted word. This limited communication annoyed him almost as much as the ridiculous mask on his face; at least his neck had stopped itching. "I meant, that would be useful for people who happened to live other places that didn't happen to be Valchondria." He used his hands to help fill in the gaps of meaning that the Maintainers had caused by their interference with language.

"You're for that?"

"I'm interested in Taldra's work. Could you show me the memory—the video chip—of *Other Valchondrias*? I didn't get a chance to see it before it was pulled."

"As long as you don't tell anyone you saw it."

Telius waved his hand outward from his chest. "I wouldn't be that heavy hazard."

"It's right there on the shelf." Jase-Dawn pointed to several shiny square objects on one of the shelves beside the wallscreen.

"Could you set it into motion for me? I'm terrible with machines."

Jase-Dawn's eyes revealed that he had just confirmed a suspicion. "Yes, but I have to leave as soon as I get it started."

"What about the project?"

"It will have to wait. Someone wants to see me."

Telius wasn't sure what to do, but he thought Taldra would come back soon, and he worried that, if he called her, Gazer might see their conversation on his wallscreen. He had to wait. Jase-Dawn started *Other Valchondrias* then left.

"Glory," she said, as the door shut.

"I'm sure," he whispered, as he sat down on the couch that faced the wallscreen.

Taldra's face appeared on the wallscreen then faded into the words "Other Valchondrias." Then she reappeared, sitting in the chair and in the room he had seen during the vision at North Edge, the control room in Life Unit.

CHAPTER 28

❀

At Signal Complex, in the studio where Taldra and Tquil had carried on their wallscreened debates, Gazer sat in the chair Taldra had always used. Silently, he watched Leader and Jase-Dawn argue about something—they argued often—while several of the Youth worked on making the video equipment run as Gazer planned. Annoyed by the noise, he finally decided to disrupt the argument.

"Is there a problem, Leader?" asked Gazer.

Leader's dark green eyes widened. "Yes, there is a problem. I don't remember endorsing lawlessness. Argen is a convicted scientist-killer, but your Youth killed one of the Maintainers while freeing him from Urloan Control. I never authorized such behavior, and I won't condone it."

"Argen can help us get Taldra."

"What is Taldra to you?" Leader demanded.

"Dangerous. She must be discredited, or the rebellion might end up in factions, with much of Valchondria following her instead of going along with the new world you've helped us create. You don't know what civil wars can do. We need to take her power from her."

"She's had nothing but negative publicity. Don't you listen to the polls?"

Gazer jerked his hulking body up, nearly against Leader. "Taldra is a force for change, something your people know nothing about.

When change begins, they will embrace it. Some will embrace her along with it."

"They will embrace me. You said you'd take over the SSC and the Maintainers."

"The SSC was easy. Many of the Maintainers will have to be killed. They actually have a bit of warrior spirit. Pity."

"But then the killing will stop. I am Leader."

"No longer." Gazer looked away from him, choosing instead to watch Jase-Dawn helping the Youth. With her gentle manner, she seemed so unlike her mother, his mentor. In fact, Jase-Dawn seemed more like Taldra than like any Degran.

"But, we agreed you would give me full control over Valchondria, as long as the Degran people would be able to live their faith without fear of persecution from the government."

"The book calls us to be the government. To allow your bookless nation to continue would be persecution of Degranon. The book calls us to rule over the evil ones. Today, I will give you Valchondria, but tomorrow, Valchondria will become New Degranon. This is the last day of Valchondria. Enjoy it."

"No!" Leader reached for Gazer's neck with his aging hands, but Gazer casually drew his laser pistol from his shirt pocket.

"Now, Leader, you can't enjoy this special day if you're dead."

Leader laughed at the threat. "I saw that it was coming to this. I saw how wrong I've been to trust you. Sadly, I trusted the wrong person."

Gazer cocked his head. "What are you babbling about?"

"This morning, I rescinded my appointment of you as my replacement. Instead, I appointed Taldra. The recording has a Maintainer lock on it. Even I can't erase or rescind it. There are sensors in my credit box and throughout Valcine Plaza. As soon as they detect my death, they will activate the recording, which will appear on every wallscreen in all of Valchondria."

Anger rose up in Gazer's body. No one had ever defied him this way. Since that day his father had slashed his face, he had allowed no one to harm him or threaten him. Even his superiors in the Degran military had feared him. He would not tolerate defiance. "Then I will kill Taldra."

"I don't believe you could do that. Any fool can see that you've never stopped loving her."

Leader was right, of course. But it didn't matter. The Valchondrian government would soon be no more. Gazer put away his laser pistol and touched Leader on his shoulder. "Appoint whoever you like as Leader. I will still rule."

Gazer's hand moved swiftly from Leader's shoulder to his larynx. Just as in his training, he pressed down until he could no longer feel a pulse.

After Leader's body fell away, Gazer smiled at Jase-Dawn.

"Your mother taught me how to do that," he told her.

Jase-Dawn shuddered but then swallowed the words of disgust that she obviously wanted to voice. She was nothing like her mother. She couldn't understand Gazer's contempt for any threat to the Degran way, the only way. Her Degran faith seemed impure, re-filtered.

He could see in her eyes that he might have been wrong to trust her so deeply as to give her this assignment. Even after seeing him kill both Tquil and Leader, she still seemed more like a Valchondrian than a Degran. He wondered, what had Taldra done to her?

Another image disrupted Telius's viewing of *Other Valchondrias*, but it gained his interest when he saw Gazer's face on the wallscreen. The picture expanded to include his entire body while his voice grew from a muffle.

"...your new Leader. The man you thought of as Leader gave unlimited power to the renegade who created Project Life Unit. She should call it Project Death Unit, for all the destruction it has brought to society. Fortunately, I have come to save you from evil. You only need turn to and accept the man who will be your next Leader: me. Dr. Lorfeltez is the one you need to fear most; she is heavy anti-glory, a threat to Valchondrian values. Highly reliable sources tell me that Life Unit is very dangerous and unstable. Everyone in the Valcine area is advised to leave as soon as this transmission is over. We will destroy Life Unit, and then we will allow you to return to your homes when it is safe.

"Your children have already accepted this world as a new Degranon; soon, you will also. As some of the gossip masters have reported, the virus hasn't been keeping people alive as long as it used to. That's because it mutates with every generation, consuming not only the viruses that threaten your body but also the viruses and organisms that your body needs, that it can't live without. Soon, your life span will be less than twenty years, and most people will be born sterile.

"You might not feel inclined to believe me, but think back. Remember the reports of people keeping their youthful appearances beyond their sixtieth year? How many sixty-year-olds do you know today? If you're over forty and your parents are still alive, you're an exception. I know that's difficult to handle, but it's the truth, because I only speak the truth.

"The virus wasn't found on Valchondria, as the SSC claims, but on another world. The colonists there thought they had discovered a miracle cure for aging, but it nearly wiped them out, not that Valchondria ever knew. Valchondria deserted all the colonists, left them to die in the cold vastness of outer space.

"Some scientists experimented with a cure for the virus. The first cure made it worse; the second destroyed every trace of it. I have both cures. I also have access to your water supply. I would like an answer by 5 solar. Oh, and Dr. Lorfeltez, please report to Life Unit if you want to see Argen alive. We have him, and we're going after Telius next."

Argen, though looking somewhat unnerved by Gazer's threat, came to his side at his beckoning fingers. Telius stood looking at the screen as the picture faded and Taldra's video resumed. She now stood behind a tiny version of Life Unit, explaining the reasons for its triangular construction. *I need to go there,* he thought. *My family needs me.*

He went to the exit, looking for a button to open it, the way he'd seen Taldra open other doors. He couldn't find the button. On the wallscreen, a Top Maintainer agreed to Gazer's demands and urged everyone else to do so as well. There, on the ornate frame that surrounded the door! He touched the button; the wall consumed the door.

A crowd of people, releasing strange glass objects that flew toward him, lunged forward, asking, "Are you Argen?" Several young men, without the glass objects, tossed him down on the walkway. They jumped on him, tearing off his mask then punching him, kicking him. One of them got on top of him and squeezed his neck; Telius pushed his thumb into the attacker's wrist then felt his grip loosen.

As more of the people with the glass objects lunged forward, they pushed his attackers back, asking him questions about Taldra, Hachen, and Life Unit. Despite being trampled on several times, he managed to pull himself up and jump through the doorway just as the door began to close.

Taldra cradled Telius's head, wiping the blood from her son's bruised face with a warm cloth. She couldn't lose him, not so soon after getting him back. His eyes opened, and he moaned. "What happened?" she asked.

"I opened the door, and there were all these people outside."

Taldra rolled her eyes. "The gossip masters. I landed over the top hatch and came through the roof before they could get to my hovercraft. They've got two hovercrafts up there, and I don't know how many of them are outside. They think you're Argen, and that I helped you escape."

"They kept asking me all these questions. Then some other people started hitting me. It was insane! I can't get used to all of these modern customs." He tried to get up, and she guided his bruised body until he managed to stand. The suit she'd bought him was torn at the chest, revealing a series of scratches on his red skin. "I could use that healing mask now, but they tore it off."

"It might have been the Youth, or just some patriots. Do any of your bones feel broken?"

"No, I've had worse falls without breaking anything."

"What?!"

Telius breathed in. "You probably don't need to hear about that right now. Did you see Gazer's wallscreen talk?"

"Yes, at Urloan Control. Fortunately, the Maintainers were fascinated enough with it that I was able to sneak out before they got too manipulated by Gazer's danger speak. He isn't making any improvements on my reputation, and they weren't interested in helping me anyway." The house began to shake. "I was afraid this was his aim. They have Life Unit; Gazer knows that it can cause damage to the ground beneath us, cause a dangerous quake. I have to go."

"I'm going with you this time."

She held her hands out. "No, it's too dangerous."

"He's my brother. I might be able to help you get him away from Gazer. You can't go by yourself, and you can't trust the Maintainers or Jase-Dawn."

"Jase-Dawn?"

"She's working for Gazer. I heard her talking to him with the wallscreen, using the old language and referring to Degranon."

Taldra braced herself against a plastic wall as the reality of Telius's words tore into her. She had given Jase-Dawn complete access to every corner of her home, every corner of Life Unit. She had trusted her even more than she had trusted Gazer. Was everything she had ever done in the name of Degranon? Had she developed a weapon, rather than a life-giving machine?

"Hopefully, the quakes have scared off our visitors," she said, opening the door to a scene of utter chaos. "Let's get your brother."

CHAPTER 29

The quake became too violent for even the most devoted wallscreen watchers to ignore. Buildings shook, windows shattered, and walls and hoverlanes collapsed, crushing the people who tried to escape on the crowded walkways. Gazer had given them no time for the evacuation he suggested.

The power flashed off and on several times before the walkway grew almost dark, with no light but the little bit of sundown that could twist through the smoke, the buildings, the hoverlanes, and the vines. The quake looked and sounded like a terrible storm, filled with the rumbling of an injured planet and the screams of its people.

Life Unit began to glow, shooting random beams of light into the darkness. Taldra felt like she was walking into a furnace when they stepped over Life's fence. She placed her hand on Life's glass entry panel but heard no hand-scan response. Then she pressed her hand against the panel so hard that she could feel the panel cracking and her hand bruising. Though she couldn't hear the recognition signal over all the chaos, the door raised up, sending smoke into their faces.

"They're probably in the control room," she said. "Follow me."

"What if they try to escape?" asked Telius. "Is there another exit?"

"Only if Gazer can create a doorway in the battery room. He seems to have more control over the doorways than he clearly spoke."

"I'll check there." He ran past her. She tried to stop him but dared not shout. Across the hall, she saw the door to the control room lifting, and she saw him run through it, behind everyone's back. When she walked in, they turned around. Jase-Dawn aimed a laser pistol at her while the Youth surrounded her. Taldra had immediately believed her son's accusations against Jase-Dawn, but seeing those accusations verified hurt even more than hearing them.

"Do come in, Taldra," said Gazer, grabbing her left ear and pulling her in.

"Gazer, you have to withdraw Life Unit's tentacles," she said, trying to ignore the pain, and trying to resist the temptation of punching him in the crotch. "You'll kill everyone."

"If that's what it takes to humble Valchondria, then I'll do it, for everyone's good. But I will rule this world, as well as my world. I know what's best for humanity. We'll return to the stars, and unite the colonies. We'll have free trade, free exchange of knowledge, freedom to explore, everything you wanted. Have you abandoned all you believed in? Are your convictions so expendable?"

"Are human beings so expandable? I never believed in killing people in order to reach my goals."

"But Valchondria does. Or have you forgotten what would have happened to Telius? Have you not wondered why Hachen's mother died in hospital the first time she had a heart condition, or why Hachen's father and uncle both died so suddenly in hospital? Have you not wondered why so many people come up missing when they reach a certain age, or when they speak their danger thoughts, or when they've been walkway people for a while?"

Taldra fought back the tears, though she didn't know why she would want to cry in such a situation. Some of what he said made sense. "Were you telling the truth about the virus?"

"Yes. There's no reason for me to lie about it. I could destroy Valchondria many other ways, Life Unit included."

"Where is the cure?"

"They're both right here." Letting go of her ear, he pulled two tiny boxes from his pants pocket: a red one and a blue one. "The red box has a signal to release the proper cure. The blue box has a signal to release the less desirable cure. Both formulas rely on self-replicating nano-technology, so the one I release will spread quickly through Valcine's water supply. You'd soon be able to transfer some of that water to other cities, all across Valchondria." He shook his hand a little. "I thought Life Unit's bracing would protect us from the quake, but I seem to be shaking."

He dropped the blue box. The room grew silent. Taldra wanted to speak but couldn't. Still, she kept thinking of her advantage: no one knew that she could see in color.

When Telius entered the battery room, the door shut behind him. He saw the visions there, the visions from North Edge. He also saw his brother there, watching the visions. Argen glanced over at Telius, seeming only vaguely aware of his presence, but didn't speak until his identical twin approached him. Argen was wearing the same loose-fitting outfit as when Telius had seen him in the North Edge visions.

"See the works, brother," said Argen, mumbling as if he were half-awake. "These are the works of evil."

They saw wars, elderly people pushed into dark rooms, giant hover-crafts flying past the stars, villages, other worlds, strange creatures, oceans of glass, fiery rain.

"It doesn't all look evil," said Telius.

"It will be. The evil ones destroy everything."

"They didn't destroy me."

"You are the secret evil. Ignorance is one of their greatest weapons. They can't help but love secrets. They hate me. Our parents hate me."

"You're wrong, Argen. We're the only siblings in our generation. That's nothing to hate. Think about how special we are. Think about who you are!" He put his hands on Argen's shoulders.

"I am Gazer's friend. Gazer hates the evil ones and their agendas." Pulling away, he slapped Telius's face, and then turned to look at the image that suddenly caught Telius's attention.

"Father?" asked Telius, seeing the vision appear of Hachen crying, the one he'd seen of Hachen at North Edge.

"Hachen!" shouted Argen, as he reached into the image. It threw sparks and fire, tossing Argen across the battery room.

"How can you expect me to follow you?" demanded Taldra, pointing at Gazer. "You destroyed my son and my life. You helped cause my spouse's death."

"Oh, I can't settle with partial credit," said Gazer, closing his hands and crossing his arms. "I killed Hachen. His skin was only singed during his struggle with Argen. He wouldn't have died if not for me shooting him on the way to the hospital."

"You're sick!" A tear rolled down Taldra's face.

"Perhaps. But I kept thinking you would come to me when no one was left."

Taldra crossed her arms, mocking Gazer's posture. "And do you still want me?"

"Yes." He smiled, showing his yellowish teeth.

"You still can't have me."

"And you've mocked me for the last time." He picked up the blue box, then tossed both boxes to Taldra. "Choose or die."

Taldra looked over at Jase-Dawn, who still held the laser pistol, pointed at her heart. Taldra dropped the blue box and pressed the button on the red one. "If we were allowed to speak about such matters, you would know that some Valchondrians can see in color, myself included."

Gazer's tiny eyes bulged in disbelief.

Before Taldra could enjoy her victory, Life Unit's danger signal started buzzing. Taldra warned, "Life Unit will overload if you don't let me intervene. The batteries are all full to capacity."

"Don't worry, I'm never a casualty." He motioned to Jase-Dawn. "Shoot her."

Jase-Dawn held her laser pistol steadily, aiming at Taldra's heart. Their gazes locked together; Taldra could see the doubt, the uncertainty in Jase-Dawn's eyes. Despite the charade, they had become friends. Taldra could see that carrying out the mission now meant betraying that friendship.

"This is no time to get squeamish, Jase-Dawn," said Gazer. "Shoot her."

Taldra's heart felt like it would explode. She noticed the welding torch she had left on the control panel. Could she jump that far?

A hologram materialized from Gazer's credit box, telling him about a new line of programming, available only with expanded wallscreen features.

Jase-Dawn's arm twitched and jerked; a beam of light shot from her laser pistol, into Gazer's chest. He fell against the control panel, then to the floor. Some of the Youth stood in shock, while the others stared at Jase-Dawn, looking ready to tear her to pieces.

She waved the laser pistol at them. "I suggest you leave, before Life Unit explodes." They complied, quickly. As they were leaving, Taldra could hear them chanting something about "the evil ones."

After they locked the main door open, Taldra and Jase-Dawn tried to manually override Life Unit's survival instinct before Taldra addressed her.

"Life, you must shut down," said Taldra.

"Life Unit must survive," she responded. "My program says survive, so the colonists can survive. Creation is continuous."

"Your batteries are damaged, and you're taking in too much energy. You must shut down to keep from exploding. Then I can repair you. It's the only way for Life Unit to survive; it meets your survival instinct. If you don't shut down, you'll die, and you'll take the entire city of Valcine with you."

"Must be repaired. You give life, Taldra. You give life."

All of Life's sensors buzzed for a moment, before silence and darkness overtook the two women.

"Are we safe?" asked Jase-Dawn, finding Taldra's hand and squeezing it.

"I can't be sure," said Taldra. "There might be more quakes." She called out the names of her sons. "Are you in here?"

As the back-up generator came on, giving them limited lighting, they went into the battery room, where they nearly tripped over the body of one of the twins. From the baggy clothes, they knew it wasn't Telius. Taldra touched Argen's wrist, found a pulse.

"He's alive, but where's Telius?" she asked.

"Right here," said Telius, from behind them. They turned to see Gazer holding a laser pistol against Telius's head.

"You failed my test, Jase-Dawn. The laser pistol I gave you won't go past its sleep setting, though its settings show otherwise. But this laser pistol doesn't have that limitation. Argen needs a healer, or he'll die. The two of you can drag him out of here, but don't try anything, or Telius gets a bad headache. I'm willing to call this day a defeat, but I have spies throughout the Supreme Science Council and all over the media. Every time the sun rises, you'll need to wonder if this world still belongs to the infidels."

Sweat poured down Telius's face. "Taldra, please don't try anything. Just get my brother to a healer. I'll come back to you. I did it before."

Taldra's heart quickened again, and she tried to believe that he could really make it back to her again. "I know you will."

Taldra and Jase-Dawn sought the entrance as if the smoke had flung them from the control room. The quaking ended, but the fires continued, and Maintainers rushed around with foam cannons, dousing the flames. One man stepped forward from the crowd as Taldra set Argen down and tried to catch her breath. It was her father, Dr. Norn. Taldra could barely make out anything in the fire, the smoke, and the sea of faces.

Dr. Norn picked up his grandson, who began mumbling incoherently, but without seeming to regain consciousness. "We'll bring him to the hospital," said Dr. Norn. "It's a long trip on the walkways, but we'll manage."

"Gra—" Taldra's voice trailed off as visions of history flashed across Life Unit's exterior, visions of the past that Valchondria had forgotten. The people who had evacuated the buildings circled around Life Unit to watch. Two men, wrapped in fur, standing on ice, gazed back at the crowd. The two men in the vision seemed to look at Argen and Dr. Norn. Only their eyes and part of their faces showed; the fur covered the rest of them. But those eyes revealed a deep connection that reached across the void.

"Telius? Alom?" asked Taldra. Somehow, this vision told her that Telius was alive. She didn't understand how it could, but it did.

The citizens of Valcine also gathered around Taldra. One of them, an elderly black woman with a hopeful smile, took Taldra's hands, gently.

"You're Dr. Lorfeltez," said the woman, in an urgent voice. "You made the visions happen."

"No, I don't know how they happened. We have to go to the hospital. My son—"

"You can build," she said. "You're someone who creates. And you tried to help us bring change. Help us now."

Taldra felt her face growing redder. For so long since Hachen's death, she had thought no one listened to her or believed in her.

"We'll work together," Taldra replied, as the woman released her hand, still smiling. "I have to go now."

"I'm a healer. That's my apartment there." She pointed to a complex nearby that had survived the quake. "I'll take care of your boy until the Maintainers can get him to the hospital. You might not know it, because it wasn't popular to acknowledge such things, but you've always had people who cared about you, people who believed in you."

That statement echoed in Taldra's mind as they walked to the healer's apartment, and as they watched the Maintainers using their foam cannons and the parents finding their children. She knew that Gazer would use Telius as a way of escaping, but she hoped that she would then find her child.

CHAPTER 30

❀

The visions encircled Telius and Gazer as the rumblings continued. Only one dim light remained inside Life Unit, as all of its other lights had gone out. However, many of the visions provided extra light. In the past few moments, Gazer had excitedly revealed everything to Telius.

"The ground is still shaking," said Telius. "Shouldn't you try to stop it? We'll be killed along with everyone else. You don't want to die, do you? I don't see how that could serve your plans."

Gazer kept his laser pistol pointed firmly at Telius's face while maintaining a safe distance. "You inherited your father's talent for senseless ranting; I didn't know such things were genetically encoded."

Telius spoke in a halting tone: "I don't know what that means, but the ground is moving."

"I think Taldra already shut down Life Unit. It will take a while for the motions to stop. Personally, I would rather have let this rusted city be destroyed, then rebuilt in the ways of Degranon."

"Gazer, I've never met anyone like you, anyone so cruel. How can you take such delight in violence?" As Telius spoke, he watched a new doorway forming near Gazer, seemingly attracted to him. Like all the others, it appeared out of nowhere and against the wall, but it seemed to follow Gazer as he paced about, excitedly.

The shaking stopped, as Gazer had predicted, and Gazer straightened his shirt with his free hand. Heaving his massive chest, he said, "Violence is the most creative force in the universe. The birth of the new requires the destruction of the old. A volcano erupts, killing ocean creatures, but an island is born, where other creatures will live. A star explodes, but the fragments of its planets bring new lifeforms to other worlds. On many of the worlds in outer space, the dominant lifeforms feed off human corpses, but the colonists can thank your precious Valchondria for leaving them there for that fate. A circle of Degranon grows weak; one of the other circles envelops it."

Telius raised an eyebrow. "And you accuse me of ranting."

Gazer shot him an annoyed glance but quickly continued. "Even the virus in your blood is destructive; it feeds off other viruses and even off some parts of your body. And since your body always wants something to fight, it will become easily addictive to the harmful drugs that might replace harmful viruses. Your twin brother is a good demonstration of that. And I speak clearly: he wanted violence. You want violence too. You'd like to kill me."

Telius could feel his face darken and his chest tighten as he felt the weight and the truth of Gazer's last accusation. "Yes, I think you deserve to die, but only for justice. You killed both of the men that I saw as my father."

Gazer smiled, leading Telius past a vision of strange metal objects, like giant hovercrafts, floating past stars. Still, the doorway followed Gazer, showing images of stars, then fire, then simply fog. "Justice, God, glory, progress, murder, war—call it what you will, the bloodlust is the same."

Telius's eyes bulged in his head, and his heart pounded in his chest. Hearing Gazer's words—his tribute to murder—made Telius think of Alom, and of Hachen. Gazer's words tortured him; he didn't like being compared to a murderer. He wanted to punish Gazer for such words, but he knew that was wrong. He needed to punish Gazer for murder, and he needed to stop Gazer from killing anyone else. Gazer was a murderer; he deserved execution for that.

Life Unit suddenly spoke, its voice surrounding them. "The temporal doorways are closing. A space rift is growing."

Gazer's face jerked sideways, and he nearly dropped his weapon while touching a button on the side of his credit box. "Computer, locate the doorway to Degranon," Gazer said, to his credit box.

A metallic voice answered: "Beside you, Dr. Geln."

Wonder filled Gazer's beady eyes, but the doorway beside him presented only images of fog, or possibly smoke.

"We're going in," he told Telius, motioning toward the doorway with his laser pistol. Like in the secret cave, a swirl of lights emerged from the doorway when they stepped closer to it. The lights shot around inside the room, circling each other and springing off the walls. Telius and Gazer walked inside, into the lights, but the lights soon faded into sparks.

Both men stood in shock at what they saw when they caught their balance and stepped out of those sparks. The scene that surrounded them looked even worse than the one they had just left on Valchondria. The remains of buildings, hovercrafts, and hoverlanes littered the ground, as if torn from the sky by some great beast, left in mangled heaps. But the sight of all those now-useless objects made Telius shiver much less than the sight of human bodies: torn, burned, severed, piled upon each other or hanging from the windows of the wrecked hovercrafts.

Birds descended from the sky, tearing human flesh from yielding skeletons. What few buildings remained standing also looked like skeletons. Even much of the dethua had somehow shattered and burned, leaving glowing embers all over the ground.

"What happened here?" Telius asked Gazer. His voice came out as a whisper, more from the sick feeling in his stomach than from any need for caution. He tried not to breathe in too deeply; the stench of burned, decaying flesh gave him nausea unlike anything he'd ever experienced, his stomach tightening and twisting.

"A bomb or a missile," Gazer replied after a moment, all traces of his arrogance gone from his countenance. He looked around with a creased brow and an upturned lip, looked down at the body of a little girl, her glazed eyes staring up at him. His face grew pale, and he opened his mouth as if to vomit, but he swallowed as Telius's eyes caught his own. "Where we're standing, this was my command center. It was my home."

The squawking, feeding birds provided the only sound for a moment. Their wings flapped by constantly as more arrived and fought over the meal.

"Aren't you going to welcome me to the world you conquered?" asked Telius, stepping closer as Gazer absently lowered his weapon.

"This can't be my world. It can't be."

Telius punched his dazed companion in the chin. The laser pistol fell from his hand. Telius picked it up, pointed it at him.

"You knew this would happen," said Telius. "But you acted out *The Book of Degranon* anyway. It ends with the king's adult children turning against each other, eventually killing each other."

"But before the king dies, he says Degranon will rise again."

Telius punched his own chest. "In us. Degranon rises in us, and if it becomes our kingdom, it destroys us and those around us. By my people's laws, I should execute you, but I'm going to do far worse. I'm going to leave you here in the ashes of your creation. But if you ever return to Valchondria, I will show you Degranon."

As Telius stepped back into the doorway, feeling the rush of lights through his body, Gazer lifted a burned board in the air, behind his back, ready to crush Telius's skull. Telius lurched sideways, outside the doorway, but not quickly enough to keep the board from scraping his left arm and left shoulder, burning him and sending pain through his entire body.

When Telius regained his footing, he saw Gazer stepping through the doorway, just as it began to close. Though barely able to move, Telius forced his body forward. The swirling lights seemed to reject him at first, to push him back out, but then he fell through in Life Unit, and collapsed on the floor.

CHAPTER 31

✿

Beneath the surface of Valcine Plaza, Jase-Dawn stepped over the fallen furniture and ceiling chests in Gazer's office. Despite the utter destruction of everything else in the basement, and despite the fact that Jase-Dawn had barely trusted the shaky elevator, Gazer's inter-doorway wallscreen remained fully functional. Like Degranon's people and all of the things they created, it lived for withstanding violence.

Life Unit seemed extremely Degran in that respect. Amazingly, Life had also survived the near-destruction of Valcine. However, the images faded away, both from the battery room and from Life's exterior walls.

Jase-Dawn had also survived, in true Degran fashion, with a quick mind and a quick use of a weapon. In her loyalty to a woman she had once considered evil, she had betrayed her superior, and maybe even Degranon. Gazing into the swirl of colors that towered against the wallscreen's left edges, she wondered if she could simply go through and lie about what happened on Valchondria. Maybe, somewhere past the devastated areas of her world, she could begin her teaching career.

As she activated the up-links to the satellite monitoring systems, she thought of how she could explain her failure and Gazer's demise.

The Valchondrians were more powerful. They were aware of the infiltration.

Jase-Dawn's thoughts stopped there. Her heart stopped there. On the wallscreen, she saw images of cities in flames, houses in ashes, human bodies lying in streets and fields, arenas in ruins, glaciers collapsing into the ocean, volcanoes erupting in some bizarrely coordinated fury, and storms of dust attacking the charred remains of the city where she was born. She saw everything but life.

And she realized that she had been wrong in thinking that Degran buildings and technology could survive anything. Everything and everyone had limits on withstanding violence. She had reached hers. She wanted nothing more of the word "Degranon."

Crying silently, she collapsed against the wallscreen and its flickering images of destruction, just as the doorway closed, ending those images.

Standing beside the fallen podium in the otherwise undamaged amphitheater of Valcine Plaza, Taldra watched Jase-Dawn walk up the stairs. Two Maintainers walked behind Jase-Dawn, and two more guarded Taldra from the side of the stage. No one drew rifles or laser pistols. The Maintainers were there to protect Taldra! It seemed horribly ironic, considering what happened the first time she had stood on that stage.

The Maintainers were her allies…at least for a time. But what about Jase-Dawn? Taldra had rehearsed all the words about betrayal and exploitation a billion times in her mind. Those thoughts became scattered, disjointed, as she saw the look in Jase-Dawn's eyes. She looked more devastated than Valcine.

"Your people?" asked Taldra, as Jase-Dawn walked up the stairs.

"There's no life on the planet," she replied, blankly, as if unable to believe what she had seen.

Taldra wanted to slap her, embrace her, accuse her, comfort her. "There is life on this planet, and on others. We need your help."

Their eyes locked together, and Jase-Dawn looked incredibly childlike. "You have it. Taldra, I never meant to hurt you. It was just a mission. And the things that Gazer had taught me, the things that my world had taught me, all indicated that you were monsters. At most, I saw myself as learning more about a dark time in our history. I never thought that you would become my friend, or that my world's history was over."

Taldra looked at Jase-Dawn's credit box. She now felt safe talking about colors, since everyone else could now see in color as well. "Not completely over. That green stripe on your credit box identifies you as a Degran, doesn't it?"

She also looked at it, as if she had forgotten it. "Yes. Most of the Degran spies wear a green stripe somewhere on their clothing. We found that red and blue sometimes occur in your fabrics, probably by accident, but you rarely have the color green."

"And that popping noise Gazer sometimes makes at the ends of his sentences?"

Jase-Dawn nodded. "Degran accent. Most of us have learned to cover it, but some of us can't cover the popping."

Taldra motioned at the Maintainers who had followed Jase-Dawn up the stairs. One of them pulled a hand machine from his belt and relayed the message to their new command center in Valcine Plaza.

Touching Jase-Dawn's shoulder, Taldra said, "You've always been like a daughter to me, and I can't imagine not forgiving one of my children. The Maintainers know all about you, and they're willing to work out something."

"If I hunt down the other Degrans?"

"You give us names, plots, and patterns. We'll do the hunting. I just got back from visiting Argen. The healers had to replace his heart, his liver, and some of the nerve endings in his hand. The damage to his hand was from touching the doorway when it was unstable. The rest was from those pills that Gazer was giving him. The healers said that they couldn't undo the brain damage without cleansing his memory and his identity.

"Your people killed my spouse and nearly killed both of my sons. I will hunt them down, from South Edge to North Edge, and I will destroy them. If I have to visit every home and search the files on every wallscreen, I will destroy them."

Jase-Dawn trembled, and Taldra wondered if it was because of her words or because of something else. Then Jase-Dawn's eyes revealed that it was, indeed, because of something else. She said, "Now that there is no mission and no Degranon, Geln will come for you. He's insane, and he's obsessed with you."

Taldra breathed in deeply. "Yes, I've noticed both of those things."

❦   ❦   ❦

Argen's eyes slowly opened. The mirror's reflection caused him to see himself. He began to close them again, but his brother's hand touched his face and his hair. It wasn't a reflection; it was Telius, sitting beside his bed, wearing what looked like one of Argen's favorite outfits, but it seemed different somehow.

"Are you really awake this time?" asked Telius. "I hope you don't mind. I've been borrowing some of your clothes, especially the ones Taldra bought, because they have color. I don't think the tailors even realized that they sometimes created colored materials. Most of the malls were burned up in the quake, so I had to mallwalk your closet."

Argen could see the dark red of the shirt, the dark blue of the pants, the green of Telius's eyes, the red of Telius's skin, but he didn't know what those colors were at the time. He only knew that they weren't gray or white; they weren't even the black of Telius's hair. They were new to him; he wondered what to call them.

"Where am I?" he finally asked Telius.

"In the hospital. You've been here two weeks. You acted like you were going to wake up a few times before. The healers said that you've almost recovered from the energy that hit you."

"Have you been here all this time?"

"When I wasn't here, Taldra or Dr. Norn came in."

"Dr. Norn, our grandparent?"

"One of them. Taldra said she's still working on the other one. Argen, you almost died. Dr. Norn helped you get to a healer's apartment. Everyone has been helping, working together. You should see it!"

"Where is Taldra?"

"At Valcine Plaza, helping the Maintainers hunt down the Degran spies. They're putting together...." He motioned about with his hands. "I'm still trying to learn all your modern terms. I believe she said that they're putting together a task force to catch all of the Degrans. Taldra said they're treating everyone in the media and the SSC as a suspect. Gazer killed Leader, but Leader had already made Taldra Leader."

"Taldra? I don't understand."

"I'm not sure I do either, but I think Valchondria is better off with her as part of the government."

"What will happen to us?" Argen looked into Telius's eyes, still amazed at the resemblance. Even with his hair cut a little shorter than Hachen would ever allow, Telius looked exactly like Argen. "Will we be killed? No bro—"

Telius interrupted. "Taldra won't let that happen. She's working to change the laws, for more freedom. A lot of the other Youth For Valchondrian Reform have been helping to rebuild; most of them believe in Taldra's vision. You'll be needed too."

"What about Gazer?"

Telius looked away.

"He's dead, isn't he?" asked Argen.

Telius shook his head. "No, but the Maintainers are tracking him down."

Argen wasn't sure how to respond. Gazer was his friend, but only seemed to bring death, and he brought death to Kryldon. Suddenly, Argen forgot about Gazer, forgot about everything but a single thought.

"I'd like to hear music, Telius. Would you bring me some music? No. Bring me someplace where there's music all around. I think people will hear it, and they'll want to dance."

Telius's smile revealed the dimples that had always endured Argen to his parents and his friends, often getting him out of trouble. "Soon."

"Telius, will Taldra allow us to say if we see in colors?"

"Yes, and I know you do. We all do. It's part of our new world. No virus. No population control. No legally un-permitted language. And I don't think we worry about linguistic terrorism anymore, but I'm still trying to figure out what that means." A buzzer went off, near the door. "I think my visit time is over, but I'll be back soon, and you'll be going home in a few days." He stood up, making eye contact once more before turning away.

As Telius walked out the door, Argen whispered, "Brothers, friends."

❦   ❦   ❦

Jase-Dawn grabbed Telius by the arm as he walked out into the hall. "Is he doing any better?" she asked.

Telius's eyes grew big at the sight of her gesture, more from surprise than disapproval. To his regret, she let go.

"He's talking, and he was aware of my presence. That's much better than my previous visits. The healer I spoke with this morning said it might take a while for him to learn independent thought again, and that he still might have cravings for the confidence pills, but that he has a very strong will."

"Like your mother?"

Telius laughed. "Yes, the healer did mention that."

"I am a little worried about her. She seems obsessed with uprooting the remaining Degrans. I've seen the results of crusades."

"That's why we need to be her counsel," said Telius, touching Jase-Dawn's shoulder. "She's a wise person. I wouldn't worry."

"You're right. After all, she made sure I wasn't exiled or imprisoned. I should recognize that." As the outer doors opened, Jase-Dawn looked around again, at all the devastation, and at all the people working to rebuild.

"I noticed you had already left when I awoke this morning. I checked your bedroom door. Did you get called in for another meeting?"

Jase-Dawn nodded. "You'd think the Maintainers would slow down, considering that their cameras, their headquarters, and most of their arsenal are shattered. Some of them were a bit upset about Taldra blocking the charges against me."

Telius shook his head and sighed. "The Maintainers are always upset. The uniforms must itch or something."

Laughing, Jase-Dawn replied, "Maybe so, but I see their aim. Imagine if the leader of a world just started disregarding the efforts of law enforcement and pardoned wanted criminals."

"Nothing like that could ever happen on a civilized planet. You're just a special case, a very special case."

Obviously feeling a bit embarrassed by his flattery, Jase-Dawn turned away slightly, then asked, "Well, are you ready for work?"

"I think so." Telius walked outside with her, holding her hand as they stepped over the bent-up metal debris that surrounded them. But he released her hand just as quickly.

"Good. I start my teaching job at Argen's school in a few months, after the rebuilding is done. But for now, Taldra has assigned the two of us to the same rebuilding crew."

"Imagine that."

Jase-Dawn smiled, but then her smile faded as she admitted her concerns. "I wasn't sure how you would feel about me, considering that I betrayed your family."

"Truthfully, you betrayed the one who wanted to hurt my family. I'm only saddened that you can't go back to your world. Are you sure it was completely destroyed?"

"Yes, the satellites encircle Degranon, and they would detect energy usage in the underground facilities. There was nothing left. If only we'd followed the wisdom inscribed by Zaysha, our planet would be peaceful and thriving."

Telius creased his brow. "Who is Zaysha?"

She breathed out forcefully. "I'm not sure I believe everything in the book literally or in all the legends about its creation, but a priest named Zaysha supposedly traveled Valchondria saying that it was real, and that an apprentice priest was taken away to serve the last of the great kings. That was during your time."

"That wasn't just my time."

"Forgiveness?"

Though her words filled him with apprehension already, Telius couldn't help but ask the obvious question: "Did Zaysha, by chance, see something in a cave?"

"She found enlightenment in a cave, yes! So did you know Zaysha? She was real?"

Telius waved his hands. "She was real, but Degranon only existed within a book! I had never heard of anyone believing it until Gazer came through time and attacked us. Zaysha was the other apprentice priest. She must have followed me to the cave again."

Jase-Dawn nodded, her dark brown eyes wide with amazement and childlike curiosity. "Are you saying that Gazer's time travel created Degranon?"

He continued, "Well, give the writer some credit. I hear it took most of his life for him to finish it. He lived in a village near ours. Alom's grandfather knew him."

"It's just a book?"

Telius nodded. "Just a book. But one of my favorites."

Though Jase-Dawn had already rejected Degranon on many levels, Telius's words about the book obviously brought her sense of reality into question. She struggled to change the subject. "Well, at least there isn't a doorway anymore. According to Gazer's monitors, most of the doorways and windows on Valchondria somehow shifted to Life Unit during the overload, and they all soon burned out. That's why we saw the window image of you and your guardian at Life Unit, even though you were at North Edge."

Telius leaned his head forward. "And in the past. I'll never understand time travel, or doorways and windows. I'm just glad it's all over, so none of the other colonists can come here."

Her breasts heaving slightly, Jase-Dawn twisted a strand of her braided hair. "Except by spaceship. Maybe one day, we'll dismantle enough of the shielding to allow space travel and colonization again, and to allow peaceful commerce with the existing colonists. It's what Taldra wants."

Telius looked up at the yellowish blue sky and breathed in the now-common smell of ashes. "It's what she's always wanted. And I think she'll succeed one day."

The fires had died out, but the remains of the buildings and the hoverlanes surrounded them like boulders after an avalanche. The flaky residue from the foam cannons had dried up, leaving a grayish crust on the edges of everything that had caught fire. Still, even with that familiar gray, Telius noticed and treasured every color of every object and every person. It occurred to him that they were creating the future from the visions he had seen at North Edge, that they were building something new and hopeful.

Over the next several days, Telius became increasingly closer to Jase-Dawn. Besides working with him and living with him, she also went with him after their shift to work with the priests who helped the walkway people. Amid the destruction of so many buildings, the walkway population had increased, driving much of Valchondria into the undermall. Telius knew that he wanted to keep helping these people who lived beneath the busy world of the future. Argen even discussed joining in those efforts, after his time with the healers finally ended.

And the search for Gazer continued. Telius rarely took the stairs down beneath a walkway without passing a Maintainer or two. Argen had told him that the Maintainers never bothered with the undermall, but they were there now: a gray uniform on every corner, always with a rifle or pistol in hand.

Sometimes, he would even see them under the walkways with Taldra…or, Leader, as everyone called her now. After all the discomfort he felt from calling her by name, he found relief in her change to a formal title.

But that title bore heavily on her. Just after nearly losing both of her sons again, she had learned that the man who once worked for her had killed her beloved spouse and let one of her sons take the blame. She had also learned of how the Degrans used her in their plans to conquer Valchondria. While trying desperately to restore order—and utilities—to the world, she also tried desperately not to let vengeance consume her.

Telius could see the bloodlust in her eyes and hear it in her voice. He could even imagine Gazer, somewhere in the undermall, delighting in the walkway talk about her fanatical crusade, mocking her loss of innocence and idealism. Both ideas hurt: the one that Gazer remained loose, and the one that he had turned Telius's mother into someone who spent all her time hunting for traitors. Argen and Jase-Dawn had both told him what people used to say about her, that she needed "to be maintained." Now she was like the very group that had introduced that term into the Valchondrian lexicon: the Maintainers.

And the vengeance, it did consume her. One night, while Telius and Jase-Dawn were having dinner with her, Taldra began listing the homes that she and the Maintainers had personally checked for Degran spies.

Suddenly having his fill of docle bread, and of such talk, Telius pushed his platter away, nearly knocking over his drink. He loathed the dethua walls in Taldra's Valcine Plaza quarters and couldn't understand why she didn't just meet them at their family home. The idea of ugly colors had never occurred to him when he had only seen in black and white. During his first day of colorsight, he had wandered about Valcine, just looking at people and things, in order to experience their colors. But dethua offered a hideous splashing of green hues that nearly hurt his eyes!

Of course, it wasn't really his colorsight that bothered him. He had rarely questioned Alom and had yet to challenge Taldra, but this vendetta of hers sounded too unlike the ideals of freedom, progress, and opportunity that she constantly espoused.

"Ta—" He almost said her name, after so many times of forcing himself to say it, but he caught himself this time.

She swallowed a bite of her synthetic vegetables. Despite her beautiful dress and the careful braiding of her hair to one side, she looked terribly ragged and frazzled. Bags formed under her reddened eyes, and she looked much thinner than only a few days before.

Smiling approvingly, she told him, "It's all right to use my chosen name. This isn't a formal meeting—just dinner with two of my favorite people."

Jase-Dawn smiled graciously at the compliment, but her big brown eyes revealed that she could see Telius's concern, the same concern she had voiced to him outside the hospital. Living and working together all the time, Jase-Dawn and Telius had quickly learned the meanings behind each other's looks and gestures.

Telius continued, pressing his hands down against the mock-wooden table. "You have the entire world to govern. You can't spend your time or risk your life bursting into people's homes with the Maintainers. I don't even understand your alliance with the Maintainers. As I recall, they've always wanted to silence you, and they wanted to kill me."

Her countenance became even more troubled, more severe. "Telius, those people today had books in their homes, maybe even *The Book of Degranon*."

Telius jerked up, nearly knocking his chair over. "Good! They need books! They need something other than the wallscreen, not that most people have electricity right now anyway. And I owned copies of *The Book of Degranon*, which I distributed to the Dalian villagers. In fact, I made one of those copies myself, from a manuscript passed down by Alom's parents.

"Books are good things, Taldra. Freedom is a good thing. But these Maintainers of yours, I'm not sure that they're good. And this obsession of yours, I know it isn't good. You—" Telius stopped as he suddenly realized two things: he was speaking in a harsh tone to his mother, and she was leaning forward to hide her swelling tears. She looked so fragile that even words could break her, even his words.

Silently, Taldra pulled away from the table and stood trembling in the corner, lightly touching an arrangement of plastic docle flowers that an attendant had placed on a stand. She seemed oddly like a gardener who had just discovered their artificial nature and felt deluded by that falseness.

Telius couldn't remember seeing an actual plant since leaving Alom's time. The people of modern-day Valchondria constantly sought to duplicate and replace the world of their ancestors, the world they had buried beneath the hoverlanes, the walkways, and the buildings.

Taldra raised her eyes to meet her son's eyes. Her voice rose quietly from her mouth, forcing him to listen even more intently. "The Degrans took my family from me. And they used what your father and I built to devastate Valchondria."

Telius walked around to his mother's side of the table. "I can't imagine what it's like to lose your spouse, but I've lost both of the men that I saw as my father, and I won't lose you or Argen. Now, we might not be all that 'maintained,' but we are a family."

As Telius stepped forward and embraced Taldra, he held out one hand, inviting Jase-Dawn to his side. It was a gesture often made in his village, one that showed friendship, or even a desire to be married with someone. He wasn't sure if Jase-Dawn would accept or even understand, but he still found himself making the gesture, and hoping she would heavy honor him.

While Taldra wept on Telius's shoulder, Jase-Dawn stood up and embraced them both. She told them, "And I would like to be a part of that family."

"You always have been," assured Taldra, touching one of the interlooping earrings she had given Jase-Dawn. "And always will be."

Backing away slightly, Telius smiled. "Then you won't disown her when you learn that she's been plotting with me?"

"Plotting?" Obviously intrigued, Taldra pushed away the tears that now flowed from her eyes. "And what is it you're plotting?"

Jase-Dawn replied, "Something for Argen's homecoming tomorrow. We'd like for you and Argen to meet us at the amphitheater, 7 lunar."

Taldra cocked her head and eyed them both quizzically. She obviously took delight in how well the two of them were getting along. The idea of them planning something together seemed to delight her even more. But they managed to keep their plans secret until the next morning.

The music filled the amphitheater. While most of the musicians on the stage were elderly, the swelling crowd represented every age. The people stood in amazement at the discovery of the forgotten music, some of them swaying ever so slightly as the rhythms grew faster and more exuberant.

In the middle of that crowd, Jase-Dawn kissed Telius on the cheek. "It looks like genius runs in the family," she told him. "This is exactly what your people needed."

"Our people," he replied, emphasizing the first word. "And could you do that again?"

She pulled on the back of his head so that his lips met hers as she kissed him. It felt intensely pleasant, in a way that Telius had never imagined.

"Like that?" she asked.

He stammered for words. "Yes. I—I've never kissed before. I know I'm a bit old not to, but Alom discouraged me from getting romantically involved with anyone, because he was sure that I would be able to go home one day."

Smiling, she told him, "I'll have to thank your mentor, when I see him in the Higher World."

"You believe in the Higher World?"

She tilted her head slightly, obviously surprised by his question, and perhaps a bit offended. "Well, yes, most of my people do. But I'm not in any hurry to get there. This world is getting interesting."

Feeling emboldened, Telius started to kiss her again, but a muscular body slammed against his.

"You did this for me?" asked Argen, his wide smile fully creasing his dimples. He looked stronger and happier than Telius had ever seen him.

"Well, we did it for everyone, but especially for you. Where's Leader?"

"On the stage, talking to our grandparents. She said she liked your surprise."

"We thought she would," said Jase-Dawn, casually slipping her hand into Telius's hand.

Argen pointed back and forth. "Are you two—?" Instead of finishing the sentence, he stopped and pinched one of his earlobes. Telius worried that it might be one of the black-outs or seizures that had plagued all the surviving Youth For Valchondrian Reform, thanks to Gazer's so-called "confidence pills." But it was something else: a sudden fascination, a sudden observation.

Telius asked, "What is it?"

Argen touched at the air. Even though several passing citizens brushed his hand down, he lifted it back up. "Telius, I don't think I ever liked music so much. It sounds so different now, so alive. It's like I had never really heard it before."

Jase-Dawn told him, "Another good reason to reject the virus. It didn't let you hear certain musical tones, including some of the most inspiring ones."

As Jase-Dawn said that, they noticed that some of the people had started dancing, and the dancing spread through the crowd until it became almost everyone dancing.

"I told Telius that the music would make people dance," said Argen, tapping one of his feet. "Didn't I, Telius?"

Telius replied, "Yes, but I never expected anything like this."

"Kryldon would have liked this." Argen looked sad for a moment, but then he slapped Telius on the chest. "Let's go see Taldra. Her guards won't let her into a crowd this size."

"All right," said Telius. "But let's not get into the habit of hitting each other." He smiled playfully and acted like he was going to punch Argen with his free hand. He pulled on the other hand, the one that Jase-Dawn held. "Are you coming with us?"

"Certainly, but I'll expect a dance later."

❧   ❧   ❧

When they pushed through the dancing crowd and walked onto the stage, their grandparents told them that Taldra had gone to a backstage control room. They were both playing stringed instruments, and stayed seated as they spoke. "She needed to accept some emergency wallscreen message," their grandmother said, shouting above the music from the gathering of musicians and tonal androids that surrounded them.

Telius couldn't stop staring at the tonal androids. While helping the Power Holders restore utilities, Jase-Dawn had reactivated the strange machines. According to the Power Holders, Valchondria's children had once used them as companions, long before they were all abandoned and sent to the Power Holders' scrap rooms.

They looked like metal versions of people, but with multi-colored lights streaming up and down the left side of their bodies, producing strange but pleasant sounds that reminded Telius of the chirping and singing of birds in the Lisuadian Forest. Suddenly, he realized that Jase-Dawn and Argen had walked ahead of him.

Jase-Dawn used a button to open the backstage door, but Argen was the first to burst inside, in what Telius had already recognized as his generally reckless nature. Argen and Jase-Dawn both nearly tripped over the bodies of Taldra's guards as they entered the tiny control room.

Through the doorway, Telius saw Gazer, his laser pistol pointed at Taldra. All five of the guards were dead. An emergency signal flashed on the wallscreen, making a buzzing noise.

"Come in and slide the door shut," Gazer shouted, in a firm and threatening tone. The music was too loud for anyone to hear beyond the doorway. "Don't make me kill her."

Telius walked inside, found the door's button, and pressed it. At the same time, though, Taldra spoke defiantly to Gazer: "We've already established that you won't kill me." She didn't seem the least bit afraid, but her countenance revealed her disgust at seeing Gazer again. Telius also felt disgusted, and regretted his decision to spare Gazer's life.

Gazer sneered. "You're right, as always, Taldra." Stepping over the guards, he stood with the laser pistol against the face of a new target:

Argen. "But these ungrateful children are another story. I risked everything to protect them, and to give them opportunities, and they've only hurt me, just like everyone else."

"What about how you've hurt us?" demanded Argen. "You killed many of the people we loved, and countless other Valchondrians. You told me 'No brothers, no sisters, no friends.' But you're the one who destroys families and takes away people's friends. You are all the things you taught me to despise."

"Argen!" screamed Taldra, who now looked very much afraid. "Stop it! Don't provoke him!"

The music reached a crescendo, then suddenly stopped. Sweat poured down Gazer's trembling face as he began whispering something beneath his breath. Telius wasn't sure, but it sounded like a name: R'zrn.

"I can't hear you," said Argen. "Speak clearly!" While he had Gazer off guard by daring to address him that way, Argen yanked the laser pistol by its barrel and jerked it from Gazer's hand.

The others all screamed Argen's name.

"R'zrn," said Gazer, the skin beneath his eyes twitching. "I had a brother too, and a family. You don't know how I've suffered."

Argen pressed the laser pistol into Gazer's chest. "No, I don't. But I know how you've made us suffer. Do you remember that day, when you made me think I did this to my father?"

"Yes!" Tears poured down with the sweat on Gazer's face. His tiny eyes looked crazed. "I remember."

"Good! I wanted it to be your last thought when I did it to you." Argen jabbed his free fist into Gazer's stomach, doubling him over as a laser blast shot through his chest and into the ceiling. The Maintainers burned through the sliding door as Argen pushed Gazer's lifeless body away. Telius took the laser pistol from his brother and hugged him tightly, glad that Argen had finished what needed finishing, but hurt that Argen had to feel the pain of killing someone, even someone as loathsome as Gazer.

"It's over," Taldra said, to herself, and to the Maintainers. "Disable the fire system, before we get foamed."

Another song started, this one peaceful, gentle, reminding Telius of the streams that ran near Dalii. Argen trembled against him as Telius tenderly stroked his hair, making sure his trembling didn't turn into a seizure.

"Leader, are you harmed?" one of the Maintainers asked, as he sprang to her side.

"No, I just want to go home and be with my family. But please send me information about the guards' families, so I can personally console them."

"We'll do that, Leader. You should—"

She touched his shoulder. "I need to do it."

Obviously realizing that it was useless to argue with Taldra, the Maintainer nodded in resignation, and stood aside for them to walk by.

As the other Maintainers marched in front of them, escorting them safely outside, Telius thought about two of the words Taldra had just used: "home" and "family." He had found them both.

Afterword

T hank you for reading my first novel! Please tell others what you thought about it; just look up *Degranon* at Amazon.com or bn.com to post your comments. If you liked *Degranon*, then I encourage you to also look for the following books.

1984, by George Orwell

Brave New World, by Aldous Huxley

A Clockwork Orange, by Anthony Burgess

Dune, by Frank Herbert

The Earthsea Trilogy, by Ursula K. Le Guin

Fahrenheit 451, by Ray Bradbury

The Handmaid's Tale, by Margaret Atwood

Space Trilogy, by C. S. Lewis

The Time Machine, by H. G. Wells

0-595-21371-5

Printed in the United States
1499200004BA/94